CAFÉ

VENGEANCE

BY CLARISSA R. COTTRILL

Tea With Coffee

— Media —

*F*or my mother, without whom I wouldn't know the value of light in a world of darkness.

Acknowledgments

T hank you to my partner, Justin. Thank you for your love and understanding every day. You have taken my hand as I trekked into the darkest corners of my mind, and never let go even when you had to lead me back. For the proofreading, the brainstorming sessions, and for listening to me ramble about hellfire and Latin translations – thank you. I love you.

Thank you to one of my dearest friends, Shannon, who is the epitome of encouragement. All writers should be so lucky to have a friend like you. You are a voracious reader, an excellent critic, and it is an honor to be someone you love. For reading, critiquing, answering those late-night texts with strange questions and hypotheticals, and for always being someone who is there for me. Thank you. *Café Vengeance* would not exist without you.

I'd also like to thank the entire team at my publisher, Tea With Coffee Media. Tyler Wittkofsky and Kelsey Anne Lovelady, who saw something in my manuscript for *Café*

Vengeance and took a chance. To Designer Victoria Moxley, for crafting the cover I'd always imagined. To every single designer, editor, and member of this amazing corner of publishing who worked hard to bring this novella to life. Thank you.

I owe this book becoming a reality to everyone out there who has supported me over the years and who has fed my earliest inclinations toward writing and the horror genre. Teachers who showed me no matter how dark, prose could still be beautiful: Mr. Ponton, Mrs. Seeders, Ms. Crisler as I knew them then. Friends both in real life and virtually who have cheered me on and offered advice. An aunt who introduced me to horror and opened up this world for me. The writers I admire, especially of dark fiction and horror, whose stories I've pored over since childhood. Thank you.

And finally thank you to my mother, to whom I've dedicated this novella. Thank you for your unabashed belief in me and for allowing me to explore so I might grow and evolve as a storyteller. I know it must have been difficult for you to relate to my interests. I looked closer at the scary movies from which you hid your eyes. I enjoyed diving into the darkness you avoided, if only to understand it better. But you never deterred me from these endeavors. You bought me Stephen King novels and Edgar Allan Poe collections that you would never read. You nurtured me, even the parts you didn't understand, and for that I will be eternally grateful.

At the end of the day this is a story of evil, which is a real monster walking among each and every one of us. I believe I've seen evil with my own eyes, and it's rarely in the form of a supernatural creature. It can follow and even live inside any one of us, but so can good. And for teaching me that, I also have to thank my mother, without whom I could never have learned the depths of good and evil in this world and in my own life.

Contents

CHAPTER 1

F ire was everywhere.

Glowing orange flames and billowing black smoke had filled every corner in Dane Roman's eyes mere seconds ago. Stifling heat had kissed his skin until sweat prickled his upper lip and hairline, with the droplets still gliding down his face to prove it. Even after the flames were extinguished, he still couldn't take a full breath without tasting thick, smoky ash on his tongue that almost forced a gag from deep in his diaphragm.

He smiled.

It wasn't the kind of tooth-bearing grin one would plaster on for a photo. It wasn't even the tight-lipped polite smile for exchanging pleasantries. Instead, the corners of his mouth only twitched up for an instant in a cool, collected smirk that wasn't visible to the naked eye.

"Sir? Sir, are you the owner of the building?" The timid questions from over his shoulder interrupted the beauty before him. Stifling a sigh and un-gritting his teeth, Dane turned around to a man standing at least a foot shorter than his six feet with layers of firefighting gear seeming to weigh him down even closer to the ground.

"Yes, I'm the owner. I'm Mr. Dane Roman," he said, holding out a steady hand. With careful precision, he unraveled every muscle and nerve above his neck and built a new expression from scratch. His groomed and arched black eyebrows knitted together, and he put extra weight into his forehead, like he was holding the world on top of it. His eyes, which were rich black like the smoke behind him, turned glassy and tired with the illusion of tears and his thin lips shifted from that devilish smile to a sad grimace. Every inch of his face, from the wrinkle of skin to the tautness of a muscle, became a brushstroke in the piece of art he had worked on for years: the face of a man deserving of sympathy.

Dane watched the scrawny excuse for a fireman fold his lips into his own mouth, widen his big blue eyes, shake his head, and drop his shoulders all at once like a man defeated before offering his own hand in greeting.

It worked. It worked every single time.

"Mr. Roman, I'm awful sorry to have to tell you this, sir, but this fire is nothing short of a tragedy," he said, a tremor hiding behind his words. He kept those wide, almost infantile eyes glued to Dane's as he spoke and it took every ounce of restraint Dane had not to roll his away. "I... I've never seen anything quite like this. The top three floors went up so quickly that almost no one up there was able to make it out. We have at least sixty casualties from those floors alone, only about twenty-five of whom have been identified. Most of them burned to death, but several tried to jump out of the building and essentially committed suicide. It's, well, it's just awful, sir. We've got several bodies of children as well, and on the lower three floors we're looking at least another twenty or twenty-five dead and many injured. Those mostly from when the building began to collapse on itself." Dane inhaled, deep and continual, through his nose and blew the breath out of his mouth several seconds later — being sure to curve his lips into an "o" shape and make the exhale audible. "Yes, a tragedy. Just a tragedy," he said, finally taking the opportunity to avert his eyes from the firefighter. "And the building? It's a total loss, I assume?"

The firefighter nodded, rambling through what Dane knew was a rehearsed, textbook speech about how the fire department would likely determine this a total loss once all was said and done. Dane kept his face blank and understanding, but with every word he wished he didn't have to hear all this from the fire department equivalent of an intern. It wasn't anything he hadn't already learned for himself.

"I know it's still early and clearly you all are still focused on tending to the tenants... the victims, but I wonder if we have any idea about the cause yet?" The fireman curled an eyebrow at Dane's interrupted question, and for just a moment, Dane worried his sympathetic mask had slipped. But it was just that — a slip — and that couldn't unravel the concocted appearance Dane had created. He especially didn't worry about fooling this weakling, who was already crumbling under the weight of his sadness and empathetic feelings for all those victims.

"I know it's so early. I just... I really care about my residents. They're like members of my family, and I know so many of them are hurting and reeling in loss right now. I want to be able to give them the answers they deserve," he explained, plucking each word and inflection from the dictionary inside his brain's left hemisphere. Well-timed head shakes and chest-rattling sighs were his punctuation. Only when he saw the firefighter's compassionate stance return beat-by-beat did Dane add a finishing touch to his elucidation. "And the sooner I can get the insurance company involved, the sooner I can hopefully find some resolution for these people and all my employees. I know it won't mean much in the grand scheme of what they've lost, but I just want to do whatever I can."

"Of course, sir. Well, from what we can tell so far, we're fairly certain that the fire originated from an open flame. So maybe a candle or match or even a fire on the stove. It's also possible a crystal or piece of glass was left in direct sunlight and sparked – I mean, that one's unlikely, but it is possible and we can't rule anything out," he said, flipping through a clipboard of notes to find the details. Dane ate up the words like sugary candy hitting a craving. He already knew. "Our response team also thinks they are close to pinpointing where this flame might have started. Based on the damage and how it evolved, it looks like the fire broke out inside one of the units on the fifth floor, which would explain why those top floors were engulfed so fast."

As the young fireman spoke, Dane's own version of the story unfolded behind his veiled eyes. In the fog of early morning, Dane had skulked through unit 511 with three of the local grocery store's Virgin Mary candles. He was sure to crack shards of glass out of all of them, chuckling when the fissures cut through the Virgin's face, and place them on a rickety oak coffee already in the apartment. Finishing his display, Dane added a few, inconspicuous pin pricks of gasoline around them like a well-organized ritual. He knew just from looking at the table it would be pretty flammable on its own, and his accelerant drops would be simply for good measure. He was nothing if he wasn't thorough.

The table was in the exact same spot as when he entered the apartment a day earlier, right next to the body of the unit's longtime tenant, a decrepit woman he remembered to be always draped in shawls and dark shades of black and olive green. Every time he saw her alive, the mane of wiry, gray hair fell well below her backside and poked out from the edge of her shawls. That day, however, it was uncovered and spread all around her frail corpse like a halo. She had to have been at least eighty, and Dane knew without looking at her file that she had no family or emergency contacts. He could count on one hand how many times he had seen her leave the building, let alone her apartment, in the years since he owned it. According to the previous owners, it had been that way for close to a decade.

Mrs. Castiglione.

That's what the old owners had called her. They said missus even though she had no husband, past or present, and never had children. Her first name was something Dane had never heard before, even though he had grown up with a hoard of Italian and Roman Catholic aunts and cousins. It was Terina, or maybe Terita, but definitely not Theresa. He had made that mistake more than once. She was a superstitious old woman who seemed to have come to that apartment straight from the boat from Italy, and was known to have so many candles, crystals, and herbs burning that neighbors sent up false fire alarms for years. He only went to check the apartment that day after an annoying middle-aged woman down the hall cornered him and begged someone to stop Mrs. Castiglione from burning such strong, rotten-smelling sage.

And there she was on the floor — pale, smelling and swelling with death's putrid bloat. Bloody, yellow pus-like foam had seeped from the corners of her closed lips. Her eyes were open, but the brown irises and eyeballs looked shriveled and dry like they could be plucked out with a toothpick. Her wrinkled paper skin had gone glassy and almost translucent, and the stench of her rotting insides emanated as far as three feet away from the body.

Dane remembered nudging her face with his leather loafer-clad foot, and grimacing when more of that blood-streaked foam gushed out of her nose and onto the linoleum floor. The tongue that had been tucked in her rotting mouth fell out, discolored with death. There was a slit just past the tip, as if she had bitten it before tumbling down to the floor. He wondered if that came before or after the infamous death rattle, but only shrugged at the passing thought. Taking a few steps deeper into the apartment, Dane opened the door to the living room closet and scanned the contents. He wasn't sure what he was looking for; in fact maybe he was looking for nothing. But he knew no one would notice anything missing from the old spinster's storage.

The closet had been filled to the brim with the usual geriatric junk: Boxes of paper and scraps, musty and moth-ball-covered sweaters, an assortment of canes, what he assumed were forgotten mementos, and random spillover sat piled on the closet floor. He saw more of the Virgin Mary candles, matches, a stack of phone books, and in the center an empty, grimy old gas can.

The lid was missing and probably had been for years. The label had faded into streaks so he almost couldn't see what it was supposed to be. He didn't recognize the brand from any store shelves. It probably had not been in business for decades. But there it was. Within seconds of staring at it, pages began to turn in Dane's head as he concocted a story that would define the days to come.

"I was afraid something like this could happen," he said, interrupting the firefighter's explanation. He could have laughed. He almost did start chuckling at his use of the word 'afraid'. Fear was as far from the truth as he could imagine. "That's why I made sure every tenant's lease agreement had a clause against burning candles and incense."

He didn't have to contort his face or tune his voice to make those words ring true. The clause was real and tucked in the inner pages of every tenant's lease agreement — as of about twelve hours before. The ache in Dane's upper back served as proof of the hours he spent hunched over the property manager's computer into the night, amending the standard lease agreement and sending it to every tenant's email under the guise of a clerical change. Notifications poured in with pings and dings announcing hundreds of freshly signed leases.

Dane had laughed then, leaning back in the discount office chair and savoring the cracks echoing from his spine. Not one tenant who responded would have had time to read that lease and notice the change, but still just tapped a few buttons as if they had. He knew it would work, because he knew these people. All of them, even ancient Mrs. Castiglione with her dilapidated gas can and phony prayers, lived glued to their cellphones and used them for everything from paying rent to signing life-changing documents. They couldn't possibly have the patience to read nearly fifteen pages of legally binding copy. And they didn't.

"That was mighty smart on your end, Mr. Roman sir," the fireman said, tugging Dane back into the present. "It's a shame people don't take fire safety seriously enough. Maybe now they will."

"Yes, maybe now they will," Dane said.

They.

The cone of silence that had encapsulated Dane and his talks with this baby firefighter melted away. He could feel the heat and soot clawing at the back of his neck again while sirens and screams assaulted his ears. Dane looked over his shoulder at the crowd surrounding the still blazing building. Men and women were huddled together, clawing at one another to stay standing while they wailed in tandem. Children were crying and clinging to police officers and firefighters while their parents became phantoms to the disaster. The shrieks were deafening, and even through the smoke he could see every face twisted in agony.

A young woman, no older than twenty-two, was separate from the crowd with two firefighters flanking her. She had fallen to her knees into a fetal position with her face less than a foot from the pavement as she screamed into the asphalt. Dane recognized her as one of the residents from the top floor. He always thought she was beautiful, but today she looked different. The long blonde locks that often fell into perfectly sculpted curls were dirty and disheveled. Her skin usually glowed like marble, but was blotchy and ash-stained. Ruby red lips had turned pale and chapped.

Looking up, Dane realized why she appeared as a different woman today. One of the firefighters held what looked like a wad of dirty sheets bridal style in his arms. If it weren't for the tiny, charred hand dangling from beneath the sheet, Dane would have had no idea he was carrying a body — a child's body. He didn't have to see the camouflaged face to know it was a little boy with blonde curls that matched his mother's and big blue eyes he assumed must be tokens from an unattached father. Any time he saw that beautiful woman in the building, Dane only had to look down to see the toddler at her side; but not today.

Today he saw a woman broken, trying to bury herself alive in the concrete as she saw her baby son's body sizzling and burned to death. He saw a world shattered. He saw a heart broken. He saw a child's chubby fingers coated in black soot and red sores.

And he felt nothing.

His chest was as empty as the moment he set eyes on Mrs. Castiglione, dead and alone on her living room floor, and then stepped over her into his scheme. His chest was as empty as when he buried both his parents more than a decade ago.

In his next breath, Dane excused himself to make a call. Putting as much distance between himself and the mob of mourners as possible, he scrolled through the contacts in his cell phone until he landed on American Dream Insurance. He rehearsed the call at least fifteen times since the night before, and from the minute the nasal-voiced secretary greeted him, he didn't deviate from the script once.

He didn't have to hide his smile anymore in the face of now fluttering flames as his insurance agent confirmed what he already knew. Dane would receive the full insurance payout on the building once he passed along paperwork confirming it as a total loss, and since the residents and "human error" had been the cause, no other investigations would delay the payment.

"You may actually have grounds for litigation against whoever's candles or whatever started the whole thing if the fire department can pinpoint that," the insurance pundit said. "From what you told me, it sounds like they have a pretty good idea where those first flames were. If they can narrow it down to an apartment number, and those residents are still alive, you may just have a case since it's clear as day in this lease here."

Yet again, Dane bit his lip and choked back his reaction. He could still see Mrs. Castiglione's ripe corpse with her black and bitten tongue lobbed out of her mouth. The phantom smell of that rotting corpse cooking in the blaze's birth tickled his olfactory nerve. Her dry eyeballs would have turned to ash and her wrinkled folds of skin would have burned off layer by layer. All of her trinkets and treasures had to be destroyed. Her body was a charred piece of meat no one would go looking for, and her very existence had faded into nothing — not even a memory.

He thanked the insurance man for the tip, but didn't dwell on the advice as he ended the call. He had taken all he could from Mrs. Castiglione.

CHAPTER 2

As clocks ticked past 6 p.m., dusk had already draped over New York City, filling the highest sky with city lights and casting dingy shadows along the lowest sidewalks. Dane's feet were heavy, pulling at his sore calf muscles with every step toward his luxury condo in Soho. Even by town car, the journey from the now burned building in the Bronx was a long one, and these last few paces home felt the longest.

Turning the final corner, the futuristic tower came into view. In the darkening sky, the low iron-glass exterior looked more like layers and layers of glittery mirrors. Lights from inside shone out onto the street, casting a harsh glow on each shorter building and passerby who couldn't call it home. His body started to relax as he reached the door, but Dane, weighed down by the day's events, still moved in slow motion through the pristine lobby. He didn't bother to acknowledge the elderly doorman's 'good evening' or any futile smiles from others in the elevator up to the twelfth floor. The walnut door at the end of the hallway beckoned him like an old friend the closer he came and, by the time he wrapped his hand around the sleek silver knob, he felt as though he could collapse into the threshold.

But Dane didn't get the chance. Instead, he had to catch all his weight on his heels and retreat when the door swung open without his push. A collage of raven hair and tan skin tumbled out of the doorway and crashed against him. Smooth arms twisted around his neck like a chokehold gone wrong and meticulously manicured nails dug into the base of his scalp, just above his neck. He didn't need to see them to know they were painted with glossy red polish.

"Oh my God, I'm so glad you're okay! I saw the fire on the news. I was scared to death you might be inside!" the woman who landed on Dane's chest said, tripping over words and unreleased sobs hiding in the back of her throat. He buried a smile in the crook of her neck and wove his arms around her waist so they intertwined across her backside, pulling her a little closer against him. She did the same, twirling a few strands of his hair in her fingers before shoving her body away from his.

"Why the hell haven't you answered your phone?" She seethed, loud enough that any neighbors close to their front door would have heard. "I've called and I've texted at least ten times and you just what? Ignored me during a fire? What's wrong with you? I thought you were dead, for Christ's sake!"

"I went from talking with the fire department, to the police, to the insurance company during the whole ordeal," he answered in the softest voice he could muster, wrapping his fingers around hers to lead her inside the condo, closing the door behind them. With his free hand, Dane twisted all three of the locks on the front door and pulled it hard against its frame, as if testing their strength. "By the time I was headed home, I didn't want to even look at my phone."

It wasn't a good enough excuse. He knew that before he said it. And sure enough, her mouth opened in protest before he even got out the end of the sentence.

"I know. I still should have answered you. I'm sorry, okay? I'm sorry you were worried," he said, reaching out to bring her into another embrace. If it were any other argument, she would have resisted, stiffening her shoulders and holding her hands up like a crossing guard, but not tonight. Those sobs he sensed at the doorway weren't hiding anymore, but had clawed their way higher in her throat. Shallow, shaky breaths fell against his chest as she let her anger melt and reveal the panic she had been concealing. Smirking when he felt her relax, Dane used his index finger to tip her face up to his. "I'm sorry, Pilar. But I'm okay, right? I'm fine, and I'm right here."

She smiled, just barely twitching up the corners of her full lips, and Dane knew she had gone back to normal. It was in moments like this, when she let go of her emotions, that he could take in every inch of her beauty. Pilar Ramos had dark tan skin speckled with beauty marks and freckles all over her face, deep brown eyes with lush lashes surrounding them, and voluminous black curls that went to the middle of her back – although she usually kept them pinned in a neat bun atop her head. The top of her scalp reached just below Dane's neck and curves accentuated her full figure. His hands rested on her round hips as he looked into her eyes, which were softening by the second, and repeated that he was fine.

"I'm glad," she said, separating their embrace after a few moments and taking a seat on their ivory leather sofa. "So what happened? The footage on the news looked crazy — like a bomb went off or something."

"Eh, nothing too out of the ordinary. No bombs," he replied with a shrug, pulling off his suit jacket and wrinkling his nose when smoke residue wafted from the fabric. Grimacing, he tossed it toward the glistening white kitchen tiles. "Some fool had candles going or something and, big surprise, started a house fire. Except when you live in a cheap apartment building, a house fire becomes a huge apartment fire really fast. Reap what you sow if you ask me."

He stretched his arms over the back of the sofa as he spoke and propped his now bare feet on the coffee table, shuddering when the cool glass tickled his heels. From the top of his head to the tips of toes, Dane's body was exhaling. In his meditation, he didn't notice Pilar shrinking away from him into the opposite couch corner with every word he spoke.

"Dane, don't talk like that," she said, her voice gritty and hushed like a mother scolding a child in church. "That's a terrible thing to say. Those people, your tenants, lost everything. People died."

"People die every day," he retorted with a wave of his hand, not even bothering to open his eyes and look at her. "It's common sense. Who the hell is dumb enough to burn candles ... or incense or whatever in a building like that where hundreds of people live within feet of each other?"

"Literally you two days ago when you lit those awful musk scented candles all over the bedroom," Pilar snapped back, rolling her eyes at the memory. "As if those would have gotten me in the mood. They smelled like they came free with your shitty, overpriced cologne."

A tiny bubble of anger popped in Dane's chest when he heard the attitude lacing his girlfriend's voice. He couldn't tell if it was because she insulted his taste or because she had the gall to compare him to his tenants, but he had to gulp back venom before he spoke again.

"You know what I mean," he said through his teeth. "You asked what happened, so there's your answer. It might be terrible, but it's the truth, and at least I ... I mean, we get to reap the benefits."

Pilar gasped in response, and her arms crossed over her chest so tight it looked like she was restraining herself. She shuffled her body so far away from Dane that her left leg was hanging off the sofa and her toes were pointed into the next room.

"Benefits? What the hell kind of benefits could there be from one of your buildings burning to the ground and literally killing people?"

The slick smile he had been tucking away all day long reappeared before Dane could stop it. He was still looking up at the ceiling, and there was no way Pilar could really see his face or just how deeply his smile curved — or so he thought. The conversations with the insurance agent replayed in his head. The word millions flashed behind his eyes like neon signs in the city of sin, blinding him to Pilar lifting her body off the couch and taking purposeful strides away from her boyfriend as she asked again.

"Come on, Pilar, you know I own ten other buildings all over New York City – not to mention the casinos in Jersey.

This one didn't even make a drop in the bucket, and was the worst one to maintain. I'm going to make more money from the insurance payout in one day of it being burned down than I ever did while that bitch was standing," he said. "This time tomorrow, we will be millions of dollars richer without having to do a damn thing except cash the check. It's fucking beautiful."

"Do you hear yourself? Dane, you sound like a psychopath," she said. Her voice was quiet and steady despite the harsh words, and her eyes grew wider by the second. "People died and lost their homes, and those are people who probably don't have much else to get back on their feet with. That money is going to go toward helping them or rebuilding the place, isn't it?"

Dane rolled his eyes.

"Don't be naïve," he spit out, curving his neck forward to face her for the first time since he sat down. All the admiration for her beauty and heart-warming concern about him had vanished — soft eyes had gone fiery and his jawline, once relaxed in a gentle smile, was rigid like he was holding something sour in his teeth. "It would be ten times more expensive to try and rebuild, especially with today's regulations. No, this is pure profit."

"But what about all those people? What if they have nowhere to go? They could have lost everything today."

"Look, they were supposed to have renter insurance, okay? It was a requirement in the lease, and it's just common sense. If they had that, then I'm sure they would probably be fine. If they didn't, then that's their stupidity and really not my problem," he said with a sigh, leaning forward so his elbows rested on his knees. He finally noticed how much distance had grown between the two of them as a new emotion swirled in Pilar's eyes: Fear.

"This money is for me — it's for you. It can be for anything you want. We could redecorate the bedroom like you've been wanting to do? Or we can take a vacation down to Puerto Rico to see your cousins?" He rattled off the list, bringing his voice down a few octaves, so it sounded smoother as he closed the gap between them and took Pilar's trembling hands into his own. "And maybe I'll use a nice little chunk of it for something special from Tiffany's? Like maybe for this finger right here?" Dane caressed her left-hand ring finger as he spoke, but she pulled away before he could continue.

"I can't believe you think I would want to do anything with that money, or that I would want anything — especially an engagement ring — bought with that money. It would be like literally having blood on my hands," Pilar said. "You're actually scaring me, Dane. If I didn't know better, I would think you set the fire yourself just to collect the goddamn insurance money."

The truth appeared in his eyes, but only for a second as he remembered staring down at the old mystic woman's gruesome corpse and deciding she would be cremated where she lay. His leg twitched just like it had when he pushed her face to the side and then stepped over her body, not flinching when his heel crunched the bones in her arthritis-warped hand. His knuckles clenched as they had when he rummaged through her belongings for the hell of it. His tongue tingled as he recalled the taste of death dancing against it when he stood too close to her rotting shell.

But, standing face-to-face with the woman he said he loved who had stumbled upon the truth, Dane swallowed those memories and kept a comforting, unassuming mask in place.

"Honey, you're getting hysterical, and you're talking crazy. You know I wouldn't do something like that," he said, trying and failing to retake her hand. "Let's just calm down, okay? How about we go out and get some dinner, and just forget this ugly conversation? We can go anywhere you want, my treat."

Pilar shook her head, blinking over and over before bringing her eyes back up to meet his gaze. She was smiling, but it was one of those small weak smiles people plastered on when they were fighting back tears.

"No, I... I'm pretty tired. I don't really feel like going out, plus I had a late lunch at the office," she said. "But you should go, really. Try and unwind from the day you've had and get some food. I'm just going to take a Xanax and go to bed, I think."

Dane hesitated, searching Pilar's eyes for any sign of deception or ulterior motive. But he found none. She was head-over-heels in love with him. They had no aggressions toward one another, and she basked in the life of luxury she earned from their partnership. Even if she were unnerved after the day's events and conversations, she would never leave him over something so trivial. He knew that for sure. Her last attempt at a smile and a growl from deep in his stomach sealed the deal for him, and Dane nodded his head.

"Alright, if you're sure, then I think I will go sit down and have some dinner somewhere," he said, kissing her cold cheek before grabbing his jacket and wallet from the kitchen floor. "I'll try and bring you back something. Get some rest."

CHAPTER 3

The second Dane stepped back outside his beacon of a condo building; a sharp gust of autumn's chilly air blew through him and sent his thin designer sport coat flapping in its path. He grumbled, folding one arm over the other as his eyes wandered back to the lobby with the thought to go grab a coat, or even to just stay in for the night.

The expression Pilar left him with, however, kept him in place. The defeat and uncertainty pooling in her brown orbs had been more striking than Dane had ever seen in their three years together. He knew there wasn't anything he could say to ease the tension. Shaking his head, he turned away from home and took his place in the sidewalk traffic. Focused on the path ahead of him, Dane took swift and hurried steps past at least five bustling restaurants. Spicy scents and warm steam wafted out of every rotating door, but no hunger-laced ideations came to mind. The only thoughts Dane could muster were of Pilar and a Rolodex of words he should have said but didn't.

"She knows me. She knows how much I love her," he thought, keeping the words under his tongue so as not to draw onlookers' stares.

"You could have explained yourself a little better, though, idiot. She thinks you burned down a building. She thinks you killed people. She looked afraid of you," he chastised himself, rolling the second layer of the statement — the truth — behind his eyes.

The mental film he was salivating over for hours, from finding Mrs. Castiglione's body to the moment he struck the match that lit those cracked Catholic knock-off candles, had left his personal theater. The memories were still there, but fuzzier than before, and Dane had disappeared from the scenes. He could still see someone: a man stepping over the woman's corpse, his foot landing on her hand and nudging her face, glancing through her belongings and spying the gas can, leaving her body forgotten there for hours before coming back with candles, matches, and a plan. But this time, that man wasn't Dane.

The leading man was dressed in Dane's perfectly pressed designer suits. He moved with Dane's decisive steps, always squared shoulders, and gliding gesticulations. His hair was the same shade of black and adorned with systematized spikes. He even wore Dane's many smiles down to the millisecond delays he took to pick the right one. Every other part of his face, however, was abstract. It was as if the remaining features had been scrambled and thrown back onto his face out of order, like a Picasso portrait gone wrong. Dane couldn't see who the man was in the images now, but he certainly didn't see himself.

Again he shook his head, pushing the thoughts out with vigor, and turned his gaze back to the road ahead. Shoulder after shoulder brushed against his own as tightly packed rows of people pushed past each other in both directions. Dane stiffened his posture, steadied his arms just a few inches from his sides, and took larger strides. The sounds of his Italian leather loafers scratching against the pavement and the weight of what he knew were hundred dollar bills packed against one another in his pocket pulled his spine a little straighter.

A glittery veil a few blocks ahead caught Dane's eye and with a few more steps, an extravagant jewelry store display came into view. A large, diamond encrusted ruby ring with a silver band sat in the center of the window. Every other trinket surrounding the ring paled in comparison, even the sparkling diamonds in which Dane could see his reflection.

The first time he and Pilar even discussed weddings or marriage was after her stepsister, Trinity, got engaged.

She was the polar opposite of Pilar: Tall, supermodel thin, short blonde hair angled around her jawline, and always wearing ivories and creams that disappeared against her white skin. She wasn't someone Dane would look at twice, but he had to admit she was a pretty woman. It wasn't any wonder she won the attention of a career stockbroker twice her age looking for a second trophy wife. Trinity seemed ready to fill the role when Dane met her at their engagement party as she alternated between showing off the three-and-a-half-carat princess cut diamond ring and gushing about plans to take leave from her interior design career.

"Well, they seem good together," Dane had said on the cab ride home, trying to make conversation with Pilar, who slumped against the window in exhaustion. "Plus, you've got to admit the ring is pretty impressive."

"Eh," Pilar scoffed, casting her eyes further out the window at the passing headlights. "I mean, it is beautiful and good God, it's massive. I'm sure it cost a fortune, even for that man. It's just not my style at all."

"Oh, no?" Dane asked as he pulled her legs into his lap, pressing his thumbs into what he knew were aching calves that had spent hours propped up in stilettos. "And what's your style, then?" Her eyes crossed, but then her lips twisted into a smirk as she questioned his intentions.

"I don't know, just thinking I may need to know what to look for ... some day," he said, shrugging and averting his eyes.

"Well, in that case," she said, sitting up a little in her seat and settling her legs deeper into Dane's lap. "I definitely don't want a diamond. Yeah, yeah they're beautiful and traditional or whatever, but I just don't like them enough to wear one every day. No, I would want a gemstone like an amethyst or maybe a big, bold ruby. I'd love to have a ring that looked like it came straight out of another time, but still sparkled like new. If that's even possible."

She chuckled at the end, shaky with insecurity. Looking at her face under the taxi's dull back seat light, he chose a simper that didn't quite reach his eyes as his next expression. He wanted her to feel safe and to let her guard down enough that she didn't feel that quiver of uncertainty about him or their future. He wanted her to feel like she was his, because she was — even if she didn't know it yet.

A year after that first exchange, talk of weddings and engagement became commonplace, and Dane was staring at the exact ring Pilar had described that night on the ride home. Every nerve in his legs fired with the unshakable urge to march inside and make it his — make it hers. He grabbed the handle to the store, but met resistance. Still, he tugged again and again, thinking if he tried with just a little more force, then the door would have to open. But the lock didn't budge.

Dane sighed, grumbling under his breath when he looked back at the ring in its perfect display. This time, there was a human hand reaching into the window from inside the store and pulling items away. Hope propelled Dane's heart into his throat.

Without a second thought, he hammered his knuckle against the glass until an elderly clerk poked her head through the other side. He became a mime, pointing over and over at the ring, then back at himself and even pulling out his wallet. After a few seconds, she seemed to understand which piece he wanted, grabbing the ring and holding it closer to the window. Dane nodded so quickly his neck vertebrae cracked beneath the skin, but groaned again when she pointed to the closed sign.

"We open up tomorrow at 9 a.m.!" She must have shouted the message, but it sounded like a whisper through the dense glass and iron bars. Dane twisted his face so disappointment and desperation dripped off of every crevice, and something in his eyes tugged the old woman's lips into a sympathetic frown. It was similar to the ones he received hours before from the scrawny firefighter. "I'll keep it locked up until 10! Come by before then, and it's yours!"

He mouthed thank you and clasped his hands together like a beggar during prayer, savoring the brighter smile and nod she gave in return before disappearing into the store with the ring.

As soon as he turned away, his usual smirk returned in tandem with his decisive steps. He would be millions of dollars richer by 9 a.m. and could pay for that ring in cold hard cash — a thought that sent even his thinnest hairs to their edge. He could almost see Pilar's face when he gave her the perfect ring and asked her to be his wife. The uncertainty plaguing her eyes tonight would be a ghost, and the word no would vanish from her tongue. Where the money came from wouldn't matter, and she wouldn't see any blood on her hands. She would only see the ring and him.

The fantasy was as vivid as reality in his mind and carried him several blocks forward until his stomach stopped him. It growled again, louder than it had back at the condo, and Dane realized he needed to find somewhere to eat before it got too late and he ran out of options. He stepped to the skirt of the sidewalk so as not to hold up the city's never-ending foot traffic and darted his eyes around, trying to get a better bearing on where he had landed.

As he stood under the subtle glow of a street lamp, a rich aroma filled his nostrils and stole his attention. It was savory and full of delectable spice, but had a tang of sweetness he could almost taste on his tongue. The scent drew a nearly forgotten memory from deep inside Dane's head: Sunday dinner at his Nonna's house. Loud and familiar Italian voices — his aunts, uncles, and parents, chitter-chattered in his ears and the most delicious robust marinara sauce filled his belly. He hadn't ever tasted or smelled anything like it since those younger days until now, standing on a New York City street in the opposite direction of Little Italy.

CHAPTER 4

D ane was never more certain he was lost than he was in that moment. Nothing around him seemed familiar, and there was no hope in retracing his steps. He couldn't bring himself to care about anything except the smell.

The titillating scent lingered and hypnotized his eyes open and up. Dane saw a glistening, ebony storefront of a restaurant. In gold embossed letters, *Café Vengeance,* shined against the dark exterior and, from what Dane could see through the petite and ivy-frame windows, the interior was elegant and reeked of wealth and exclusivity — and that mesmerizing sauce straight from his childhood.

He swung open the matching black and paneled doors, walking into the classic and ornate foyer where gliding, but distant piano notes greeted his ears. The walls were such a bright, sparkling white they seemed to have flicks of diamonds embedded in the paint, contrasting with the restaurant's dark exterior. Shimmering silver and crystal chandeliers hung from the ceiling. The way the lights reflected told Dane every piece was real, and each one must have cost a fortune. Deep and robust cherry wood floors welcomed his feet further into the establishment, and with each step he noticed another opulent fixture or piece of décor. Crystal and gold figurines sat in purposeful patterns on shelves all around the entry, the restaurant's name appeared once again, this time in crimson, over a wall and set of sliding doors he assumed led to the dining room. There was a tall host's stand in the corner of the room rich with baroque carvings and a row of encrusted red rubies across the center.

The gems, so similar to the one in the ring he committed to buying for Pilar, were spellbinding Dane as he stepped closer to the host's stand. His face reflected back in what had to be fifty stones, glazed in glistening red. He couldn't stop staring.

"Sir?" A profound, but almost melodious voice interrupted Dane's gaze. "Good evening, Sir?"

Dane ripped his eyes away from the rubies and set eyes on the host. A tall and almost sickly thin bald man stood straight faced behind the counter dressed in a traditional, rental-house worthy tuxedo. He must have been blond in a previous life, because Dane saw no trace of colored eyebrows, lashes, or facial hair. Dane cleared his throat and asked if a single table was available for dinner, and the host's face broke into a grin.

"Ah, yes of course. We would be honored to have you dine with us this evening. Come with me, Sir," he said as he slid the partition open to the dining room and beckoned for Dane to follow his lead.

The dining room was just as stunning and tasteful as the foyer. A handful of tables covered in crisp white linens and black lace overlays were spaced around the area, none too far or close together. Each one had a hand-blown red glass vase full of black rose bouquets. Gold inscriptions of *Café Vengeance* and lines written in another language, maybe Latin, decorated each of the four walls. The space was small — what a more polite person would call cozy — but its visual beauty made up for its lack of square footage.

"This is a gorgeous place — very elegant. Did you just open?" Dane asked, looking around like a child at the zoo while the host guided him to a table in the heart of the dining room.

"In a manner of speaking," the host answered. "We do our best to cater to a particular class of clientele. Sometimes we find ourselves in a bit of a purgatory waiting for the right opportunities to serve."

Dane nodded, his chest puffing out a few inches as he offered his understanding about wanting to keep *lower class riff-raff* out of more prosperous places. The host didn't agree, but continued to smile until all of his yellowing teeth were in sight.

"Have a seat, Mr. Roman, and open yourself up to all we have to offer. You will be served momentarily."

"Wait, I'm sorry," Dane called after him once he turned his back. "Did I give you my name? I don't recall giving my name."

The host didn't turn around to face his customer, just stood like a statue and stared back toward the foyer with his hands clasped behind his back.

"How could we not know you, Mr. Daniel Roman? Wealthy property owner and developer, investor, and casino operator — why, your reputation precedes you," he said. "Dare I say, you are a perfect example of that special clientele we aim for?"

Pride stoked coals deep in Dane's belly, spreading a warm blaze all the way up his chest, throat, and into his face. He struggled to keep his expression stoic, but the light in his eyes smoldered as he sucked a satiated breath through his teeth. His head dipped into a curt nod, and he muttered *yes of course, thank you,* as a signal for the host to carry about his business.

With that, the man disappeared out of the dining room and left Dane to truly take in his surroundings. His eyes landed a few feet ahead beyond the last of the tables where a raised platform filled the corner of the room with the makings of an orchestral quartet. A grand piano sat in the center with a large, antique silver candelabra ornamenting its lid and holding at least ten unlit candles. A violin, cello, and clarinet had been placed on surrounding stands, but no musicians were there to play them.

Quirking an eyebrow, Dane checked his watch. It was already 8:30 p.m., and the dinner rush around the city should have been in full swing, yet Dane sat alone in this lovely dining room with no music, even though he was sure he heard some when he entered.

"Odd," he muttered behind his lips, glancing at the tables again for any sign of recent diners — a dirty plate, ruffled tablecloth, or rogue napkin left on a chair. There was nothing. Every table and chair was immaculate as if never used. "Must be a hell of a bus boy working here."

An icy chill crept up his spine as he excused the peculiarities, almost forcing him to shake his head against his own thoughts. Jerking his neck from left to right, Dane focused on the table in front of him for the first time since sitting down. The black roses in the center vase resembled indulgent silk and sparkled with artificial dew in the chandeliers' glow, as did something closer to Dane's table setting. Looking down, a silver and black place card rested where his plate should have been. He picked it up and squinted to read the engraved, metallic caption: *Vindicta expectat dignis*

As his eyes scanned over the words, the lighting around him dimmed several shades. The candles atop the piano sparked one by one as a vivid, glowing spotlight basked over the instruments, now complete with four musicians.

All were men with the same lanky, almost skeletal stature of the host and wearing tuxedos just like his. He couldn't see their faces in the darkness. The musicians were playing a gloomy, mournful tune like something one would hear at a funeral — nothing like the airy melody Dane heard when he entered Café Vengeance.

"Good evening, Mr. Roman."

Dane jumped in his skin, which was prickling with a cool sweat, and yelled into his own throat. The host, or at least a man who looked identical to the host down to the hairless features, stood smirking just behind his left shoulder and adding distance between Dane's table and the quartet.

"Lovely to make your acquaintance, Mr. Roman," he said just above a whisper. "I'm honored to have you dining with us this evening."

"We met. I mean aren't... aren't you the host?" The waiter smiled a little wider, showing off dingy, almost brown teeth and closing his eyes while he shook his head no. Dane squinted back at him, trying to catch a glimpse behind his eyelids and recall what color the host's stare had been.

"I, Mr. Roman, will be serving you this … breathtaking evening," he responded, casting his still ambiguous eyes down to a silver name tag that read *Virgilio*. "I'm happy to guide you through your entire experience here at Café Vengeance. Can I get you a menu? Or perhaps you are interested in hearing about our evening's special dishes?"

Trapped in a state of perplexity, Dane stared at the server still trying to decipher if Virgilio was the same man who had seated him. Within his mind, Dane retraced his steps from pavement to dining room, and remembered what made him choose the café in the first place. As if on cue, the same hearty marinara spices tickled his senses and his mouth filled with saliva. The chill in his spine didn't feel so cold anymore.

"Virgilio, huh? You must be more Italian than me, so I bet you'll know your stuff. I'm not sure if it's one of the specials, but on my way inside I smelled the most amazing dish. I'm ashamed to say though, I'm just not sure what it was. Maybe you can help me figure it out," he said, waiting for Virgilio's nod of acknowledgment before continuing. "It smelled like marinara sauce, but a very specific kind. To be honest with you it smelled like the marinara sauce my grandmother made back in Italy when I was a child. So it was a sort of rustic, rich Italian marinara. I think she often made it with eggplant."

"Of course, Sir, I think I know precisely what dish you're meaning," Virgilio said. "One of our specials tonight is an authentic Eggplant Parmesan, and I believe the sauce is an old family recipe from the kitchen — all the way from Rome."

"That's where my grandparents lived. We visited all the time after my parents came over, so that probably is it," Dane replied, trying not to falter when the server's smile curved into something a little eerier. "What a coincidence. I'll have the Eggplant Parmesan special then. Oh, and could I actually get one to go before I leave as well?"

Virgilio chuckled and cast a hurried, almost unnoticeable glance toward the quartet before facing Dane again.

"I'm not sure what will still be available by the time you finish your meal here, Mr. Roman, but I will leave word with the kitchen to save an extra serving if they can."

Dane again scanned the still empty dining room, unsure how the kitchen could run out of anything at this rate, but resigned to thank the server before he disappeared from sight.

Piano keys clashing together drew Dane's attention to the quartet once again. They had left behind the funeral-appropriate song, and the notes gained volume as they played faster and with more vigor. Dane didn't recognize the music as anything close to classical. It was haunting and gratingly melodic, like something out of a carnival fun house. But the more he listened, the more he realized this tune was far too dark for any such setting.

Dane studied the men on stage. Even straining his eyes through the shadowy lighting, he saw they had lost any semblance to lively humans. The musicians looked thinner than moments ago, with their tuxedos barely clinging to bony bodies and their skin turning morose and waxy. The longer Dane stared and the faster they played, the sicker their faces appeared.

Dane's pulse quickened beneath his ribs, and his lungs shrunk with each breath he tried to take. He was repulsed the more he watched the musicians play, but he couldn't tear his eyes away.

CHAPTER 5

G *et out of here.*

Dane repeated the command in his mind at least fifty times as he sat paralyzed in thedining room chair, watching gaunt and emaciated men play music that nettled the back of hisbrain. The pianist's bony and elongated fingers flitted across the black and white keys at aninhuman pace. Dane tried to follow the furious rhythm in an effort to decipher anything aboutthis music, but even trying to keep up made his stomach churn and his head spin.

The cellist and violinist moved their bows at the same quickness, and it looked as if theywere seconds away from flinging their shoulders out of place or missing the instrument andslicing their own throats. Desperate for any reprieve from the musical motion sickness, Dane casthis focus to the clarinetist.

The man on the clarinet was perhaps the sickest looking of all as he struggled to push airinto the instrument. His eyes had no colored irises, but only shone white as they bulged andcontorted out of their sockets, red and wiry with popping blood vessels. Tears spilled from thelower lids and looked black against his yellowing and peeling skin. Still, he managed severallong and low notes that sounded more like groans of pain — his pain.

As Dane connected his own black eyes with those tortured and bloated orbs, themind-racing melody faded away. All he heard were those groans, louder and louder until theystruck him more as deep screams. His consciousness of sitting in the restaurant vanished intospectral darkness as Dane started to fall. At first it felt like falling in a dream, where the onlyimpact would be muscles jolting against one's mattress – but the rescuing tremor never came ashe continued to tumble away from reality.

It was a slow descent, matching the tempo of the clarinet's song, deeper and deeper intonothing. Like swirling in a drain at a snail's pace or tipping backwards at someone else's hand,Dane was lost to all his surroundings except for the chair secure beneath him. He wanted to yellfor help, but still didn't scream. He wasn't even sure he made a sound at all. He just fell and felland fell until the sluggish rotation stopped.

At some point in his plummet, Dane must have closed his eyes. After a few immobileseconds, his body and stomach stopped spinning and the screams in his throat died. Quivering eyelids fluttered open and revealed the clarinetist's swollen eyes just inches away and now fully opaque with a shadow of death.

But they weren't the clarinetist's eyes anymore — at least not entirely. His eyes had no color, and these had chestnut irises that struck a familiar chord in Dane's memory. They were too light to be his, and not round enough to be Pilar's.

Mrs. Castiglione.

As the whispered memory fell into Dane's ears, the eyes in front of him shriveled like dry and crumbling paper. They squished and sloshed as some invisible fist throttled every ounce of fluid out of the organs. Gags echoed from Dane's diaphragm as oozing green and yellow pus exploded into the darkness and landed at his feet. He watched it pool in a perfect circle around his loafers and shuddered a sigh of relief when none touched him.

Suddenly, the smothering darkness lifted, and Dane could finally see his surroundings. The hard surface he perceived beneath his chair was gone, and the floor was a raging river of the same septic pus throttled from the eyes. It was just like the chunky, foul smelling, and blood-tinged discharge coming out of Mrs. Castiglione's face a day earlier, and it was swallowing him whole.

The liquid scorched his nose as it clung to his shoes and ate away at the expensiveleather. It climbed his legs, soaking into the fabric of his pants and burning his skin as it workedits way into every pore.

Dane's throat was on fire, every muscle and vocal cord burning white hot betweenshrieks and retches. This had to be what drowning felt like. The grotesque sludge rose higher andhigher on his body. He was submerged, screeching in disgust every time a steaming, diseased chunk slithered over his chest, across his shoulders, and then crept up his neck. Pus dripped from his jawline and then bubbled to the very corners of his lips. He forced himself to stop screaming. If he even twitched, Dane knew the bloody and festering muck would seep into his mouth.

"Mr. Roman? Sir?"

Dane howled, waiting for the pus to pour down his throat, but felt nothing. In a moment, everything had disappeared. The dark cavern was gone. The raging rapids of decay vanished. He was warm, dry, and on solid ground, once again staring at the Café Vengeance place card.

"Apologies, sir, I seem to have interrupted a moment of ... profound thought," Virgilio said. "I wonder if I could interest you in a glass of wine while your meal is prepared?" The words were gibberish in Dane's ringing ears. He stared back at the waiter, who presented a bottle of merlot. "Sir? Would you like a drink?"

"What just happened?" Dane spoke finally, darting his gaze around the room. Everything looked just as it had before — immaculate, empty, and home to that haunting tune from the quartet. The only difference was that the lights were no longer sultry and dim, but so bright his eyes stung with tears. He tried again to connect with the musicians one-by-one, ending with the clarinetist, but none would return his looks. "I was... I fell and there was... have I just been sitting here this whole time?"

"I've been gone a matter of minutes since taking your order, Mr. Roman," Virgilio responded. There was no color or depth in the waiter's eyes, just transparent windows to nothing but stony obscurity. There was no jovial smile creasing the lids or glimmer of humanity bouncing off his irises. Any memories of their previous anecdotes or musings had disappeared, for now he addressed Dane as a stranger. Virgilio no longer looked human. "You did appear rather static. I thought perhaps you had fallen asleep, or at the least were drowning in your own curiosities."

Drowning.

He had been drowning in putrid human filth no more than five minutes prior — death's waste sucking away his skin and forcing waves into his mouth. Wafts of rotting flesh filled his nostrils with each breath.

"Wine, sir?"

Dane gagged, struggling to push down gallons of vomit, and shook his head. He opened his mouth just long enough to ask for water instead, which appeased Virgilio, who walked away to fetch some.

"Oh my God," Dane whispered once he was alone, dipping his clammy forehead into his

hands. "What the hell is going on with me? Did I just hallucinate?"

Before Dane could answer his own question, the waiter returned with a glass of tepid water. In one swift motion, he placed the glass on the table and turned on his heel, saying he would be right back with Dane's eggplant dinner. The idea of eating, especially something so heavy, churned his stomach. But even as his diaphragm threatened revolt, the sauce's familiar aroma won a battle with his senses. If anything could make him forget what he saw, tasted, and smelled in that waking nightmare, it would be his grandmother's sauce.

So he sat up straight, blew out a breath that felt more like a sob, and reached for his water. The weighty glass cooled his quivering lips on contact, but nothing came to quench his thirst. Dane pulled the glass back, cocking his head to the right as he inspected it. Water swirled and sloshed inside the crystal, and condensation pooled around his fingertips. Again, he attempted to take a sip, but his mouth remained dry. Dane replaced the glass on the table, crossing his arms and tipping back in his chair a few inches. His instinct was to summon Virgilio, but to say what?

"I can't figure out how to get the water from the glass into my mouth. Be a good chap for me and fix it?" It sounded even more ridiculous in his head than asking about the pus flood.

His mind must have been playing tricks on him. From the hallucinations to the inability to drink a glass of water, no other explanation made sense. Maybe he was fatigued into a mild psychosis, or perhaps he had inhaled too much smoke and chemicals at the building fire. Maybe this place had fast-acting, toxic mold blossoming beneath those pure white walls.

A stretched, whining violin note interrupted Dane's considerations. He craned his neck, showing the incredulous look on his face to the band. There's no way they thought this actually sounded pleasant, did they?

The violinist cocked his head and cackled — loud and howling like a wild banshee. He never looked away as he laughed, but kept his stare transfixed on Dane, as if he had heard the rhetorical question. The piano music became nothing more than clashing against the keys that mirrored the maniacal laughter, and seconds later, the other musicians followed suit. Dane clasped his hands over his ears, but the commotion only got louder and more piercing.

"Stop! Oh God, please stop! I'm begging you, please, you're going to burst my eardrums," Dane pleaded to no avail, scrunching his eyes shut as if he could hear through them as well. He didn't realize he was crying until he tasted salt on his lips. "Please!"

He opened his eyes, hoping something in the desperate weeps might convince them. But no musician or stage was in front of him — nothing was. Dane wasn't sitting anymore either; in fact, his chair had vanished along with everything else. The screeching music was still coming from somewhere and surrounding him. It was as if he was trapped in one of those Reiki meditation sessions Pilar was always begging him to join.

Another ear-splitting cackle echoed in the space, and Dane looked up to see the quartet hovering above him. He stood in some sort of hollow trench with a path that seemed to go on for miles behind him. Before fear could take hold, Dane's hope swelled when a flicker of light sparked in the distance. There might be a way out.

Dane turned on his heel and let his reflexes take over. He pumped his knees as hard and fast as he could, slamming his feet into the dingy ground to try and get more power behind each step. The screaming siren song above him got louder, and the men played quicker, weaving his every move into their rhythm, but Dane didn't stop. His heart thundered against his chest and his lungs seared, but he ignored all the pain as the light got brighter with every stride.

"Can't be long now," he huffed, raising his knee even closer to his chest, only to have it pulled down into the trench. Something caught his ankle with so much force Dane was sure that his leg joints were dislocated. Still, he tried to keep running even as his other leg met the same resistance. The weight was overwhelming, like someone had poured concrete into an elliptical machine's gears.

"No!..." he wailed, unable to hold in his cries as the taunting laughter and music became overwhelming. Hot, sticky blood trickled out of his ears and coated his jawline as he collapsed in place. "God, no why?"

"You can never leave us."

An eerie choir whispered the answer from behind him, and Dane's previously racing heart stopped mid-beat. A thousand eyes stabbed into the back of his head, sending his hairs into hard quills and turning his skin cold with terror.

"You will never leave us," the voices said again. Dane locked every muscle, fighting the urge to turn around and meet his obstacles, but it didn't work. His head moved as if independent from his body, turning over his shoulder.

Clinging to his left leg were mangled and interwoven bones from at least ten human skeletons. The bones bent into a sort of boulder behind him, but what should have been bare skulls on the end were coated in rotting flesh and features he recognized. Dark brown, almost black, eyes that matched his bore into him and familiar voices repeated that he could never leave them behind. His grandmother's wrinkled skin hung in shreds on her skull and her once flowing gray hair had decomposed into random strands that looked glued in place. A maggot-infested man's face that mirrored his own mouthed the word *'son'* through scaly, rotting lips. His mother, whose once rosy red lips and beautiful high cheekbones were now skeletal spurs with bloody backsplash, grinned and croaked his full name: *Daniel*.

He wanted to feel something other than crushing fear and disgust — sorrow, grief, or warped joy at seeing his family again. But no emotion spilled or even trickled through the floodgates of Dane's soul, and those familiar corpses said nothing else. He only saw a pile of rancid meat and bones.

"You can't leave us behind."

The words sounded in his right ear, buzzing like an insect had flown in and gotten trapped against his eardrum.

Gulping back another wave of terror, Dane twisted his head to the other side and prepared for more dead relatives.

Again, he saw a mass of skin and bones, but these weren't quite as wasted. Warm flesh and bloody tissue still clung to the bodies. The skin he could see had its top layer burnt off to reveal a raw, spongy pink surface. Others were crusted in bubbling black ash. The eyes staring at him were crimson with blood and burns, and smoke poured from at least fifty mouths as they screamed anguish in his face.

"You will never leave us," they hissed in unison. "*Vindicta expectat dignis.*"

Dane stared at the monster before him in disbelief, unable to find any words to say back to them. The more he stared, silent and stupefied, the tighter they clung to his ankle. Heat from the fatal blaze was still trapped in their hands and leached into his skin. He attempted to pull his leg free as his own flesh cooked in their grip, but their hands pressed harder and scaled further up his limb.

As he struggled, a face from deep within the sphere pushed forward, spattering blood and embers all over him as it emerged in the front and center of the boulder. It was a woman whose deep wrinkles were caked with shattered glass and steaming burn blisters. Billowing streams of smoke replaced strands of hair, and her face was disfigured — nose pushed back through her skull and mouth scorched into nothing but a bleeding crater. Her light brown eyes were shriveled in their sockets, just like when he last saw them lifeless on a cold apartment floor. But now they were white hot knives in his soul.

"Mr. Roman? Your dinner is served."

CHAPTER 6

D ane had not one second to collect himself — to feel the smooth leather chair against his thighs or hear the now placid orchestral music cooing in his ears but still swinging too quickly to be comfortable. A warm, bubbling mound of chunky red sauce on a gold-trimmed plate was thrust in front of him.

"Yes, here we are, sir," Virgilio said, the announcement like lyrics against the haunting melody. "Your Eggplant Parmesan special complete with a rustic *marinara inferno.*" Virgilio fluttered his fingers in the air and thickened his accent with the last two words. Dane didn't speak or acknowledge him. He just stared into the dish, trying to decipher one layer of tomato sauce from the layers of smoldering flesh that had swallowed his ankle moments ago.

"I will warn you, it will be just a tad spicy," Virgilio added in an undertone, leaning close enough to Dane's ear that his hot breath bristled the back of his neck. "Of course, I'm sure you could infer that based on the *inferno* and since this seems to be a familiar recipe from your past. Enjoy, Mr. Roman."

He snapped his wrist forward, presenting Dane with a gold-plated fork and then vanishing behind his back. His brain replayed images of bone shards smashed into globs of blotchy lifeless bodies, but the amalgam of aromatic spices and herbs working its way into his nostrils acted like an eraser — overpowering one morsel of decay at a time.

A drip of drool trickled from the corner of his mouth, and Dane could no longer resist the food in front of him. He snatched the fork and stabbed into the middle of the dish, flinching when a drop of marinara squirted onto his cheek. He licked it away with the tip of his tongue, a sudden ravenous monster roaring beneath his ribcage. Ripping off a hefty chunk of eggplant, he swirled the bite a few times in the sauce before shoveling it into his mouth. Without stopping to chew, Dane scooped in another and another, anxious for the seasoning to light up his senses. Once he stuffed his face to capacity, he finally sunk his teeth into the dish's core.

Whatever was in his mouth wasn't eggplant. The firm outer coating split on impact and a gritty, gelatinous sludge gushed out. Dane's jaw collapsed into his neck, and out poured viscous, iron-heavy blood peppered with a scream.

"Everything to your standard, Mr. Roman?" Virgilio's question exploded into the dining room like an animalistic snarl, echoing from one ear to the other and sending a biting chill down Dane's back. "Anything not quite up to snuff?"

With a long and yellowing fingernail, Virgilio caressed the crux of Dane's jaw and neck, forcing another surge of blood down his face.

"What the hell is this?!" Dane screeched, his vocal cords scraping against his throat.

"Who are you people?"

Virgilio laughed, and the floor seemed to rumble in time with his chest. Every member of the quartet joined in his laughter, harmonizing together like an ethereal chorus. Music that had faded to background noise revved up again into an overpowering presence — sound bathing every corner of the dining room space. The tune was ominous and continuous as it amplified with every swing of the horrid melody and sharp note bouncing off the piano keys. It drowned an already horrified Dane into pure panic, blood still dripping from his teeth and slipping down his gullet.

Virgilio's thunderous laughter clapped again from behind Dane while an almost identical form appeared in front of his eyes. It was as if Virgilio the waiter had split in two, becoming less human with each iteration. As he continued to guffaw, his face disintegrated into something more gaunt and pale until waxy jaundiced skin was melting off the bone. A gag full of bloody vomit ruptured from Dane's mouth and onto the floor.

The candles on stage ignited for the second time, now with rouge flames that cast a demonic glow across members of the quartet. Every jawline burned red and their eyes melted out of the sockets, first into inky black orbs and then down their faces like tears. Their laughter grew louder and more maniacal as each musician played faster and faster — their flesh turning to slime and dissolving just like Virgilio's had until only skeletons remained.

"Mr. Roman," Virgilio said, a sinister joy overtaking his voice. "I would ask how else I could serve you, but you see I already know." He disappeared and reappeared behind Dane's chair. "This, Mr. Daniel Anthony Romano, is Café Vengeance, where you always are served exactly what you deserve. You've made a life order of gluttony and excess from cruelty, thieving, deceit, manipulation, and now the darkest of Hell's sins — fraud and murder. It's time to pay your bill."

Tears mixed with drying blood on Dane's cheeks, but he refused to accept the words. Garnering all his strength, Dane tried to jump from his seat and bolt to the door, but the act was impossible. Whatever demonic force was ruling over Café Vengeance kept him bound to that chair.

"Are... are you going to kill me?" Dane asked, the question catching on a lump in his throat while his eyes desperately searched for some escape path. He cringed when all the surrounding skeletons broke into another chorus of mirth that sounded more like scraping screams in his ears.

"For such a smart man you think quite small, Daniel," Virgilio said, suddenly re-materializing at the front of the room. Dane's chair squawked against the floor as it rotated in the same direction — no movement from Dane required. "Death is far from the end of man's journey. There's no need for death to bring final judgment. No, for you it's only just begun."

Virgilio pressed his index finger bone to the tip of his thumb over one of the candles, snuffing it out into darkness.

"So I'm dead? What happened? Did I die in the fire?" Dane rattled off the inquiries like they were accusations, his still quivering voice gaining volume by the second. "Was any of tonight real — at home with Pilar or the jewelry shop? Did I... I don't know, did I stroke out waiting for dinner? Or did you kill me with a rogue bus outside like some freak accident, destiny bullshit?"

Silence draped over the restaurant. The musicians stopped playing their troubling tunes, and all their laughter ceased. Virgilio's neck bones crackled as he twisted his head all the way to the left and tensed, like a snake about to attack, staring at Dane. The waxy white pseudo eyeballs in his skull boiled into a pool of black in which Dane could see his own reflection. If lips still lived on his face, their corners would have pointed to the floor in a scowl.

"You fool! Everything that has happened to you, Mr. Roman, has been by your own hands. The same hands that counted filthy money and tossed your family name aside instead of caring for loving parents on their deathbeds," he said, gravelly poison dripping off each syllable. Reaching out his arm, tuxedo sleeve falling off the bones, Virgilio clenched his skeletal fingers across Dane's fleshy trembling ones.

"Those same hands that recoiled from showing any kindness or dignity to an old woman who died alone. The same hands that tampered with the dead, destroyed what another held sacred, and lit the first flame of loss and despair in countless lives. These hands have committed arson, murder, despicable fraud, and held treasonous puppet strings for those you claim to love and those who trusted you. Those whom you have betrayed in the worst of ways. These hands, and nothing else, have sealed your fate this evening."

Fury raged in Dane's core, and unspoken words of indignation occupied his internal dialogue. No one had ever dared speak to him with such malice and disrespect. This was not his story. This was not the story of a formidable, crafty hero. Dane Roman was great. He was the child of hard-working immigrants who died early, leaving him to make his own way and name in the world, which he did. He was tactical, resourceful, and a natural businessman who had to claw his way into opportunities others had from birth. He was the hero of his story.

Sometimes he may have acted a little less than saint-like to make necessary moves — lied a little, cheated here and there, took advantage of a prospect — but Dane Roman had earned more respect than this. He fought for it with every breath he took, and he wouldn't accept less.

"I worked for everything I've ever had! Show me one man who never lies or cheats or even steals to get what he wants – what he *fucking deserves*. You can't!" he raged, staring daggers into the black emptiness that had overtaken Virgilio's eyes. "I deserve everything I have! I knew I deserved to live a life of means, and I'll be damned if I didn't make one for myself!"

Virgilio's mandible grinded against his maxilla, revealing every one of his fully rotted teeth as he sneered at Dane's claims.

"*Damned* indeed," he whispered, snapping his fingers over the same candle he extinguished moments ago. The flame sparked once again, and everything else faded to black.

CHAPTER 7

D ane shut his eyes and clenched every muscle and tendon in his body in preparation for fire, brimstone, and demons whipping his bare back. Like a fetus still in utero, he curled into his own form for moments, hours, maybe even days, waiting for impact in the darkness. But he felt nothing — not a gasp of wind or spark of heat. He was entrenched in nothing.

"D...Dane?"

The breathy call was softer than a whisper, but clattered like church bells within Dane's state of sensory deprivation. His frontal lobe kicked into overdrive, pleading with his body not to react and become susceptible to pain and punishment. Again, someone muttered his name. The voice was gentle, but scared and shaking like a child lost in the woods. There was too much depth and knowing to be the calls of a child, however. Whomever this was knew Dane and knew he would answer.

"Dane? Dane, please, I need help."

His eyelids unsealed, springing open as if someone had pulled a lever. His heart warmed even as he sat abandoned in this desolate wasteland. He knew that voice just as well as its speaker knew him.

"Pilar?"

And there she was. Standing not two feet away from him, hunched over with her arms crossed over her stomach. She was shivering and when Dane finally acknowledged her presence, a stray tear trickled from her eye.

"Oh my God, Dane, where are we? What is this place?" The relief that had washed over her wavered as she looked from left to right. Dane followed her gaze, and the same quiet horror simmered in his stomach.

Rich, suffocating blackness stretched to infinity all around them. This was an otherworldly darkness no sunlight or otherwise could penetrate. Dane was still sitting in the leather-upholstered chair from Café Vengeance, while his now bare feet sunk into layers of sand so rough it scratched and blistered his skin. Looking up, desperate for some sliver of reprieve, Dane could have cried or even prayed. But he did neither. Above him, there were only more layers of crushing abyss and an icy rain pouring into his very core.

"Dane, I'm scared," Pilar said, regaining his attention. "How did we get here? Where even is here?"

"I don't know. Oh God, Pilar, I don't know where we are," he said, wrestling his way forward in the chair while the sand sliced deeper wounds into his feet with every move. "Are you okay? Did you follow me to the restaurant? Tell me they didn't hurt you!" The rain turned to sharp sleet and plagued his skin with thousands of tiny paper cuts as he writhed, and his cries grew from fervent to hysterical once he realized he was still bound to the chair.

"What are you talking about? Who is 'they'?" Pilar stood a little straighter as she asked the question. She, unlike Dane, was wearing shoes, and her covered feet seemed to stand on solid ground instead of cutting quicksand.

"The skeletons," Dane answered, struggling to catch his breath in the downpour. "The skeleton people in the restaurant captured me. I don't know if they're like, fucking demons, or really skeletons or... they could be psychos wearing costumes. I just don't know, but they must have drugged my food or something. I saw the worst things. They're torturing me."

"You torture yourself."

Dane couldn't breathe. The retort from somewhere deep in the darkness wrapped around his throat like a noose. Virgilio was watching him, but neither the man nor the skeleton stood anywhere in sight.

Shuddering, Dane looked back to Pilar, who was watching him with nothing short of bewilderment behind her eyes. He didn't need to ask. She hadn't heard any voice except his.

"Her only crime is enabling your sins with her own ignorance," Virgilio said, his explanation dancing on the glacial rain. *"She shares none of your pain and none of your punishment — only wallows in the despair you've created on Earth."*

Tears pooled in the corner of Dane's eyes but froze before they could flow down his cheeks, collecting like slush at his waterline. Pilar stood in his gaze, not weighed down by the shackles of misdeeds and whatever evil entity tied him to that godforsaken dining chair. She was tall on her feet with her back straight and shoulders out, while her disheveled curls fell into her face. Even as terror brushed every crevice, Dane found himself admiring her beauty and remembering every time he had painted a smile across her full, ruby red lips.

He had seen this face, touched her skin, and kissed her every day for years. He never hurt her, at least not on purpose, and couldn't live without her. When he thought of love, he only thought of Pilar.

"Why is she here?" Dane asked the question in silence, ignoring Pilar's continued peppering of frantic queries. "What are you doing to her?"

Everything stopped. The rain vanished. The sand no longer stung his feet. Pilar froze – tongue-tied and immobile as Virgilio appeared once again, standing between the two lovers. His tuxedo was gone, and he stood as a skeleton whose only covering was sporadic patches of gruesome decay.

"You brought her here, Mr. Roman. You tied her to your soul and seduced her into a life built on lies of transparency and love. You — "

"I do love her!" Dane bellowed, fighting against the chair's bonds once again. "You're wrong. It's not a lie. You got me, okay? I never loved or liked or gave a damn about anyone out there. They were all just pawns or means to an end. But not Pilar. She's the only one who has ever been different. I love Pilar. I swear, I love her."

Dane's defense devolved into impassioned blubbering while memories of his and Pilar's love affair flooded his thoughts. His heart strained as he openly sobbed for the first time since childhood, wails morphing into screams as layers of frozen tears forced his eyes to remain open.

"Then set her free," Virgilio said. "Tell her the truth, and you can untether her soul from your own and wash all secondhand blood and ash from her hands before it's too late."

"Too late? No, you're not going to hurt her, are you? Are you going to kill her, too? No please," Dane said, still cycling through mania. "Please don't kill her. She can't die. I need her."

"She lives, Mr. Roman, as do you," Virgilio said, exasperation seeping into his speech. "I told you that death is only a small step in man's journey, and you have yet to take that step — as has your beloved."

Dane's breath hitched in his throat, and his face flushed with heat strong enough to melt some of the ice encrusting his eyelids. Raising his head for the first time in what felt like eons, he gazed into Virgilio's empty sockets, searching for some grain of truth.

"Do...do you really mean that? I'm still alive?" Dane stuttered through the questions, chest swelling with a strange tingling sensation when Virgilio's neck bones crunched up and down in confirmation. "And Pilar is still alive, too? She's safe?"

"She is, but that reality is yours to protect," Virgilio answered. "You must confess your treachery to her and reveal the darkest truth you carry, or I fear you will condemn her to a fate worse than death."

"The fire?" Dane asked, already knowing the answer. In his mind, he re-lived their exchange from earlier that evening, which seemed like several lifetimes ago. She judged his coldness and cruelty and suspected him of foul play. Dane could still see her fill with disgust as she listened to him and rejected his idea of a wedding ring from the newfound riches.

"It would be like literally having blood on my hands. You're actually scaring me."

Those were among the last words she had spoken to him on Earth, but Dane truly heard them for the first time in shadowy damnation. She guessed the truth right to his face, but whatever was swirling in her eyes stopped her from believing it. There was uncertainty, fear, dejection, and crippled hope, which Dane neglected to notice before he walked out of their home.

"Her love for you and the image you created for your life together have shielded her from the ugliest truths. She has believed in you, but that is no longer enough," Virgilio said, interrupting Dane's introspection. "Only you can free her. And if you're going to do it, then you must do it now."

Dane cried out as the heavy sleet resumed above him and thousands of tiny glass splinters impaled his feet, punctuating Virgilio's departure. The bleak beach in the pit of Hell reanimated in one fell swoop, and Pilar was awake and standing before Dane once again.

"What is it? Baby, are you okay? Are you hurt?" Pilar tried to come toward him when he yelped in pain, but her steps were in vain. They stood on different grounds.

"Please tell me what's happening," she said, drawing her feet back together and knitting her sculpted brow in confusion. Her lower lip quivered for a split second and tempted Dane to cry again. "Dane? I love you, please, tell me what's happening to us."

"I love you too," he said, casting his eyes to the sand. "Nothing is happening to you, Pilar. It's happening to me, and I'm sorry you're dragged into it."

Dane paused, taking a shaky breath as his mind raced for any other solution to save Pilar without exposing his deeds and dropping his mask. No perfectly calculated smile or papier mâché poker face could save him from her judgment.

Grimy, bony knuckles tickled the back of Dane's neck while he wallowed in hesitation. Dane stiffened, unsure if the presence lurking behind him was true or trapped inside his own mind, until Virgilio's putrid breath once again steamed against his ear.

"A fate worse than death."

Dane gulped, pushing more air down into his chest and forcing himself to sit up a little taller and face the woman he loved.

"I hate that I have to tell you this, but it's the truth. You know how earlier at the condo you said if you didn't know any better, you'd think I set the apartment on fire on purpose?" He lingered just long enough for her to nod. "Well, I did it. I started the fire to get rid of the building and cash in the insurance policy."

Pilar's gasp was sharp enough to slit Dane's throat, and for a moment, he thought it had. Cold despair penetrated his skin, deeper than the frozen rain could reach, and all the surrounding darkness cloaked his shoulders. The division between him and his partner had never been clearer as he sat soaked, trapped, and hunched under a shroud made of evil and she stood upright on solid ground.

"No," she said, desperation thick in the plea. Her eyes were wide and swimming with the same cocktail of emotions he remembered, but this time they welled up as tears and spilled down her cheeks. "No, Dane, how could you do that? You couldn't do that."

"I did it," he snapped, facing the sandy ground again. "I got the idea yesterday after I ... found something, and I realized how easy it would be and how much it would pay off. So I bought a bunch of candles, and I lit them in a unit I knew had several already and improperly stored gasoline in it. I set the fire on purpose with every intention of it burning the building to the ground."

"Inside a unit? Was it empty or did you knowingly burn tenants alive? Did you frame someone? Oh my God," Pilar gasped for full breaths. It was a simple answer, but Dane twirled the technicalities in his head. At least in that apartment, no one would be burning alive.

"Answer my question!" Pilar shouted him out of his thoughts, fists forming at her sides. "And tell me the truth! I deserve to know just how much of a monster you are."

Dane's heart sank, and one crumb of resentment settled on his tongue.

"I'm not a monster. I was never a monster to you. I love you, and I've done everything for you," he said, attempting to lock his eyes with hers even as they blazed with fury. "Have I done some bad things? Yes. But I never did them to you. If anything, I did them so I could do more good things for you. I love you, Pilar, so much and — "

"You're insane! Do you hear yourself? You burned down a building because you loved me?" She raged rhetorical questions at him, taking tiny steps backward. "I'm supposed to ignore the fact that you burned a full apartment building down to commit insurance fraud and murdered people because why? Because you didn't light me on fire or kill me? Because you were going to buy me something pretty with the blood money? You're a psychopath!"

"I'm sorry, okay? I'm sorry that you're so hurt. But I'm trying to be honest, and I really never did try to hurt you. I've done everything I can to make you happy and to make you mine and me yours, and I would never do anything like that to you."

"You already have, Dane," she said, cold and unforgiving. Frantic yells and squeals were now a thing of the past. Her eyes went still and her lips curled over her teeth. "You hurt me. You might as well have locked me in that apartment and lit me on fire, too. Now, answer my question. Did you try to frame someone for this?"

Dane's stomach lurched, and he was certain he would vomit if he tried to tell her no. The unfamiliar sensation terrified him almost more than his disturbing surroundings. His pulse pounded in his ears, sweat tickled his hairline, and his gut gurgled with such ferocity he thought it could never settle.

"Not exactly," he breathed out, wincing when Pilar yelled Spanish obscenities at his response. "Okay, okay yes. Basically yes, that's what I did. I went into one of the apartments yesterday to check on a complaint, and the tenant was dead in there already. She was an old woman, real superstitious and always lighting candles for saints and burning plants — I don't know, mystic shit."

Dane held up his hand, forcing Pilar's continued silence as he caught his breath to spew the rest of the story.

"She must have just had a stroke or something and been dead for a few days, and I found her candles and the old gas can, so I set it up with fresh gas and more kindling and started the fire in her apartment. She had a reputation of being really irresponsible with that shit, so I knew it would be easy for people to assume she started the thing and just died in it," he explained. "And I retroactively changed the leases to include a clause that made it against the rules to burn candles and forged her signature, so there would be no loose ends. That's it, that's everything."

Pilar wasn't looking at him anymore. She was looking through him, shaking her head, and pressing her tongue against her cheek. Dane opened and closed his mouth several times, trying to come up with some line of consolation or bargained promise that would gain him at least some conditional forgiveness. But nothing came to mind. He couldn't save himself from her.

"You disgust me," she said finally. "I never want to see you again. Go to Hell." Forcing her neck up to look back at him, Pilar's mouth twisted into a tear-soaked sneer as she cursed Dane one last time. And in the blink of an eye, Pilar ceased to exist.

CHAPTER 8

D ane's face deflated, tears rushing from his eyes, only to once again freeze against pallid cheeks. He opened his mouth, microscopic ice crystals dropping onto his tongue as wordless cries escaped. He didn't try to stand or thrash in his chair. Even if his bonds had been broken, every limb on his body felt too heavy to lift. Maybe this was heartbreak. Maybe this was death.

"Mr. Roman, I must admit I didn't think you had it in you," Virgilio said as he appeared in Pilar's place. "Well done."

"Where is she? Where did you take her?" Dane swallowed his emotion, trying to demand a straight answer. Virgilio held his skeletal hand up, just as Dane had done moments ago.

"She is safe on Earth, free to live the rest of her life in peace unless or until her own actions disrupt that," he answered, stepping closer. "Her memory of this will look very different. It will be much more realistic to the mortal mind, but the impact is the same. She is free of you. The honesty, which tastes like venom on your lips, was the elixir that saved her soul."

Dane smiled for the first time since sitting down at Café Vengeance. Cries ceased, and the ice drifts staining his face stopped growing.

"So Pilar is alive and you won't hurt her?" Virgilio nodded. "Am I still alive too? Even after all that?"

"Yes, Mr. Roman," he said. "You won't face death tonight."

Dane's cautious, hopeful smile grew into a grin — perhaps the first one of his life he hadn't constructed from social cues and mirroring others. Leaning back in his chair, Dane let out a single bark of laughter and peeled frozen tears from his skin.

"Oh, I can't believe it," he said, shoulders straightening as invisible weights crashed onto the supernatural beach. "I did it. It's over. Oh, thank God, this has been a nightmare."

"Ah-ah-ah," Virgilio interrupted, wagging his finger bones in Dane's face. "Don't misunderstand, Mr. Roman. I told you death was inconsequential. If this is your nightmare, as you call it, nothing about it is over. And I hate to tell you this, but God certainly isn't on your side."

Dane shut his eyes as a refrain of Virgilio's sickening laughter clattered against his exposed ribcage, filling the atmosphere around them. Dane heard his own voice shouting 'no' as if he were in a vacuum, and every part of his body disjointed from the other. Skin peeled back and bared his own bones while they dislocated from their proper sockets. Blood ran like rivers from his shoulders, his waist, each knee as it twisted away from his thighs, and from his neck as it crunched backward — forcing his own blood into his mouth.

Screams weren't enough to describe the tortured, animalistic bellows coming from his lips. His chest split in two as he tumbled mid-air, not looking at what surrounded his mutilated body, but unseen claws peeled his eyelids from his own face, so he had to watch every inch of the so called nightmare below. Writhing bodies burned in sky-high piles on the ground while thousands of skeletal demons like Virgilio poured white-hot coals on top to brighten the flames. Waves crashed onto ash and corpse-covered shores as seas of darkness raged like monsoons. Even with the wild stormy surfs, no fetid water reached countless trenches where tattered bodies marched through lava as monstrous centaurs threw spears at their backs.

Sour fumes of anguish reached Dane as he turned his wounded face toward the sky to try and escape. As he did, a murder of crows flew past him in a smear of black, but then circled back to his body as it barreled through the channel between Hell and Earth. Once they approached, Dane realized they weren't crows at all.

They were winged monsters with a bird's beak, a rattlesnake's tail, human skin that had been painted in inky black grease and smeared with crimson blood, and oblong ambiguous heads made of translucent glass. Dane saw his own mangled, screeching reflection in each creature encircling him. Cawing in an abject tone, two of the monsters swarmed at his chest cavity. Their talons stabbed into his remaining flesh, ripping his heart from its chamber and shredding his lungs to pieces. Two more took turns teasing closer to his face until they used their beaks to pluck out eyes.

Blood, sweat, waste, and pus all from inside his own body covered what was left of Dane's outer shell. Pieces of his brain hung where his ears once lived, but somehow he could still hear. Among the shouts of pain in the gutters below, he heard echoed chants of *Ptolomaea* and *vindicta expectat dignis.*

"This is death," Dane thought. "Virgilio lied. I'm dying." He stopped fighting, screaming, and praying for release. Dane succumbed to his myriad of torture, trying desperately to thrust any semblance of life or consciousness from his being.

Still, he remained awake even as a corrupted mass of bloody tissue and bone, much like the ones that held his parents and victims in another circle of Hell. He had nothing left, and yet he continued to exist in agony as if this suffering would never end.

Until it ended.

Everything was still in the sudden conclusion. Pain dissipated, fear evaporated, and the only noise was pleasant orchestra music and the hum of quiet conversation. Coming back to full awareness, Dane realized he was under the temperate glow of sparkling chandeliers in Café Vengeance's dining room.

Golden etchings still adorned the pristine walls, the sullen group of musicians still played their respective instruments, and red vases full of black silk roses remained as table decoration. Those tables, however, were full.

Wealthy New Yorkers wearing luxury suits and dresses sat circled around several of the restaurant's tables as they chatted, laughed, drank wine, and dined on rustic Italian meals. No gushing blood filled their cheeks and no brain matter dribbled down quivering chins. Dane scanned the smiling humans around the room, stopping when he landed on a familiar and fully intact face.

His body sat at the same table from which he had vanished, legs crossed over one another as he nursed a tiny mug of espresso. A portly man with a full brunette beard and mustache Dane recognized as his American Dream Insurance agent was seated opposite to him. He pointed out passages on a document, while Dane's body nodded along and wore a soothing smile across its lips.

The exchange continued for about five more minutes before the agent pushed an envelope toward Dane's body, shook his hand, and left the restaurant. Dane watched himself shed the silhouette of a smile and scrunch his eyebrows as he opened the envelope and pulled out a check laden with zeroes.

"Curious, isn't it?" Virgilio's slithering voice entered Dane's cognizance. He stood mere feet away from Dane's body at the table, that leathery, sickly skin and cheap tuxedo from earlier covering his skeleton once again. "How could a man be in two places at once?"

"You said I was still alive before," Dane answered, not looking away from his reflected form in the dining room, afraid it may disappear if he gave it the chance. "Maybe this was a crazy dream, or a premonition to warn me about my behaviors and the consequences. Or I suppose it could have been real, like a spiritual war to test me and my conscience."

Dane was reasoning with his own mind as much as he was with Virgilio, keeping his stare centered as the quartet transitioned into a song with a livelier tempo.

"A test, you think?" Virgilio asked, sucking in a sharp breath of air.

"Sure, a test. There are so many in the Bible — like Daniel in the lion's den," Dane explained. "They threatened him with death and torture, but he stayed steadfast and strong. God judged him for that, and he was saved. He became a hero."

Dane paused, shifting his vision to Virgilio's figure for an instance before looking back at his own. Virgilio's exposed ribs vibrated beneath his suit as he wove a chuckle in with prodding Dane to continue.

"I proved I could be honest and seek mercy," he said. "I showed how much I loved Pilar and told the truth so we could be together again. I mean, I saved her life and her soul, according to you. So now I must have a second chance, right? A second chance to live a good life and delay death?"

Virgilio's once clandestine laughter amplified and grew more evident. The diners should have been able to hear him, but none stirred away from their meals and conversations. Behind him, the musicians moved their thinning fingers faster against their strings and keys. The violin and viola swung their sound toward the other in a furious tandem. The clarinet's notes bottomed out into a hollow baritone hum, and the piano's feverish sharp notes clattered against each other like shattering shards of glass.

"I've already told you, Mr. Roman, death is inconsequential to affairs of the damned. You clearly haven't died. Your earthly body is there before us. It is eating, drinking, and steeped in malicious merriment," Virgilio gestured toward Dane's body, flashes of bone showing under the hem of his tuxedo sleeve. "But vengeance, I'm afraid, is a fickle beast. Your core — your soul — descended to the depths of damnation at a pace your body couldn't match. You, Daniel Roman, have diverged from yourself."

Dane watched in disbelief as his body rose from the dining chair that had imprisoned him for what felt like eternity. His hands brushed over his slacks and sport coat, and he bent at the waist to make quick work of signing the check for his meal.

"This body you see, the one which you once inhabited, is now a vessel for something even more evil than your worst deeds combined," Virgilio continued. "Hell has commandeered the physical form you squandered. A creature, a demon from the molten center of the afterlife, will walk the Earth until that human body reaches its natural end."

As Virgilio spoke, Dane's body straightened back up and cast a glance over its shoulder. It moved and held its posture like Dane. Its hair and lower features resembled the ones he remembered from the mirror and fell in the same patterns. Its black stubble covered the same path Dane recalled from his own jawline. But its eyes were no longer the same warm shade of brown. Pupils and irises fused and bled into the whites, casting the entire orb in immortal darkness.

A cold smirk, identical to the truest smile Dane ever wore on Earth, crossed its face and a crimson shimmer shone in those eyes as it looked back toward the quartet. The eyes lingered, just for a moment, to where Dane was watching before walking through the dining room and disappearing into the streets of New York.

"Vengeance waits for no man and spares no soul once he's had his chance," Virgilio's words reverberated through Dane as the music's pitch heightened and a melodic chant of *vengeance* filled the air, smothering him from every direction. Breath by breath, he lost his humanity and inch by inch, the floor disappeared beneath him. Dane parted his lips to scream, to cry, to plead for another chance or to pull another word from Virgilio but no squeal or screech emerged. The dining room scene flickered all around him like a movie struggling to start, buzzing in and out of focus against the droning sound of the orchestra as Dane's soul plummeted back through the channel to Hell.

THE END

C larissa R. Cottrill is a horror and literary fiction author who hails from the rolling hills of West Virginia. Café Vengeance is her debut novella. In addition to writing, she is the producer and co-host of the millennial lifestyle podcast "30, Dirty, & Dying", where she and her co-host explore the ups and downs of being a thirty-something in today's world. Clarissa resides in the Mountain State with her partner and cats whom she treats like children. In her work you'll find infusions of her Appalachian roots, complex history with mental health, and things that go bump in the night.

Printed in the USA
CPSIA information can be obtained
at www.ICGtesting.com
JSHW062149151023
49994JS00009B/62

Soli Deo Gloria Publications
P. O. Box 451, Morgan, PA 15064
(412) 221-1901/FAX 221-1902
www.SDGbooks.com

*

*

ISBN 1-57358-118-6

God's Call to Young People

A Call to the Rising Generation to Know and Serve God While They are Still Young

by

John Barnard
William Burkitt
William Cooper
Charles Chauncy
Jonathan Edwards
Cotton Mather
Increase Mather
Jonathan Todd

Edited by Dr. Don Kistler

Soli Deo Gloria Publications
. . . for instruction in righteousness . . .

Contents

God's Concern for a Godly Seed

by William Cooper

(A sermon preached in Boston, March 5, 1723, on a day of prayer, called by the congregation usually meeting in Brattle Street, to ask the effusion of the Spirit of grace on their children, and on the children of the town)

"That He might seek a godly seed." Malachi 2:15

I presume there are none in this assembly who need to be informed of the reason and design of the solemnity of this day, which is to supplicate the God and Father of our Lord Jesus Christ, the Father of Lights, from whom cometh down every good and perfect gift, for the effusion of His Holy Spirit upon the rising generation of this town and land, more particularly upon the children and young people of this church and congregation, that they may be a godly seed. And surely there can be nothing more worthy of the prayer, care and concern of the people of God than this, that there may be a godly seed to serve the Lord, that shall be accounted to Him for a generation, when they themselves shall be gone off the stage of this world and be silent in the dust. For this is what God Himself shows great care and concern about, that a godly seed may be raised up for Him, from among the successive generations of

1

men, even to the world's end; as appears from the
words I have now read unto you.

In our context, God, by His prophet, charges the
people of Israel with, and reproves them for, profaning
the ordinance and violating the covenant of marriage.
They, at least many of them, not only slighted and grew
cool in their affection to the wives with whom they had
been lawfully joined according to God's ordinance, and
whom they were bound to love, but they misused them,
and treated them harshly and cruelly; so that the poor
women fled to the temple of God, there to pour out
their sorrowful hearts before Him, and to complain to
Him of the injuries which they received from their base
and wicked husbands. In doing this they even covered
God's altar with their tears, as in verse 13. Nay, many of
them took other and more wives to themselves of the
idolatrous nations, which is called in verse 11
"marrying the daughters of a strange god." By this they
not only violated the covenant of marriage, but profaned their covenant of peculiarity, whereby they were
formed to be a holy people to God, separate from other
nations: "Judah hath profaned the holiness of the Lord
which he loved." Of this their treachery to their wives,
their companions, and the wives of their covenant, the
Lord Himself was a witness, as in the verse before our
text.

Now to convince them what a sin and transgression
this was, they are argued with from the original law and
institution of marriage, as in the verse of our text. "And
did not He make one? Yet had He the residue of the
Spirit. And wherefore one? That He might seek a godly
seed. Therefore take heed to your spirit, and let none
deal treacherously against the wife of his youth."

And did not He make one? It is the original and fundamental law of marriage that it be of one with one, of one man with one woman. To be sure, God never intended that one man should have more than one woman, for in the beginning He made but one pair, Adam and Eve. When He saw it was not good that Adam should be alone, He made Eve and gave her to Adam, but no other.

Yet he had the residue of the Spirit. He could have made more as well as one. He could have made two or more women, as amiable and beautiful as Eve, if He had seen it good and fitting. But as He saw it was not good for man to be alone, so He saw it was not good that he should have more than one wife—therefore He made but one for him.

And why only one? To what end? With what intent? For what cause? Upon what ground and reason? Why, truly, a very great and worthy one, namely, this in our text: "That He might seek a godly seed," or "a seed of God," as the word is.

Some think Christ may be here referred to, who is by way of eminency the seed spoken of in Galatians 3:16–19, the seed of God, yea, the seed who is God. But a religious offspring, a perpetual succession of religious persons in the church and in the world, seems to be the thing intended; the seed *of* Christ rather than the seed which *is* Christ. Irreligious and wicked men are called the children or seed of the devil, but the religious and godly in the world are the children or seed of God. They are so called, in opposition to the children of men and the seed of the devil (Genesis 3:15; 6:2).

More than legitimacy is intended by a godly seed in the text. For the end and design of God in the institution of marriage, the appointing to every man his own wife and but one, was not only the increase of the world with a legitimate issue, but the supply and increase of His church with a holy seed. In it He sought a race or set of men in the world who should have something more in them than the nature of men; who should be made partakers of the divine nature and bear God's own image; whom He would not be ashamed to own as His offspring, in a sense proper and peculiar to them. Matthew Poole, in his *Annotations,* says that the phrase "That He might seek a godly seed" means "That there might be a holy seed born unto God in chaste wedlock, and brought up under the instructions and virtuous example of parents living in the fear of God and love of each other, which in polygamy cannot be expected." Matthew Henry's take upon that passage is this: "That the nature of man might be propagated in such a way as might make it most likely to participate of a divine nature."

The words may then afford us this doctrine:

DOCTRINE: Great is the care and concern of God that a godly seed may be raised up and continued in the church and in the world.

In speaking to this doctrine I shall do the following:

1. I shall say who are a godly seed: who the persons are who may bear this character and denomination.

2. I shall say why these are called a seed.

3. I shall say why they are called a godly seed.

4. I shall show the care and concern of God to be great about this matter, that there should be a godly seed raised up.

5. I shall say why the care and concern of God is great about this thing.

1. First, we are to say who are a godly seed, who these persons are who may bear this character and title.

Briefly, the godly seed are to be sure an instructed seed. Knowledge necessarily lies in the foundation of true godliness. Some indeed, who withhold the key of knowledge from the people, pretend that ignorance is the mother of devotion, but this has been justly exploded by Protestants as false and pernicious. The unerring oracles of God teach us quite otherwise. Proverbs 19:2: "Also that the soul be without knowledge is not good." We must not expect to find real goodness in those who are destitute of divine knowledge. The devotion of such is only superstition and false worship, like that of the Athenians in Acts 17:22–23.

There can be no true godliness without faith and repentance, and both of these are grounded on and flow from a doctrinal knowledge. It must then be supposed, concerning this godly seed, that they are informed in the revelation which God has made of Himself and of His mind and will to the children of men, and so know what they are to believe concerning God, and what duty God requires of them; that they are acquainted with the doctrine which is according to godliness, and know the truth as it is in Jesus. And hence it is a precious promise respecting the godly seed, the seed of Christ, and of the church, that they shall all be taught of the Lord (Isaiah 54:13), implying both a literal and doctrinal and also a spiritual and saving knowledge.

The godly seed are a holy seed. This divine character is given of them in Isaiah 6:13: "So the holy seed shall be the substance of the land." And in 1 Peter 2:9

they are called a holy nation.

They are holy, not only as they were brought under a holy consecration to God in baptism, when those great and awful names—the name of the Father, and the name of the Son, and the name of the Holy Ghost— were named on them, and by the personal, actual dedication of themselves to God as a living and holy sacrifice. They are holy as they have a real, inherent holiness wrought in them by a renewing work of the Spirit of God in and upon their souls whereby all their powers are formed anew, framed after the divine image, and ennobled and beautified with the saving graces of sanctification.

And as they are holy in heart and soul, so in life and conversation. Being renewed in the spirit of their minds, they put off, concerning the former conversation, the old man, which is corrupt according to deceitful lusts, and put on the new man, which after God is created in righteousness and true holiness (Ephesians 4:22, 24). As they once followed after sin and served their lusts, so they now follow after holiness and are the servants of righteousness. They are other manner of persons than the rest of the world are, and than they themselves once were, in all holy conversation. None but such as these are to be accounted a godly seed, or a seed of God. God will be ashamed to own any relation or affection to those who are not cleansed from defiling lusts, and who don't keep at a distance from the pollutions of sin. "Be ye separate, and touch not the unclean thing, and I will receive you" (2 Corinthians 6:17).

The godly seed are religious and pious towards God. Their hearts being touched by grace, they stand rightly affected to God. They love Him with all their heart, soul, and mind, choose Him as their portion, and delight in Him as their chief good. They fear God; they fear to offend Him, and are careful in everything to please and glorify Him. They reverence God in their hearts, and never mention His great name but with a holy awe. They live a life of devotion to God and communion with Him; they live a life of trust in, resignation to, and dependence upon Him.

They are, to be sure, a praying seed. By this they are known and distinguished almost as much as anything. Psalm 24:6: "This is the generation of them that seek Thee, that seek Thy face, O Jacob's God." And we have them thus characterized in 2 Timothy 2:22: "Them that call on the Lord out of a pure heart." They pray in secret, in private, and in public. They pray always and in everything. There is no long intermission between their prayers. The various occasions of life and providences of God set them on and keep them praying. They pray for all men. If there are any who restrain prayer before God, who are strangers to frequent, serious, and fervent prayer, nothing else is needed as evidence that they are not of the godly seed. Psalm 32:6: "Every one that is godly will pray." It is truly said that we can as soon find a living man without breath as a living saint without prayer. "Prayer," said one, "is the natural language of the godly seed. 'Abba, Father,' are the first words they learn to speak." As soon, therefore, as Paul was converted it was said of him, "Behold, he prayeth" (Acts 9:11). And they continue herein. Of the hypocrite indeed it is asked, "Will he delight himself in the Almighty? Will be always call upon God?" (Job 27:10). No, it can hardly be thought that he will persevere in this holy, heavenly duty. But the sincerely godly resolves with the Psalmist, "I will call upon Him as long as I live" (Psalm 116:2). His last breath shall be spent in praying, as did Stephen, who died calling upon God, "Lord Jesus, receive my spirit" (Acts 7:59).

They are careful, holy Sabbatarians. They remember the Sabbath day, to keep it holy. They take pleasure and pains in Sabbath-sanctification. They call the Sabbath a delight, the holy of the Lord, honorable, and honor Him on it; and they are no less careful to do the works of God on His day than they are to do their own works on weekdays. They are, or endeavor to be, in the Spirit on the Lord's day, in spiritual and heavenly frames. They lay aside temporal cares and worldly thought so that they may have close converse and communion with God. They endeavor on this day to get above the world and above themselves. Now they mount up as upon eagles' wings, and make their sallies, at least, into the suburbs of heaven. Loose and careless Sabbatizers don't act like the godly seed. The Pharisees were not out in their rule of judging, but only in the application of it to our Savior, when they said in John 9:16: "This man is not of God for He keepeth not the Sabbath day."

Furthermore, they frequent God's house and public worship. It has been foretold concerning them, " 'From one Sabbath to another shall all flesh come to worship before Me,' saith the Lord" (Isaiah 66:23). They love the habitation of God's house, the place where His honor dwells; they prize the communion of saints, and would not so much as seem to turn aside by the flocks of His companions (Song of Solomon 1:7). They don't forsake the assembling of themselves together as the manner of some is, but continue steadfastly in the apostles' doctrine, in fellowship, in breaking bread, and in prayers. So did the first Christians (Acts 2:42).

Additionally, they keep up religion in their families. They who keep up personal religion and devotion will keep up family religion and devotion too; where there is the former, there will ordinarily be the latter. Wherever the godly seed have a house, God will have a church in it. Their houses will be little churches, places wherein God is acknowledged, served and worshipped. We can turn to none of the godly seed, but we shall find them examples of family religion. Abraham was one of them, and God Himself gives this testimony concerning him that he would command his children, and his household after him, that they should keep the way of the Lord (Genesis 18:19). Joshua was another of the godly seed, and he resolved that, whatever others did, as for him and his house, they would serve the Lord (Joshua 24:15). David also was of the godly seed, and he piously resolved that he would walk within his house with a perfect heart (Psalm 101:2). We read that Cornelius was a devout man, one who feared God with all his house, and prayed to God always (Acts 10:2). Prayerless householders are not to be accounted of the godly seed; no, the Scripture puts them among the heathen who do not know God (Jeremiah 10:25). Thus the godly seed are religious and pious towards God.

They are good and kind, just and righteous towards men. They conform to the precepts of the second table of the Law as well as the first. As they love God with all their heart and soul, so they love their neighbor as themselves. They do justice and love mercy, as well as walk humbly with their God. They put on, as the elect of God, "bowels of mercies, kindness," and so on

(Colossians 3:12). They exercise themselves to keep a conscience void of offense towards God and towards man. They renounce the hidden things of dishonesty, and will not go beyond, nor defraud their brothers in any matter; they render to all their due; and as they would that men should do unto them, so will they also do unto others. Wherever there is true piety towards God, there will be this charity and righteousness towards men. They can't be sincere in their observance of first-table duties who do not have a conscious regard to the duties of the second table also. The neglect of these is sure evidence of a hypocrite in religion. Such may seem to be religious, but their religion is vain; they have only the show of religion, and nothing of the substance of it. See the character of the citizen of Zion in Psalm 15.

The godly seed endeavor to serve their generation according to the will of God, and labor, what in them lies, to promote and advance the interests of Christ's kingdom. Religion forbids and condemns a private and selfish spirit; it would have us to look, not everyone on his own things only, but on the things of others also (Philippians 2:4). And indeed the truly godly have such a divine temper in them, such as disposes them to seek and embrace opportunities to do good to others. They are sensible that they are not born only for themselves; they desire and endeavor that others, even all about them, may fare the better for them.

According to the station they are in, the powers and talents that are bestowed upon them, they seek the good and weal of the place and people with whom they live, and endeavor to promote all their truly valuable interests. And whereas religion is the first and highest interest of any people, and the kingdom of Christ among them their greatest beauty, safety, and glory, to maintain and promote these the godly seed will bend their chief and utmost endeavors. They will therefore openly profess religion themselves, and endeavor to set a bright example of it before others for their imitation. That they may help to build up the church of Christ, they will join themselves to some holy society of Christians, attend and help support the worship and institutions of God our Savior with them, and endeavor to promote peace and good order, the truth, purity, and power of religion among them. They will endeavor to propagate religion in places that are destitute of the means of it, and to transmit the precious privileges of Christ's kingdom to succeeding generations.

David and Nehemiah were some of the godly seed. Of the former we read that he served his generation by the will of God before he fell asleep (Acts 13:36), and of the latter that he did good deeds for the house of his God among his people. Some are the curse and plague of their generation, and the burden of the places where they live. But the godly seed are not so (however a wicked generation may sometimes be weary of them), but they are the best servants of, and the greatest blessings to them. And happy the place that has many of these to show!

Thus we have said who are the godly seed; who the persons are who may answer this divine character.

2. Why are these called a seed?

It is, in a word, because of their propagatory virtue, their being designed and used for production and increase. From seed come plants and trees of the same kind. So the godly propagate their godliness: they communicate it to others, beget children to God, are spiritual parents, and have a spiritual offspring.

Not that godly parents can give grace to their children. Let none understand me to mean that. No, that is God's work, and His alone. But as these do more than others to have their children be godly, so God often blesses their endeavors, so that many more of their children are godly, it may be, than of others. We have more ground to expect godliness from the children of the godly than from the children of those who are of a different character.

As I said, they do more than others to have their children be godly. They carefully teach them the way of godliness, charge them to walk in it, and endeavor to go before them therein. They are much in prayer for them; they wrestle with God for the blessing for their children, that blessing of blessings, the Holy Spirit; they even travail in birth again with them till they can see Christ formed in them. And God often has such regard to their prayers and cries, and so blesses their faithful and painful endeavors, that their children are wrought upon thereby. The Spirit of God sets in with and gives efficacy to these means, so that they become effectual to their saving conversion.

It must indeed be acknowledged that many children of godly parents live and die ungodly. They prove to be degenerate plants, bear none of the fruits of godliness, and are at length plucked up out of the church and out of the world, and cast into the fire, the fire of hell. We read in Scripture of many very ungodly children who descended from very godly parents. There was a scoffing Ishmael in Abraham's family, a profane Esau in

Isaac's, an incestuous Amnon and a murderous Absalom in David's, and so on in others'. On the other hand, the grace of God sometimes lays hold on the children of wicked parents, converts them from errors of their parents' way, and makes them truly godly among the rest that are accounted to Him for a generation. The reason of these dispensations I may not now inquire into. Only, it teaches us the freedom and sovereignty of God in bestowing His grace. He is not obliged to let it turn in this channel and not in another. He will be gracious to whom He will be gracious, and will show mercy to whom He will show mercy.

Yet this does not alter the fact that most who belong to God come from parents who are themselves godly. It is thought that God has so cast the line of election that, for the most part, it turns through the loins of godly parents, and that, so far as can be observed, there are more of the children of these converted than of others in proportion. The second epistle of John is directed to the "elect lady and her children," as being partakers together of the same grace. Timothy had the same unfeigned and saving faith dwelling in him that dwelt in his grandmother Lois and his mother Eunice (2 Timothy 1:5). The promise is to believers and to their children (Acts 2:39). And as it takes place in all of them as to outward church membership, so it does in many of them as to real saintship. "The mercy of the Lord is from everlasting to everlasting upon them that fear Him, and His righteousness upon children's children" (Psalm 103:17). Thus sweetly and graciously does God's covenant with His people run. " 'My Spirit that is upon thee, and My words which I have put in thy mouth, shall not depart out of the mouth of thy seed, nor out of

the mouth of thy seed's seed,' saith the Lord, 'from
henceforth and forever' " (Isaiah 59:21). Yea, it is
promised to Christ in Psalm 45:16–17, "Instead of the fathers shall be the children. I will make thy name to be
remembered unto all generations." Instead of the fathers who were Christ's, shall arise the children, and be
Christ's also, and so His name shall be remembered.
He shall be acknowledged, worshipped, and served to
all generations.

This, we have said, is why the godly are called a seed:
because they are designed and used for propagation
and increase, because it is to be supposed and hoped
that those that spring from them will be godly like
them. It is upon them that the church depends for its
future supply.

3. Why are they called a godly seed?

(1) Because they are a seed of God, begotten by
Him, born of Him, and raised by His power. They are a
divine seed, of whom God is the Father and Parent. As
they are a godly seed, they are born not of blood, nor of
the will of the flesh, nor of the will of man, but of God
(John 1:13). As they come of their natural or earthly
parents, they are not godly. Grace does not run in the
blood, as corruption does. A polluted man begets a son
in his own likeness, but a renewed and sanctified man
does not beget a son in that likeness. And as parents
don't beget their children godly, so neither can they
make or form them so afterwards. They can instruct
them indeed, advise them, and pray with and for them,
but that is all. They can direct them to the same Word
that was the means of their regeneration, and can put
them over into the hands of the same Holy Spirit that

sanctified their souls, but they cannot give their souls the same holy impressions that are upon themselves. No, this is God's work, and His alone. Regeneration, or the new birth, is owing to the Spirit of God as the great and sole Author, whatever the means and whoever the instruments. James 1:18: "Of His own will begat He us, by the Word of truth." All creatures are made by God, but none are born of Him but the godly; and, because they are so, they hear this divine character in the text.

(2) Because they are God-like. Being born of God they resemble Him, in some measure, as children do their parents. They are made partakers of His nature, life, and image. They are like Him in their minds, dispositions, and actions; they are holy as He is holy, in all manner of conversation; merciful as their Father in Heaven is merciful, and so on. The new man which they now have on is renewed after the image of Him who created him (Colossians 3:10). And they are followers or imitators of God, as dear children, with a kind of natural affection and propensity (Ephesians 5:1).

(3) Because they are for God; they belong to Him, and are employed in His service. They have been devoted to God, we may suppose, by their parents in their infancy. And they have devoted themselves to God; they have subscribed with their own hands to be the Lord's; they have brought themselves under a free, voluntary engagement to Him in an everlasting covenant never to be forgotten. Accordingly, they look upon themselves to be not their own, but His, and endeavor to live not to themselves, but unto Him, glorifying Him with their bodies and spirits—and God has more honor and glory from them than from all the world beside.

Others turn His glory into shame; they don't honor
God, and God does not own or regard them; nor does
He take any delight or pleasure in them. But these are
to Him for a people, for a name, for a praise, and for a
glory. He accounts them as His portion and His peculiar treasure (Jeremiah 13:11; Psalm 135:4). Thus they
are a godly seed.

4. We are now to show that the care and concern of
God is great about this matter, His having a godly seed
in the church and in the world. He seeks a godly seed,
says the text. He desires it; His heart is set upon it; His
mind has been employed and exercised about it, and
He has taken those ways and methods that will effectually secure it.

(1) He has from all eternity determined to have
such a seed. God (who has foreordained whatsoever
comes to pass) did, from all eternity, determine to raise
up some of the children of men from the ruins of their
fall and apostasy (which He foresaw) in whom His lost
image should be repaired, from whom He would have
service and honor here, and who, being fitted for glory,
should be at last brought to it. For known unto God are
all His works from the beginning of the world (Acts
15:18). They are laid out in order in the divine mind
and purpose.

(2) He made choice of the very persons who
would be this godly seed. He not only fixed upon the
number, but pitched upon the very persons whose
names are therefore said to be set down in the book of
life. The godly seed are, all of them, elect according to
the foreknowledge of God the Father, through sanctification of the Spirit unto obedience (1 Peter 1:2), and

therefore they are godly. They were not chosen upon the foresight that they would be godly, but chosen that they might be godly. They are sanctified, made holy and godly, in pursuance of God's eternal decree of election concerning them. Ephesians 1:4: "According as He hath chosen us in Him, before the foundation of the world, that we should be holy and without blame before Him in love."

(3) He has given his own Son that, by His meritorious sufferings and death, He might purchase for these that grace which would make them holy and godly. The end and design of the death of Christ was not only to save the elect from hell, but to redeem them from iniquity, and to purify them so that they might be peculiar people to God and zealous of good works (Titus 2:14). The sanctification of the elect to be this godly seed is one principal part of the fruit of Christ's death. He gave Himself for the church that He might sanctify and cleanse it by the washing of water by the Word (Ephesians 5:25–26). Hence we find the sanctification of the Spirit connected with the sprinkling of the blood of Jesus (1 Peter 1:2).

(4) The raising up of this seed was the end and design of God in the institution of marriage, as was said in opening the text. God instituted marriage to man in innocence. This and the Sabbath are the two most ancient institutions. He has declared this state to be honorable in all. He has commanded the marriage-bed to be kept undefiled, and the marriage-bond inviolable. He has forbidden fornication and adultery upon pain of damnation. And why has He done this? The answer is in the text: "that He might seek a godly seed," that the children born in holy matrimony, which is an

ordinance of God, might be bred up as they are born, under His direction and dominion, and so might come to be a seed to serve Him.

(5) Because God seeks a godly seed, He has taken the infant seed of believers, with themselves, into and under His gracious covenant. The covenant which God made with Abraham, the father of the faithful, was entailed; it was made not with him only, but with his seed after him. Genesis 17:7: "And I will establish My covenant between Me and thee, and thy seed after thee in their generations, for an everlasting covenant, to be a God unto thee, and thy seed after thee." Accordingly, the token, the initiating seal of the covenant, circumcision (for the sake of which the covenant itself is sometimes called "the Covenant of Circumcision," such as in Acts 7:8) was ordered to be applied to Abraham's infant seed as well as himself. Acts 7:10–12: "And God said unto Abraham, 'This is My covenant which ye shall keep between Me and you, and thy seed after thee, and their generations: every man child among you shall be circumcised. Ye shall circumcise the flesh of your foreskin, and it shall be a token of the covenant betwixt Me and you. And he that is eight days old shall be circumcised among you.' " It is with Abraham and his spiritual seed, as well as his seed after the flesh, that this covenant is made. It therefore extends and reaches to believing Gentiles under the gospel, as the apostle informs us in Galatians 3:7, 9, 14: "Know ye therefore that they which be of faith, the same are the children of Abraham. So then they which are of faith are blessed with faithful Abraham . . . that the blessing of Abraham might come on the Gentiles through Jesus Christ." So we now, and our seed, are in the same covenant with

God, for substance, that Abraham and his seed were. If we are of faith, i.e., if we are true believers, we are blessed with Abraham, as he was—not only blessed in the seed of Abraham, but blessed as Abraham was blessed.

The covenant which was made with him is, in the administration and blessings of it, transmitted to us; and our children are in covenant with God as his were, and have a right to the initiating seal of it, baptism, which under the gospel-administration is laid in the place of circumcision. Else were our children unclean and out of covenant of God, as the heathen, but now they are holy, are to be looked upon in covenant with God as part of His church, and should be admitted thereunto by the solemn instituted rite of admission (1 Corinthians 7:14). And why now does God thus take the children of His people into covenant with Him but that they might stand bound and obliged in the most solemn manner that can be to be a godly seed to serve Him, that they might be in the way and under the means of grace, and that they might have the offer of that grace which shall be sufficient to make them really holy and godly, if they heartily accept and diligently seek it? They are made federally holy so that they may become really so.

(6) He has made it the duty of parents to bring their children up in the way of godliness. This is very strictly and solemnly charged upon them in the Word of God. Deuteronomy 6:4–6: "Hear, O Israel, the Lord our God is one Lord. And thou shalt love the Lord thy God, with all thine heart. . . . And these words which I command thee this day shall be in thine heart. And thou shalt teach them diligently unto thy children."

Psalm 78:5–7: "For He established a testimony in Jacob,
and appointed a law in Israel, which He commanded
our fathers, that they should make them known to their
children; that the generation to come might know
them, even the children which would be born . . . that
they might set their hope in God, and not forget the
works of God, but keep His commandments." And in
Ephesians 6:4, parents are charged to bring their children up in the nurture and admonition of the Lord.

(7) Yea, He has made it one great and special
part of the work and duty of ministers, to labor with the
young ones of the flock that they may be a godly seed.
That no endeavors may be wanting to bring the children of his people to be a godly seed, He has appointed
them to have ministerial instruction, exhortations, and
admonitions, as well as parental ones. Christ gave it in
charge to Simon Peter, and in him to all His ministers,
to the world's end, to feed His lambs (John 21:15). And
Timothy, a young minister, is directed to exhort young
people to sober-mindedness, i.e. to practical godliness
(Titus 2:6).

(8) But because this work of raising up a godly
seed, if it is left only in the hands of parents and ministers, will certainly miscarry and come to nothing,
therefore He has put it into the hands of the ever-
blessed and Holy Spirit. He is sent forth to strive with
the children of the covenant; and, as for such of them
as belong to the election of grace, He never ceases striving with them till He has indeed rescued them from
sin, converted them to God, and brought them into a
life of godliness.

(9) And then, that He may never be without a
godly seed in the world, He so orders it that His elect

are brought forth in the successive generations of men
to the world's end. They are not brought forth in one,
or in a few generations, but some of them in every generation; so that there never has been, nor ever will be, a
generation upon the face of the earth in which God
has not a godly seed, more or less. And because there
are some of these to be converted and brought home to
God in every age and generation, there will be a gospel-
ministry continued to the end of the world (Matthew
28:19–20; Ephesians 4:11–13).

Now lay all these things together, and then ask
whether God does not indeed seek a godly seed,
whether His care and concern about having a godly
seed in the world is not great about this matter.

5. The last thing proposed under the doctrine was to
say why the care and concern of God is such about having a godly seed raised up and continued in the church
and the world.

Here note three things, briefly:

(1) It is out of regard for His own glory. The
glory of God is the sovereign end which He proposes
and pursues in all that He does, and this is His great intent in seeking a godly seed. For if He had not such a
seed in the world, what would become of His honor
and glory in it? The inferior creatures glorify God only
objectively; they are not qualified to do it rationally and
intentionally. As for ungodly men, they are so far from
glorifying God that they run His glory into shame; they
wrong Him in His honor by despising His laws, tram-
pling upon His authority, and employing their powers
and abilities, both of body and soul, in the service of
sin and Satan. It is by the godly seed only that He is ac-

knowledged and worshipped, served and obeyed. These
are they who keep up a face of religion in the world,
and who propagate it to future times. If it were not for
these, all the service and obedience of this world would
be paid unto Satan only, who is called its god. God
therefore seeks such a seed so that He may not go
wholly without a tribute of honor and praise from this
lower world.

(2) It is out of regard for His Son Jesus Christ, so
that He may see His seed, as was promised to Him upon
His undertaking the work of redemption; that He may
see the fruit of His death and sufferings, the travail of
His soul, in the many living children who are born
unto God, and be satisfied (Isaiah 53:10–11). God seeks
a godly seed in the world so that the blood of Christ
may not be shed in vain (which it would be if none
such were raised up), that He may not fail of having a
church in the world since He has so dearly purchased
one, that He may have some to serve and honor Him
since He has served and glorified the Father; to bear up
His name in the world so that it may continue so long
as the sun (Psalm 22:30; 72:17), and in whom it shall be
admired and magnified forever and ever.

Christ died that such a seed might be born. He fell
to the ground like a corn of wheat so that they might
be raised up. The promise of such a seed made Him
engage in the work of redemption; the prospect of it
encouraged Him in going through the difficulties of it;
and seeing them sanctified and glorified is, and will be,
His everlasting satisfaction and delight. It is with the
utmost pleasure that He speaks of them, "Behold, I, and
the children which God hast given Me" (Hebrews
2:13).

(3) Last, it is out of regard for the world itself that God seeks a godly seed in it. For if some such were not to be raised up in every generation, the gospel would not be preached to the world, nor the means of grace afforded to any people. If this blessing of a godly seed were not to be found in the world, God could not, and would not, spare it as He does, but would soon bring upon it that destruction by fire to which it is reserved.

It is therefore out of a regard for the world that God seeks a godly seed in it, that the gospel offer of salvation by Christ may be made to it, which is no small favor. And it may be honorably spared till the time of its destruction, the time of which is set, which will be when all the godly seed are taken out of it.

But I may not stay upon these things. It is now time for me to hasten to some application of the doctrine.

Application

1. We may hence infer the excellency of true godliness. Does God seek a godly seed, and do so much for the securing of one? Surely, then, godliness must be an excellent thing, and the godly must be the excellence of the earth. If there were not something very excellent in true godliness, God would never set so much by it, and by them in whom it is found.

2. Does God seek a godly seed? How wicked, then, are they who cast contempt upon serious godliness and those who practice it; who endeavor to prejudice others against it, and to hinder the propagation of it among those who are rising up! Alas, that we should suppose that there are any such; but it is too obvious that there

are many such in the world who not only won't practice godliness, but do what they can to disparage it and bring it into contempt; who ridicule serious piety and discourage living religion where they see it, and endeavor to lay stumbling blocks in the way of it. We read of some in Luke 11:52 who enter not in themselves, and those who would enter in they hinder. These enemies of righteousness are the children of the devil; his servants and instruments they are. Instead of praying that God's kingdom may come and His will be done on earth, as our Savior has directed us, they labor to promote Satan's kingdom, and that his will may be done. Very dreadful is the "woe" denounced against such in the Word of God. Truly it were better that a millstone were hung about their neck, and they cast into the sea. They themselves will think so in that day when our glorious Savior and Judge shall come with ten thousands of His saints, to execute judgment upon all and to convince all who are ungodly not only of their ungodly deeds which they have committed, but also of the hard speeches which ungodly sinners have spoken against Him, His servants, and His ways (Jude 14–15).

3. Does God seek to have a godly seed raised up in the church and the world? Then we may be sure this is what Satan will do all he can to hinder. For the devil hates God and godliness; he seeks to rob God of all His glory in this world, and would have the children of men be as wicked as himself. The propagation of godliness he will set himself in a special manner to oppose, whereas the hope of the church of God is in the rising generation, and among them God looks for a godly seed. Satan will do all he can to debauch, corrupt and spoil them, and to make them unfit to be the seed

of God. He will use many arts and strategies, and employ all the instruments he can to effect this. I mention this so that the people of God, who wish well to the interests of religion and godliness, being not ignorant of his devices, may be stirred up to counter him, and may have their prayers and holy endeavors awakened and more employed.

4. Therefore, see what should be the great care and concern of the people of God, namely that there may be a godly seed rising up in the church and in the world while they are passing out of it. This is what God Himself seeks, what He shows great care and concern about; and surely His care should direct ours, and we should pursue the same design and intention with Him.

I might here say that this should be the care of rulers. They should see that seminaries of knowledge and religion are planted and maintained for the training up of youth, and that such public fountains be kept pure, and be in a condition to answer the end for which they were founded. They should take care to have all manner of vice and wickedness discountenanced and punished, that the youth of the place may not be hurt by the example and contagion of it; and particularly to have all ill houses suppressed.

This should be the care of ministers. They should labor for the instruction and conversion of young ones to God; they should condescend to be teachers of babes, by catechizing of them, and sometimes by suiting and directing the Word preached unto them—letting their doctrine drop upon them as the rain, their speech distill as the dew, as the small rain upon the tender herb.

This should also be the care of elder and aged Christians. They should all of them do what they can to preserve the foundation of religion, "that that light may not die in their hands, that treasure be buried in their graves." They should therefore communicate their knowledge and experience, and recommend vital religion to those that are rising up, by letting them know what pleasure and satisfaction they have found in it.

But in a very particular manner this should be the care of parents for their own children. This should be their first and chief care for their children, that they may be a godly seed to serve the Lord. Of all concerns that relate to their children, this should lie nearest their hearts. They should therefore dedicate them to God as soon as they are born. And as they grow up, they should do their utmost to have their minds well instructed, and set right for God betimes. They should be often telling them what a miserable and sinful state they are in by nature, the need they stand in of Christ, the necessity of their being born again, and the like. They should often admonish them of their duty, call upon them to mind their souls, and lay charges of God upon them. They should watch over them, restrain them, and endeavor to keep them as much as may be out of the way of temptation. They should be much in prayer for them; they should strive and agonize in prayer to God, that He would pour out His Spirit and grace upon them. And they should set them holy examples, walk before them in the way of godliness, and think no pains too much to take, to bring them to be a godly seed.

Consider, O parents, what your children are likely to

be and prove if they are not a godly seed. They will then prove to be an ungodly seed, a seed of and for the devil; his interests will be served, and his kingdom promoted by them. And can you bear to think of begetting or bringing forth children only for the devil?

Consider also what will become of religion in this land if our children and young people don't prove to be a godly seed. It will fail and sink. God's truth will be lost or corrupted. His Sabbaths, house, and ordinances will be neglected or profaned. The work of God in planting New England will fall to the ground—that work of purity and reformation in religion for which we should pray, "Lord, let it appear unto Thy servants, and the divine beauty and glory of it unto their children!"

Consider again the judgments your children and posterity will lie open and exposed to if they are not a godly seed. They will then be a generation of God's wrath. He will pull down His judgments upon them, and drive away His presence upon which their prosperity depends. God will withhold blessings from them, or will curse their blessings to them. Prosperity, if they meet with that, shall but destroy them; afflictions and judgments will but harden them; the means of grace will be either taken from them or be penal and judicial to them; and they will ripen for a wrath unto the uttermost.

On the other hand, what blessings may you not hope for if your children prove to be a godly seed? Then, it may be hoped, they would see an end to the public judgments which have been wasting this people; and that God would make them glad, according to the days wherein He has afflicted us, and the years wherein

we have seen evil; that they shall possess this good land
which the Lord gave unto our fathers, and leave it with
the advantages we enjoy in it, civil and religious, for an
inheritance to their children after them forever; that
they shall have a safe conduct through this world till
they arrive at the promised land, that better country
which is heavenly, which our forefathers declared
plainly that they sought for themselves and for their
posterity when they left the conveniences and comforts
of their own land, and planted themselves in an uncul-
tivated wilderness.

Finally, how great will be your honor and happiness
in being instrumental in raising up a seed for God!
What a service may you do herein to the church of God,
to the town and land! And what a blessing may you be
to many generations, to those of your posterity that are
not yet born! How comfortably may you leave your children at death if you first see them godly! You may then
say to them with faith and comfort, when the time of
your departure is at hand, as Israel said to his Joseph, "I
die, but God will be with you." And then, what a joy and
crown will your godly children be to you in the day of
our Lord Jesus Christ, if you can then stand at the head
of a little spiritual offspring and be able to take up
those words of Christ, which He will speak to His eternal Father concerning the seed which He has give
Him, "Behold, I and the children whom Thou hast
given me!" Upon all these considerations, how careful
should parents be so to train up their children in the
knowledge and fear of God that they may come to be a
seed to serve Him!

But leaving parents, I come to apply the doctrine to
the rising generation: the children and young people

that are here before the Lord.

5. The children of God's people may from hence learn what should be their care and concern, their desire and ambition, respecting themselves, namely that they be a godly seed, a seed of God and for God. God seeks you to be a godly seed; we are this day seeking to God for you that you may be so. Oh, will you also seek this for yourselves? I might here argue many things with you.

You have been already devoted to God had His mark set upon you in baptism, so that you are strongly obliged to be a godly seed, and can't prove otherwise without breaking the most sacred bands asunder that you can possibly be bound with.

God expects that you be a godly seed to serve Him, whoever are not already, under the advantages of your birth and education.

If you are not a godly seed, God will be more dishonored by you than by others, and religion will suffer more damage from you.

It will be apostasy in you if you don't prove to be godly; for you are the seed and posterity of those who were eminent for godliness.

And it will be worse for you than for others. For as God has known you above most of the families of the earth, so He will punish you the more for your iniquities.

Your happiness, as to both worlds, depends upon your being a godly seed. If you are such, God will be with you as He was with your fathers, and will delight to bless you; but if you are not such, He will forsake you, and then woe to you; yea, He will cast you off forever. Oh, think, children, how dreadful it will be if you should live and die ungodly! Know that it will be more tolerable in the day of judgment for the children of heathen than for you.

To these motives and persuasions, I might add some words of counsel and advice:

Labor to be well informed in the doctrine which is according to godliness.

Take heed of being prejudiced against the ways of godliness.

Cherish your early convictions, and take heed of grieving the Spirit of God.

Abandon the company of the ungodly, and cry to God for His Holy Spirit to be poured out upon you, as we are now seeking this mercy and blessing for you. But these things cannot here be enlarged upon.

6. Does God seek a godly seed for Himself? Then it must be acceptable and pleasing to Him to have His people pray and seek that He may have such a one raised up to Him from among them and their seed. The work of this day must be pleasing to God as to the matter of it. Oh, that it may be so as to the manner of its performance! We are seeking that of God which He Himself seeks. We are sure that the thing we have met together today to pray for is according to the will of God. The consideration of this may well help to engage our faith and fervency. "For this is the confidence we have in Him, that if we ask anything according to His will, He heareth us."

And now, oh, that in answer to our united prayers this day that promise might be remarkably fulfilled, which we should be pleading and acting faith upon. Isaiah 44:3–5: "I will pour water upon him that is thirsty, and floods upon the dry ground. I will pour My Spirit upon thy seed, and My blessing upon thine offspring. And they shall spring up as among the grass, as willows by the water courses. One shall say, 'I am the Lord's'; and another shall call himself by the name of Jacob, and another shall subscribe with his hand unto the Lord, and surname himself by the name of Israel."

We shall therefore now again pour out our supplications to the God of all grace.

The Important Duty of Children

by John Barnard

(Delivered to a religious society of young men
on April 24, 1737)

"And thou, Solomon, my son, know thou the God of thy
Father, and serve Him with a perfect heart and with a
willing mind; for the Lord searcheth all hearts, and
understandeth all the imaginations of the thoughts; if
thou seek Him, He will be found of thee; but if thou
forsake Him, He will cast thee off forever."

1 Chronicles 28:9

I have today spoken some things upon these words
before many of you who are here present, and have observed that they are the words of King David to
Solomon, his son. In them we have a father's great
concern that his child may know and serve the Lord.
From these words I have arrived at these doctrines:

**DOCTRINE 1. It should be the great concern of par-
ents that their children may be such as shall know and
serve the Lord.** The words are spoken unto Solomon, a
young man under twenty years of age, and show him
what his great concern should be, namely, to serve God
with a perfect heart and a willing mind, and that because God knows the heart and will accept such to serve
Him and reject them if they do not do it now.

DOCTRINE 2. It should be the most important concern of young people to know and serve the Lord with a perfect heart and a willing mind.

In handling this doctrine I shall endeavor to show you:

1. What is to be understood by knowing God.

2. Wherein consists the service of God.

3. That God is to be served with a perfect heart and a willing mind.

4. And then I shall evidence this to be the most important concern of young people, where I shall consider the arguments made use of in the text. I begin with the first of these.

1. What is to be understood by knowing God? "Know thou the God of thy Father." Now the knowledge of God may well be understood to comprehend these three things in it: (1) That there is a God; (2) What this God is; (3) What this God requires of us.

(1) To know God comprehends in it the knowledge that there is a God. For if the mind is not first informed and does not give credit to the information that verily there is a God, some supreme and infinitely powerful and wise Agent from whom all things originate, there can be no foundation for the knowledge of Him, nor for any service to Him. This, therefore, is the first thing in the knowledge of God, to have the mind firmly impressed with the belief of the being of God. Hence we are told in Hebrews 11:6: "He that cometh unto God must believe that He is." This is the first thing of which young people should be well informed, that there is a God, a supreme Being, who is the first cause and the last end of all things; that there is a God who gave be-

ing unto all this world, that this God made us, formed us, fashioned us, and furnished us with all our powers of choice and of action.

Therefore the preacher says in Ecclesiastes 12:1, "Remember now thy Creator in the days of thy youth." So as soon as you come to years of understanding, you should remember that there is a God who is your Creator, and the Creator of all things in heaven and on earth. While your minds are soft and tender you should receive the impressions of the being of the great God so that the belief hereof may have its due influence upon you all your life. The belief of a God of all perfection, the Maker and Ruler of all worlds, and to whom you must be accountable, should be deeply rooted in your minds; and serious thoughts of this God should be often present with you. Indeed, you can look nowhere without seeing some plain evidences and proofs of the being of a God. Young as you are, you are capable of seeing God in all things, for, as the Psalmist said in Psalm 19:1, "The heavens declare the glory of God, and the firmament sheweth His handiwork." And so says the apostle in Romans 1:20, "The invisible things of Him, from the creation of the world are clearly seen, being understood by the things that are made, even His eternal power and Godhead." The first thing to know is that there is a God.

(2) The knowledge of God includes in it the knowledge of what this God is. Not that youth are able fully to understand what sort of a being the Lord is. The most ripened years cannot attain unto the knowledge of God, because there is no finding out the Almighty unto perfection. Yea, the very angels of heaven cannot so know God, for no finite mind can

comprehend that which is infinite. Yet so much of God
may be known by us as is necessary to our serving Him.
And thus young people should be concerned to know
God. For example, they should know that the Lord is a
great God, that this God has all power in His own
hands and can do whatever He pleases. What cannot
He do who made a world out of nothing? You are to
know, as Job expresses it in Job 42:2, that God "canst do
everything and that no thought can be withholden
from Him." Therefore, we know that this God can
punish severely those who dare to offend Him, and that
He is able to protect and reward those who faithfully
serve Him.

Again, you are to know that this God is an infinitely
good God, whose goodness is seen in His giving being
to you, in His constant preserving of you, and in His
bountiful supplying of all your wants. "Thou art good
and doest good," said the Psalmist in Psalm 119:68.
"Yea, God is good unto all, and His tender mercies are
over all His works" (Psalm 145:9). So as soon as you arrive at the use of reason, you should well acquaint yourselves with the goodness of God unto you so that you
may be allured thereby unto all fidelity in His service.
And need you to look to see the instances of His goodness to you? Or can you forget the Author of your lives,
your constant Preserver and Benefactor, from whom
you receive your all?

You are to know that this God is a very Holy God,
that He has no pleasure in wickedness, neither shall
evil dwell with Him, but He perfectly hates all sin and
iniquity and cannot by any means approve of it.
Habakkuk 1:13: "Thou art of purer eyes than to behold
evil and canst not look upon iniquity." You should

therefore know early and bear in mind not only that God is Himself at an infinite distance from all moral evil, but that He hates all sin wherever He sees it. And because sin is the abominable thing which the soul of the Lord hates, therefore He hates all the workers of iniquity.

You are to know that this God is everywhere present and perfectly knows all things, all persons, and all their actions. So says God by His prophet in Jeremiah 23:24: "Can any hide himself in secret places that I shall not see him? Do not I fill heaven and earth?" Young as you are, you are to know and realize that God sees you wherever you are, that He knows all your actions, words, and thoughts, and you cannot hide yourselves, nor what you do or say or think, from His view.

Finally, you are to know that the Lord is a God of truth, and that it is impossible for God to lie (Hebrews 6:18). You are to know that God is true in what He has spoken, and that all His sayings are faithful and worthy of all acceptance. And God will be true to His word, and accomplish the things that have gone out of His mouth, in fulfilling both His threatening upon His enemies and His promises unto His friends. These and the other adorable perfections and attributes of God you are to have your minds well-informed in the knowledge of.

(3) To know God includes in it the knowledge of what God requires of us, or the knowledge of the mind and will of God concerning us. This knowledge of God is attainable in two ways:

First, by the light of nature. Something of God and His mind and will concerning us is to be seen by a due exercise of our natural reason and conscience. But this is such a very dim and obscure knowledge of God, and of His mind and will concerning us, which, after all our pains, we can attain to by the light of nature that our best and safest knowledge of God and His mind is.

Second, from His holy Word. For it has pleased God to make a full and clear revelation of Himself, and His mind and will, unto the world, confirmed by many signs and wonders and diverse miracles and gifts of the Holy Ghost; and therein He has shown to us that He is, what He is, and what the Lord our God requires of us, so far as is necessary to be known by us.

Now, it concerns young people to endeavor to know God as He has revealed Himself unto them, to attend unto the light of nature, and to take heed unto the Word of God as a more sure word of prophecy, a light that shines in a dark place. Therefore, young persons should learn quickly to read the Word of God, and, being capable of reading it, they should make conscience of daily accustoming themselves to read some portion thereof and meditate on that holy Word, so that they may be acquainted with the mind and will of God concerning them and know what they are to believe and what they are to practice in the service of God. For if they know not their master's will, how shall they be able to perform it? And especially, according to the gospel revelation, they should endeavor to know God in Christ, that is, to understand the great doctrines of the gospel relating to the person, nature, offices, and benefits of Jesus Christ. They should acquaint themselves with the wonderful grace and mercy of God in providing a Savior and sending His own Son into the world to suffer and die for sinners so that He might bring us unto God, that they may be led by the

knowledge hereof to the faith of the Son of God, and to
eternal life through Him. This is to know God, and this
is the knowledge which it cannot be good that the soul
should be without.

2. The second thing I proposed to take notice of
under this doctrine is to show you wherein the service
of God consists. Young people should be concerned
not only to know God but to serve Him. And that they
may be enabled to serve Him, it is necessary for them to
know what that service is which is expected of them.
Here, then, we may inquire what is intended by and included in that service which young persons, and which
indeed *all* persons, should yield unto God. This includes in it generally a compliance with whatever the
Lord our God requires of us, doing what God has
commanded us, and living up to the rules which He
has prescribed to us in His holy Word. And so it includes in it our whole duty. But to be a little more particular, it includes in it the duties of piety, the duties of
sobriety, the duties of justice, and the duties of charity.

• The service of God includes in it all the duties of
piety which are due unto God Himself. These are duties
which young persons are concerned quickly to engage
in, to reverence God being one of the first lessons they
are to learn.

Thus they are to believe in God and in His Son Jesus
Christ; for this is the great command of the gospel, and
what God requires of everyone who hears His Word, to
believe in Him and to believe in Christ. So said our
Savior in John 14:1, "Ye believe in God, believe also in
Me." And John 6:29: "This is the work of God, that you
believe on Him whom He hath sent." This is so necessary a part of our duty unto God that without it no man

can serve God acceptably, "for without faith, it is impossible to please Him" (Hebrews 11:6). Faith in the divine Being, and in His Son Jesus Christ as the great Mediator through whom alone we have access to God and acceptance with Him, are the fundamental principles of the Christian religion. You must, therefore, get a principle of faith in God, and faith in Christ as the Son of God and Savior of sinners, into your hearts as the grand spring of all your spiritual and acceptable service. Without this you can never find favor with God, because, outside of Christ, God is a consuming fire unto guilty sinners; but in Christ He is a God who is reconciling a guilty world unto Himself.

Repentance towards God is another duty of piety which young persons should carefully attend upon so that they may serve God. That is, they should turn from all sin unto the living God. All sin is carrying the heart off from God unto the creature, unto self, unto the world, and unto the devil. Repentance is the soul's renouncing these usurpers, refusing to be any longer in subjection unto foreign lords, returning to its duty unto its rightful Sovereign, and subjecting itself unto the living Jehovah. And inasmuch as you were all born sinners, being conceived in sin and shaken in iniquity, and having lived as sinners, having broken the holy law of God many times within the few years you have been in the world, therefore you need to come to repentance. And this is what God in a peculiar manner requires, now that the gospel has enlightened the world and shown you the evil of sin, the dreadful consequence of it, and a Savior from it. Acts 17:30: "The times of ignorance God winked at, but now hath commanded all men everywhere to repent." You owe your whole selves and all your time to the service of God, and none to sin. The danger of continuing in sin is that you grow hardened therein; therefore, you should now, in your youth, forsake every evil way and endeavor after a universal conformity unto the will of God.

Also, young persons ought to pray to God. This is another duty of piety which God requires of all persons, and of young ones, that they pray to Him, that they be sensible of their entire dependence upon Him for every good thing, both respecting their bodies and their souls for time and for eternity, and that, in a sense thereof, they come humbly before Him. They should pour out their heart's desire unto Him, in all things by prayer and supplication making known their requests unto Him; they should beg God to preserve them from dangers, to lead them in a right way, to keep them from sinning, to bestow their daily bread upon them, to give them His grace and unite them unto His Son, and to finally bring them to glory. Our Savior, therefore, spoke a parable to this intent: "Men ought always to pray, and not to faint" (Luke 18:1). He directs you "to enter into thy closet, and when thou hast shut the door, pray to thy Father . . . which seeth in secret" (Matthew 6:6). And this will be a comfortable token for good upon you in whom God has begun His work, when it can be said of you, as of Saul in Acts 9:11, "Behold, he prayeth." But then remember in your prayers that you are to give thanks unto God for all the instances of His goodness, bounty, and mercy to you. How lovely is the spectacle, in the eyes of God, to see young persons thus going alone and earnestly presenting their supplications and acknowledgments to Him. This is a grateful sacrifice with which God is well pleased.

Finally, a work of piety which should concern all young persons is to do all they can for the honor and glory of God. In 1 Corinthians 10:31, the apostle gives us this rule: "Whether you eat or drink, or whatsoever ye do, do all to the glory of God." Young persons should remember that they, as well as all things beside, were made for this great end, to glorify God; and therefore they should endeavor to advance this high and noble end in all the ways they are capable of. All your natural, civil, and religious actions should be performed with a single eye to the glory of God. Be ready to do all you can to build up of the Church of God, become living stones in that temple of the Lord, and do not think it much to lay yourselves out, to spend and be spent in the service of God and to improve of your worldly interest in such works of piety as may tend to the glory of God. Thus are you to serve God in the duties of piety.

• The service of God includes in it all the duties of sobriety. And thus young persons are to serve God by behaving themselves with sobriety in the government and regulation of their appetites and passions, in the temperance, chastity and purity of their manners and behavior.

Thus young persons should be sober in their temperance and in restraining their inordinate appetites and desires after the world and the things thereof. "Exhort young men to be sober-minded," said the apostle in Titus 2:6. They are to be sober in their meat and drink, and not allow themselves in gluttony and drunkenness, nor in too great curiosity about the quality of them, but be content with what they have. They are to be temperate in their apparel, not craving every new and flaunting fashion, not hastening, if possible, to be one of the first in it, nor going to the extent of it which will be but an indication of a vain mind, but preserve a due moderation and use the world (and the things thereof) so as not to abuse it (nor themselves with it) because the fashion of this world passes away 1 Corinthians 7:31).

Again, young persons should be sober in the chastity and in the purity of their manners, behaving themselves with modesty and shamefacedness, carrying themselves with all circumspection and good behavior before their superiors, rising up at the face of the old man and giving that honor and reverence to their parents, natural, spiritual, and civil, and ready obedience and submission to them, which the Word of God requires of them. They should be careful also to remember and observe the apostle's rule from 2 Timothy 2:22: "Flee youthful lusts." They should preserve themselves pure and chaste from all unclean lusts, and learn to possess their vessels in sanctification and honor, and be careful not to allow themselves in any lewd talk and evil communication, in any impure or immodest words or actions, and, as much as may be, drive impure thoughts out of their minds, not allowing them to lodge within them.

Young persons should be sober in the regular government of their tongues. They should not suffer that unruly member, the tongue, to run at large, but lay their seasonable and prudent restraints upon it and keep it under the bit. They should hate and abhor lying as a base and odious vice, proceeding from a meanness of soul, and which renders them abominable and contemptible both in the sight of God and men. Ephesians 4:25: "Wherefore, putting away lying, speak every man the truth with his neighbor." They should always be careful to speak the words of truth and soberness. And they should be careful to banish all impious and profane language from their mouths so that their mouths may not be set against the heavens, and belch out their blasphemies against the God who made them. They should be careful never to allow themselves to take the name of God in vain by customary oaths in conversation, much less in their solemn testimony to anything, because this will dishonor God and not serve Him, and God will not hold him guiltless who takes His name in vain (Exodus 20:7). They should also guard against all reproachful and injurious talk, all whispering and evil speaking, and take care that they do not raise or spread false reports of their neighbors; nor should they suffer railing and reviling language, and bad names or cursing, to proceed out of their mouths. They should not be too talkative. "A young prating fool is an uncomely sight." Let your words, therefore, be few, sober, and seasoned with grace, so that they may minister that which is graceful to the hearer.

Young persons should be sober in the government of their passions lest they betray them into many mischiefs. Youth is naturally hot, and is very apt to be soon angry and easily provoked, and suddenly kindle into a flame. If, therefore, you would be the servants of God, you must carefully watch over your passions, and quickly suppress them when you first perceive them beginning to stir and rise. Don't allow yourselves to be soon angry, nor suffer your anger to grow up into rage and fury. But if you have just cause to be angry, as possibly sometimes you may, remember the apostle's rule in Ephesians 4:26: "Be angry and sin not," which you cannot be if your anger is without cause or exceeds due bounds in the measure or duration of it. Therefore the apostle adds, "Let not the sun go down upon your wrath." Especially take heed never to harbor malice and revenge in your hearts. Beware of doing evil unto others because you think they have done some ill thing to you. Romans 12:19: "Dearly beloved, avenge not yourselves, but rather give no place to wrath for it is written, 'Vengeance is mine, I will repay,' says the Lord." Learn to do good for evil and bless those who curse you; pray for those who curse you and pray for those who despitefully use and entreat you, so that you may be the children of the Highest. In such instances as these, young persons should serve God in sobriety.

• The service of God includes the duties of justice. For as God is a righteous God, and just and right is He, so He requires justice and righteousness of all His servants, and will not allow any designed unrighteousness in them. Young persons should therefore get established early on in the principles of justice that they may ever do that which is equal and right, and observe that "Golden Rule" of our Savior's in Matthew 7:12: "All things whatsoever ye would that men should do unto you, do ye even so unto them." Always think what you would look upon as just and right and fitting that other persons should do unto you, were they in your circumstances, and be careful to do unto them accordingly.

Thus be strictly just in your care never to wrong any man by taking anything from him without his knowledge or against his will. Are you children? Do not rob your parents, for if you take anything from them which they know not of, or are not willing you should have, you are guilty of stealing from them—and this is one of the highest instances of injustice.

Are you servants? Do not wrong your masters or mistresses by purloining and pilfering or wasting their goods, or consuming their time idly. This would be an iniquity which you would have sad cause to repent of. Young people, it is true, are ready to think that there is no great harm in these things, yet know that God will look upon all such things as breaches of His holy commandment, and will call to a sad account and severely punish therefore if such sins are not repented of. "Exhort servants," said the apostle in Titus 2:9–10, "to be obedient unto their own masters, not purloining but shewing all good fidelity." And is not robbing your neighbor's orchard or garden stealing from them, as well as robbing their vessels and houses? Yes, surely, God will esteem it so. Therefore, such young persons as would serve the Lord must be very careful to abstain from all such acts of injustice.

Be strictly just in your diligence in your business. The apostle says in Colossians 3:22, "Servants, obey in all things your masters according to the flesh, not with eye-service, as pleasing men, but in singleness of heart, fearing God." Do not be eye-servants, who will attend your business no longer than while your parents' or master's eye is upon you, but be as diligent when they are absent as when they are present; otherwise you are unfaithful and rob them of so much of the service which you might have done them. So when you are employed by others, remember faithfully to attend the business you are employed about, and do not idle away your time, spending and consuming it in vain chat and diversions, when you should be at work, because this would be to cheat and wrong those who employ you;

but show all good fidelity so that you may adorn the doctrines of God your Savior in all things.

Be just in all your dealing and commerce. "Let no man go beyond or defraud his brother in any matter because the Lord is the avenger of all such" (1 Thessalonians 4:6). Always deal fair and square and above board. Never impose upon the ignorance and credulity of anyone. Never make use of double weights and measures. Never circumvent, overreach, or trick your neighbor. Never suffer yourselves to make false entries and bring in wrong accounts, for all such unjust dealing is robbery.

Finally, let there be justice in your words as well as in your actions. See that your words are true, and endeavor to make good all your promises and engagements. Remember to make no rash promises. See to it that the thing you promise is within your power to perform, by the ordinary providence of God, and then, once your word is engaged, be exceedingly careful to fulfill what you have promised so that no man may have just cause to complain that you are not a man of your word, that you are unfaithful and not to be depended on.

All of this is included in the service of God because God very peremptorily requires this justice and righteousness and truth in all men. And the careful observation hereof will be a comfortable sign to you that you are indeed the children and servants of God; for, says the apostle, "If you know that He is righteous, ye know that everyone that doth righteousness is born of Him" (1 John 2:29).

• The service of God includes in it the duties of charity. God is love, and requires love and charity from all His servants. And therefore the apostle tells us that all our faith is nothing without charity (1 Corinthians 13:2). And Colossians 3:14: "Above all these things put on charity, which is the bond of perfectness." And our Savior gave this as a sure badge of His disciples: "By this shall all men know that ye are My disciples, if ye have love one unto another" (John 13:35). So those who would serve God must live in the exercise of the duties of charity. And therefore those young persons who would make it their concern to serve God must be careful of this as well as of all other parts of their duty.

Thus young persons should cultivate and improve their natural disposition to pity and compassion, and not allow themselves in anything that will tend to harden their minds into savageness and cruelty; for this humane affection of pity and compassion will be of great use to them in restraining them from acts of injustice and oppression, and will greatly dispose them to kindness and benignity. Therefore 1 Peter 3:8 says, "Having compassion on one another . . . be pitiful, be courteous."

Young persons should exercise this charity in their inward affection, in their hearty love and good will unto all their fellow creatures in general, but especially unto all good men, the household of faith, and those of the same family and society with them so that they may preserve the unity of the Spirit in the bond of peace, in the family, in the church, and in the state.

This charity they should also be careful to express in their actions by a kind, courteous, affable carriage and behavior, being ready unto all good and kind offices to all about them and, as they are able, to help the indigent and miserable, to relieve the poor and distressed, to assist one another in all difficult affairs, and to advise and counsel one another for their good.

Especially should this charity be exercised to the souls of others by counseling and admonishing one another in love, and by endeavors to strengthen and encourage one another in the steady, persevering practice of all religion and virtue, under all discouragements, temptations, and trials.

Particularly is this charity required and expected from you of this society who are very much formed upon this foundation, that you may assist each other by your kind watch, your faithful advice, your wholesome admonitions, and your earnest prayers with and for each other; that you may endear yourselves to one another and help one another forward in the way to Zion, to your mutual edification and comfort.

Thus, in these hints, I have shown you what it is to serve God. I trust you see that it comprehends your whole duty unto God, to yourselves, and to your neighbor, and that in all the various branches of your personal and relative duty, for so the grace of God, which has appeared to us, bringing salvation, teacheth us to deny ungodliness and worldly lust, and to live soberly, righteously, and godly in this present world (Titus 2:12).

3. The third thing I propose to consider is that God is to be served with a perfect heart and a willing mind. So says my text: "Know thou the God of thy father, and serve Him with a perfect heart and a willing mind." I will consider each of these distinctly, though briefly.

(1) You are to serve God with a perfect heart, that is, with a heart sincerely devoted unto the service of God, a heart free from all guile and hypocrisy. It does

not mean that you should serve God with an unerring, sinless perfection of heart, according to the strict demand of the law, for no man can serve God so. "For there is not a just man upon earth that doeth good and sinneth not" (Ecclesiastes 7:20). Still, you are to press after the greatest attainments in grace and holiness, and not be content with any low measures and degrees attained unto. But it means an evangelical perfection of heart, that is, a heart that is sincere, without any reigning and allowed deceit and guile. This is the character of the truly good man. John 1:47: "Behold, an Israelite indeed, in whom there is no guile." And the blessing belongs to such a man, in whose spirit there is no guile (Psalm 32:2). This perfect heart or sincerity is the very life and soul of all other graces and virtues, without which they are but vain appearances and empty shadows, and have nothing solid and substantial in them. Notwithstanding all the goodly show which any man may make, if he is destitute of sincerity, he is, after all, but a fair hypocrite, whose outside indeed is gay and splendid, but within he is full of rottenness and stench.

Therefore, young persons should take special care that in all their pretensions to the service of God they begin at the heart and see that they are sincere in what they do, lest they be found at last to have unhappily deluded themselves and their fellow creatures to their undoing. For sincerity is the only thing that will render you acceptable unto God, without which your sacrifices will be an abomination unto the Lord, being heartless and corrupt. And if men (who are often and easily imposed upon) should at length discover your hypocrisy, you will be become loathsome unto them, for all men abhor being cheated by an impostor. God

demands this of you. Proverbs 23:26: "My son, give Me
thine heart." This is what God chiefly aims at, and
without this nothing will please Him. And for the sake
of this He will be ready to overlook many imperfections.

What is there that, without sincerity, can establish
and confirm you in the service of God, and make you
stand against the temptations and allurements you will
meet withal, to turn you aside from the paths of virtue?
If there is not soundness and integrity to preserve you,
you will be more easily warped from your duty, and be
prevailed with for the sake of some worldly gain and
advantage, or to gratify the humor of some you may be
in friendship with, or have some dependence on, to
give over the service of God and turn aside from the
holy commandments. Therefore, above all things, see
to it that your hearts are right with God, and are found
in His statutes. Then you shall have no cause to be
ashamed when, in sincerity and truth, you have respect
unto all His commandments.

(2) You are to serve God with a willing mind, that
is, with a mind freely engaged in the service of God, so
that it may be truly your own choice. A willing mind is
here opposed to outward constraint, and what a man
may be compelled and forced to, as a perfect heart is
opposed to inward hypocrisy and guile. And it imports
as if David had said to Solomon, "If you only serve God
to please me, and think when I am dead and gone to
give over this service, this will be no real benefit to
you." God requires voluntariness in His servants. Psalm
110:3: "Thy people shall be a willing people in the day
of Thy power."

Thus, young people are to serve God willingly,

freely, out of their own choice, because they choose to serve Him, knowing Him to be the best of masters. They are, therefore, to renounce all others and determine with themselves to serve Him forever. Let not, then, the service of God which you, my children, engage in be only to please men. As you may not serve God only to be seen of men, but in sincerity, so neither are you to serve Him only because your parents or your masters or your friends would have you do so—but it must be with a willing mind. Your parents or masters or friends may first lead you into the thought of serving God and show you how you are to serve Him, and they may charge you to serve Him, but, after all, your service must be the result of your own understanding and choice or it will not be a reasonable service. You must serve God because you are convinced that you ought to serve Him and resolve to serve Him, that is, because God will have you serve Him, and because you are now willing to have your will resolved into the divine will, and are willing to be and do what God would have you be and do.

So Joshua puts it to the choice of the people and lets them know what his own choice was. Joshua 24:15: "Choose you this day whom you will serve . . . but as for me and my house, we will serve the Lord." He was determined with himself to serve God out of choice, and he would have all the people be free and willing in serving Him also. And just so should you choose to serve God as an act of your will and choice, moved by an enlightened understanding and the regular working of your affections, because God is most worthy of your service, and because you love God and are loath to offend Him. When the service of God thus becomes the act of your will and choice, you will then be likely to abide by it and hold on therein unto the end, and not suffer anything to move you therefrom, but continue steadfast and immovable, always abounding in the work of the Lord, till you come to the end of your faith, the salvation of your souls. This may suffice for the third head.

4. I wish to evidence this to be the most important concern of young people, thus to know and serve the Lord with a perfect heart and with a willing mind. And here, as I said, I shall consider the force of the arguments made use of in the text. Particularly, (1) God searches all hearts and understands the imagination of the thoughts; (2) if you seek Him, He will be found by you; and (3) if you forsake Him, He will cast you off forever. They are arguments of great weight, and, one would think, would have a mighty force upon the mind to determine it for the service of God. I may not now draw them out at their length, but may only hint at things.

(1) God searches all hearts and understands all the imaginations of the thoughts; and, therefore, it concerns young people to serve Him with a perfect heart and with a willing mind. The omnipresence and omniscience of God is a very good reason why all His rational creatures should serve Him faithfully, because He perfectly knows whether they serve Him or not, and He cannot be imposed upon with an external show and pretense. The Lord is a God of knowledge; by Him actions are weighed. His understanding is infinite, and therefore He is perfectly acquainted not only with all your actions, but with the thoughts and intentions of your hearts; and so He knows whom you serve, whether

God or the devil, and how you serve, whether sincerely and willingly, or only in pretense and by constraint.

God knows all your actions. Young people are very ready to imagine that if they are out of the presence of any man no eye sees them, and the thought of their being in secret and hidden from human sight is oftentimes a very great encouragement unto them to commit many sins, which they would not have the face to allow themselves in if any man were present. But remember, O young man, when you are tempted to sin under the pretense of secrecy, that, though men do not see you, yet the holy and flaming eyes of God are upon you. And God sees in the darkness of the night as well as in the lightsome day (Psalm 139:11).

Remember that God searches the innermost parts of your heart, and knows every imagination of your thoughts, so that you cannot contrive and purpose any secret wickedness in your heart, nor harbor an unclean or vengeful thought there, but God is acquainted with it. God says in Jeremiah 17:10, "I the Lord search the heart. I try the reins even to give unto every man according to the fruit of his doings." And will you dare then to sin in the presence and under the eye of the heart-searching God? Oh, serve Him in sincerity because He sees and knows what you do, and you cannot deceive God as you may a man.

(2) If you seek Him, He will be found by you, and therefore you should serve God with a perfect heart and a willing mind. If you thus seek God, by making religion your great concern, by endeavoring to know the mind of God and to sincerely and heartily practice according to His will, then God will be found by you. That is, you shall obtain that blessing from God which He

has promised to bestow upon His faithful servants: to find God, to find favor with Him and obtain the blessing from Him, to find Him to be what He has said He is, and to find Him to be unto you what He has said He will be. Thus you will most certainly find Him if you serve Him with a perfect heart and a willing mind; and the sooner you begin thus to seek and serve the Lord, the sooner you will find Him. By beginning early, you will have the longer time to serve Him in, and so much the greater will your rewards be. How strong a reason and a motive should this be unto you to serve God with a perfect heart and a willing mind, seeing that this is the way to blessing. Then God will be found by you as your God, your Friend, your Portion, and your all. You may then safely depend upon Him for the blessings of this world that are needful for you, for godliness has the promise of the life that now is (1 Timothy 4:8). Then God will bless your labor and employment, for the meek will He guide in judgment; the meek will He teach His way and lead them in a plain path. Then God will be your Shepherd and comfortably provide for you, for there is no want unto those who fear the Lord. They shall want nothing that would be good for them. Then God will be your shade at your right hand, to preserve you in times of danger and keep you from evil so that it shall not grieve you. He will sanctify all afflictive evils unto you and make you real gainers by them. Then shall you find God the Fountain of grace and comfort unto you, who will make His grace sufficient for you and strengthen you in your Christian course, so that you may run therein and not be weary, and walk and not faint. He will succor and support you under temptations, deliver you out of them, and make your tried faith to be more precious than gold. He will speak peace to your souls, afford you rejoicing in the testimony of your consciences, grant you the witness of His spirit, and fill you with all joy in believing.

Then shall you find God in another and better world to be better than your present hopes and most enlarged desires. This God will be your God forever, your Guide unto death and through it, and the unchangeable Portion of your souls. You shall then find mercy with God in the last and great day, for He has prepared rewards in heaven for His servants who serve Him. When you leave this world, a world of sin and sorrow, He will fetch you away unto Himself, to the world of purity and joy, to live in His more immediate presence, to serve Him in His heavenly temple, and to be everlastingly happy in His favor. And, oh, how abundantly will this recompense you for all the labor and toil you have taken, all the patience and self-denial you have exercised in your most constant and unwearied endeavors, to serve and honor and glorify so great and so good a God as the Lord is! Oh, let the thoughts hereof strengthen your hearts and hands, and mightily encourage you unto all fidelity and perseverance in His service, now in your youth and to the latest old age.

(3) But if you forsake Him, He will cast you off forever. If you will not serve God with a perfect heart and a willing mind, but if all your religion is mere show and pretense, and if your hearts are estranged from God while you draw nigh unto Him with your mouths, or if, after you have lifted yourselves in His service and given up your names to Him, you at length prove to be deserters and turn away from His holy commandments, know assuredly that God will cast you

off. He will not own you for His servants, nor bestow the least reward upon you, but will throw you out of His family, reject you, and cast you out of His favor, and you shall have no right to any blessing from Him.

Nay, you shall have no right to the blessings of earth. For no man can have any right to his daily bread but by virtue of the covenant of God, which they who forsake God have no interest in; and therefore they can have no good grounds to hope for any success in their business, for any daily provision, or for protection and safety in time of danger.

If you forsake God and serve sin, and walk in the ways of your own heart and in the sight of your own eyes, serving diverse lusts and pleasures, be it known unto you that God will cast you off forever. That is, He will everlastingly reject you, disown you and say to you, as in Matthew 7:23, "I profess unto you, I never knew you; depart from Me, ye that work iniquity." And what is this but the very essence of hell, the consummation of the misery of the damned! To be forced to depart from God, the only Fountain of all good, is the perfection of misery. Oh, therefore, serve God now with a perfect heart and a willing mind, so that God may not reject you forever and render your condition unhappy beyond expression.

Thus I have endeavored to handle this text and doctrine in the most practical manner, fitting it to your capacity and condition, and have been all along exhorting you unto the duties pointed at in it.

Application

And now suffer me, my children, to close all with an earnest address unto you, so that you would all look upon this as it really is, your greatest and most important concern, to know and serve the God of your fathers with a perfect heart and a willing mind. You are making some outward show and profession that you do so. For this end you are assembled together this evening, and this is the great design of your stated meetings on the evening of every Lord's day: that you may acquaint yourselves more and more with the mind and will of God, that you may be directed and assisted in serving Him in obedience to His will. We rejoice that you thus begin to be concerned for your souls and your own salvation, that you are in any measure willing to know, and desirous to perform your duty to God and your own souls. Truly, I have no greater joy, my children, than to see you walking in the truth. And oh, may this be the happy result of your meetings! May you find from your own experience that it is infinitely better for you to serve God in the duties of prayer, reading, and catechizing than to spend the Lord's day evening in gadding abroad in sport and sin, and lose the relish of the holy things of the house and day of God, as is the unreasonable and vicious practice of too many among us.

May you find God and be found by Him. May you find Him meeting with you and assisting you in your devotions, and commanding a blessing to rest upon you. May He fill you with knowledge and understanding and the fear of the Lord, and furnish you abundantly with that wisdom which is from above, which is first pure, then peaceable, gentle and easy to be entreated, full of mercy and good fruits, without partiality, without hypocrisy, and make you lovely and pleasant spectacles unto men and angels. When you have served God and your generation according to the will of God in this world, may you be received to the blessed abode of light and life and joy, to dwell in the presence of God and of Christ forever and ever.

Inasmuch as here is a great assembly of young people met together with you at this time and place, I would most earnestly call upon you all to serve the Lord now in the days of your youth.

Therefore, remember that the time of your youth is the most fitting season to begin the great work of God and of your own souls. Is it not the most reasonable and fitting thing that the great God, who made you, and on whom you depend for all, should have the very prime and best of your days and strength? But besides, it is the most fitting and proper season for you to begin to serve God because it is the time of your choice, as it is called in Ecclesiastes 12:1, and you are not yet fixed in the ways of sin, as you will be some years hence, if you should go on in a sinful course of life when it will be harder for you to alter the corrupt bent of the mind. "Youth is the age of discipline," the proper season to receive instruction and most apt to learn. A young tree is easily bent while it is very difficult to bend an old one. It is most highly reasonable to do that which must be done one time or other, when it is easiest to be done, when we may do it with the greatest advantages, and when we are likely to meet with the least and weakest opposition. Such is the time of youth, and, therefore, the fittest season to enter upon the service of God.

Remember, there is no time so pleasing and acceptable as the time of youth, though God will reject none
who truly turn to Him and sincerely lift themselves in
His service in any part of their lives; they who have
stood idle until the eleventh hour, if they will then
hearken to the call of God and enter into His vineyard
and faithfully labor in it, shall at night receive their
penny. Yet who are so grateful and pleasing and endeared unto God as those who begin to serve Him
early? A young David is beautiful in the eyes of his God.
A young Jonah seems to be the care and favorite of
heaven. Under the law, God required the first fruits and
the firstborn to be devoted to Him, to sanctify and pro-
cure a blessing upon all the rest; and so the first of your
days should be consecrated unto the service of God so
that you may enjoy His blessing in them all. Doubtless,
the holy angels of God behold, with delight and joy,
your early dedication to God, and it will be very pleasing unto all thinking persons to see young people acting prudently, behaving with discretion and sobriety,
and living religiously—but it will be much more pleasing unto God Himself. God will remember with pleasure the kindness of your youth, the love of your espousals, when you early went after Him. No disciple was
so acceptable to our blessed Lord as John, the youngest
of the disciples, who lay in the bosom of Jesus, and
whom He peculiarly loved.

Remember that, for all you can tell, the time of your
youth may be the only time that you shall ever have to
serve God. If you should foolishly think of deferring
this great work of repenting of your sins and living a
life of faith and holiness until old age overtakes you,
you don't know but that God may cut you off while you

are yet in your youth and send you down to hell; and what then will become of you? Oh, my children, you cannot begin to serve God too soon! You may defer too late because you know not how soon death and judgment may overtake you before you have seriously given yourselves up to God in Christ, and have sincerely engaged in the service of God by a fixed resolution and honest endeavor to mortify sin and lead a holy life. And if this is your case, it would have been better for you that you never had been born.

But if, in your youth, you serve God with a perfect heart and a willing mind, bring your heart and soul under a consecration to God, and make it your constant endeavor to do the things that are pleasing in His sight, then let death come when it will. The day of your death will be better unto you than the day of your birth, because it is the day of your entering upon the possession of eternal life. Oh, let the thoughts hereof awaken you now to serve the Lord while you are yet in your youth, and have the most proper, if not the only, opportunity for this!

In a word, remember that you have been baptized, and were brought under the most solemn obligations, most of you in your very infancy, to be the servants of the most high God. You have been devoted to God by your parents, and you are false to God, your parents, and yourselves if you do not serve Him. Therefore, my children, "know thou the God of thy Father, and serve Him with a perfect heart and with a willing mind, for the Lord searcheth all hearts and understandeth all the imaginations of the thoughts. If thou seek Him, He will be found of thee, but if thou forsake Him, He will cast thee off forever."

Advice to the Children of Godly Ancestors

by Increase Mather

(Given July 9, 1721, and taken in shorthand
by one of the hearers)

"And said unto Samuel, 'Thy sons walk not in
thy ways.' " 1 Samuel 8:5

In this chapter the children of Israel are weary of
the theocracy which they had been under a long time,
and ask for a king after the manner of the nations. The
reason they give for it is that the sons of Samuel did not
walk in his ways. Samuel had grown aged, and used his
sons to assist him in the government, hoping that they
would walk in his ways; but they did otherwise.
Wherefore the elders of Israel came in as a body to
Samuel, and complained to him of the bad government
of his family. It is a sad observation which we have here,
and which I present as a:

**DOCTRINE: The sons of good men do not always
walk in the good ways which their fathers have walked in.**

We shall consider this doctrine in several propositions.

Proposition 1. All good men walk in the same way. It
is that which is called "the way of good men." Proverbs
2:20: "Walk in the way of good men, and keep the paths
of the righteous." It is also called the old way, and the

61

way that is holy (Jeremiah 6:16). It is likewise called "the way everlasting" (Psalm 139:24), because from the beginning of the world good men have always chosen to walk in that way; they have chosen the way of truth, laying the judgments of God before them.

Particularly, first, the way of good men is the way of piety. They have always, like Samuel, worshipped God and Him only, and have been careful not to take the name of God in vain. They have sanctified the holy Sabbath of God. Yea, sanctifying the Sabbath is indeed so great a part of piety that it is put for all religion (Isaiah 58:13).

Second, it is the way of righteousness. They are conscientiously careful to observe the first table of the moral law, and the second table also. Therefore Paul could say in Acts 24:16, "Herein do I exercise myself to have always a conscience void of offense toward God and toward men." Thus it was with Samuel; he was upright, and could appeal to the people as in 1 Samuel 12:3: "Have I wronged any man?" And they all said in verse 4, "No, thou hast wronged no man." But then his sons, who were very unrighteous, ran after filthy lucre. They took bribes and perverted judgments, all which were quite contrary to what their father did.

Third, it is the way of prayerfulness. Thus Samuel said to the people, "God forbid that I should cease to pray for you." Good men are praying men. Psalm 24:6: "This is the generation of them that seek Him." They who seek the face of God are the generation that belong to Him. Yea, there is not one godly man in all the world but who is a praying man. Psalm 32:6: "For this shall every one that is godly pray unto Thee." As for those who are prayerless, they are mentioned among the workers of iniquity (Psalm 14:4). If they are prayer-less, they are so to be accounted. Thus we see in short the good ways that good men are forever found walking in, the ways of Samuel!

Proposition 2. The children of godly men have pecu-liar advantages to serve the God of their fathers, and walk in the good ways in which their fathers walked. They have various advantages which other children in the world do not have.

First, they have the Scriptures; they have the Word of God to direct them in the way of life and salvation. As is said concerning the Jews in Romans 3:1–2: "What ad-vantage hath the Jew? Much in every way; chiefly because that unto them were committed the oracles of God." Thus it was said of Timothy: "From a child thou hast known the Holy Scriptures which are able to make thee wise unto salvation." They have also the Word of God preached unto them; as the written Word of God, so the preaching of the gospel is the ordinary means by which true faith in the Lord Jesus Christ is wrought in the souls of His elect. Romans 10:17: "Faith cometh by hearing, and hearing by the Word of God." In that re-gard, the children of godly men have special advan-tages to know the God of their fathers.

Second, they are the subjects of parental instruc-tions. They are taught by their parents how they ought to serve God. Thus the Lord required His people of old, "Thou shalt teach thy children diligently My com-mandments" (Deuteronomy 6:7). And in Psalm 78:5–6 it is said, "They should teach their children from one generation to another." And the Lord said concerning Abraham, "I know Abraham, that he will teach his children to keep the way of the Lord" (Genesis 18:19).

Now, they who are the children of Abraham will do the works of Abraham.

So we find the servants of God have always done. David taught his son Solomon and his other children. He said in Psalm 34:11: "Come, ye children, hearken unto me, I will teach you the fear of the Lord." And his son Solomon said in Proverbs 4:3–4, "I was my father's son . . . he taught me." His godly mother was careful to instruct him. We read in Proverbs 31:2: "What? my son, and what? the son of my vows?" Said she, "I have vowed and prayed to God many a time for you, and will you not hear the counsel of her who has so often prayed for you, and vowed and offered many sacrifices to God on your behalf?"

Third, the people of God put up many prayers for their children, prayers that God would give them His grace. They pray the prayer found in 1 Chronicles 29:19: "Give unto Solomon my son a perfect heart." Thus Abraham prayed for Ishmael, and God said concerning Ishmael, "I have heard thee." Their advantages are peculiar in this respect: they are prayed for.

Last, they have the blessing of their parents, which is not a light thing. The blessing of a father is not to be despised; it ought to be regarded. We see Esau as bad as he was, yet when he saw he was deprived of his father's blessing, he wept and made a great and bitter cry. Verily, 'tis a considerable thing, a valuable thing for children to have their pious parents imploring and pronouncing blessings upon them in the name of the Lord. So the children of godly parents have advantages which other children in the world are strangers to.

Proposition 3. Many children of godly parents prove to be godly too, and walk in the good ways of their par-

ents; yet it is too often sadly otherwise. Some well observe that God has so cast the line of election that, for
the most part, it runs through the loins of godly parents. John's second epistle is written "to the elect lady
and her children." If so be the mother is elect, there is
more hope and encouragement that the children belong to that election too. We read in Psalm 103:17 that
"The mercy of the Lord is from everlasting to everlasting upon them that fear Him, His righteousness unto
children's children." Thus Paul says concerning
Timothy in 2 Timothy 1:5, "I am persuaded that faith is
in thee, that thou are a true believer, when I call to remembrance the faith that was in thy grandmother Lois,
and thy mother Eunice." It is as if he were saying, "Your
grandmother was a godly woman, your mother a holy
woman, and therefore I cannot but hope the more for
you." Doubtless, if an account of it were taken, it would
be found that the greatest part of such as belong to God
have descended from godly parents.

Proposition 4. But the grace of God is still sovereign.
It is not engaged to any particular family. God is free in
the disposing of His grace. He says in Exodus 33:19, "I
will show mercy on whom I will show mercy." So that
many children who descend from godly parents are not
godly, but much otherwise; this is a sad truth. And now,
I will first show the proof of it, then inquire whence it
comes to pass. For the proof of it:

1. We find in the Scripture that particular families,
many of them, degenerated from the faith of their forefathers. Let us look back as far as Adam's family and we
shall find it so. Adam had a godly son whose name was
Seth; the posterity of that godly son in process of time
degenerated and became as the rest of the world.

Genesis 6:2: "The sons of God saw the daughters of
men." The sons of God, that is to say the posterity of
godly Seth, degenerated and became like the rest of the
world. Noah had a godly son, Shem, but this man's posterity sadly degenerated; notice is taken that they became idolaters. In Abraham's family there was an
Ishmael who would scoff at his brother who was a godly
man. In Isaac's family was an Esau, who was a profane
person. So the apostle says, "Take heed lest there be
among you a profane person like unto Esau, that for a
mess of pottage sold his birthright." Think of David,
and how many wicked sons sprang up in that good
man's family! There was Ammon, who committed
incest with his own sister; Absalom, who murdered his
brother Ammon, and after that would have murdered
his own father to have gained the kingdom. Is it not
said of Nabal, who was a drunken sot, that he was of the
house of Caleb (Samuel 25:3)? It is a sad thing that so
vile a wretch as Nabal was should descend from such a
house as Caleb's was! Josiah was a godly man, yet all of
his children were bad! God said to one of them, "Did
not thy Father do judgment and justice? But thine heart
is for thy covetousness."

2. It is true concerning whole generations.
Sometimes whole generations have apostatized from
God and become exceedingly sinful in His sight. So
when Joshua was dead, Judges 2:10 says, "There arose
another generation which knew not the Lord, nor the
works which He had done." A whole generation degenerated from the piety of their fathers who had gone before them. " 'I planted thee a noble vine, but how are
thou degenerate?' saith the Lord" (Jeremiah 2:21).

But now, second, I will show why it is that godly men

sometimes have very ungodly children. I believe there are three reasons:

• The children of godly men are born just as sinful as are as the children of other men. They have original corruption in them as much as others have. Hence David says in Psalm 51:5, "I was shapen in iniquity, and in sin did my mother conceive." Yet David's mother was a singular good woman, a very holy woman. When David prayed to God he said, "Remember the son of thine handmaid." His father, Jesse, also was a very holy man; the Jews call him "Jesse the Righteous." They have such a high opinion of him that they hyperbolically say, "The angel of death could find no sin but that of our first parents to charge him with." The son of a godly father and a godly mother was conceived in sin and shapen in iniquity. Such are as apt to sin as the children of ungodly men; they are apt to tell lies as soon as they are born. When they commit a fault they are apt to tell a lie because of the corruption which is natural to them; yea, they are inventors of evil things (Romans 1:30). They are apt to commit such sins as never any did before them. They are apt to do amiss and to fall in with the ways of sin.

• This comes to pass from the malice of Satan, who does what he can to corrupt the churches. Among the wheat there springs up a world of tares. How does this come to pass? Why, says the text, "an enemy has done it." The devil is the enemy; the devil is an enemy to purity in churches; he would have churches to be like the rest of the world. Therefore he sows tares in the Lord's field. He does it in the degeneracy that he labors to introduce among the children of the covenant.

• It comes to pass from the removal of eminent servants of God. Thus it is that when Moses was about to be taken away he said, "I know that after my death there will be great changes among you." Thus Paul, when going from Ephesus, said, "After my departure there will come grievous wolves among you." And how often is it said in the book of Judges that, while the good judges continued, things went well; but when those good judges were dead, and removed out of the way, they presently degenerated, and became like the rest of the world; they became guilty of such sins as others in the world were guilty of. Thus we see the doctrine cleared in the particulars that have been mentioned.

Application

1. Hence we see that men ought not to set their hearts inordinately upon their children. Indeed, they are apt to do so; they promise themselves much comfort in their children. We see it in Abraham when he said, "Lord, what wilt Thou give me, seeing I go childless?" And it is threatened as a judgment that such a man shall die childless. We see it in Rachel's cry, "Give me children or else I die." God gave her children, and she died for it. And when her soul was departing, she called his name Benoni, that is, "the child of my affliction." Indeed, when the children of the faithful die in their infancy, there is cause to hope they are saved because of the covenant of God, the covenant of grace which they have not violated. But when they out live their infancy and become wicked and vile, the case is much other-wise. Wherefore parents who do not know how their children may turn out should not set their hearts inor-dinately upon their children. Who knows but that the

child you are so fond of may prove to you as Esau did to Rebecca and to his father? He was a grief of mind to them both. And Rebecca said, "I am weary of my life because of the daughters of Heth."

2. If the children of good men may prove to be ungodly, it is no wonder that the children of ungodly men do so. Children are more apt to imitate their parents in that which is evil than in that which is good. Jeremiah 7:18: "The children gather wood, the fathers kindle the fire, and the women knead their dough to make cakes to the queen of heaven." It is abominable to worship the moon! Yet when parents did so, the children did so too; and no wonder that they did. The Samaritans who succeeded those who were carried captive worshipped graven images and served other gods. "As their fathers did, so did their children, and their children's children; as did their fathers so do they unto this day" (2 Kings 17:41). Those children who mocked the holy prophet Elisha in 2 Kings 2:23, who said, "Go up, thou bald head; go up, thou bald head; thou sayest thy Master Elijah is gone up to heaven; do thou go after him"—would these children have done so if they had not seen the iniquity of their fathers? Doubtless their fathers were guilty of the like iniquity.

3. We may see by this that it is not in the power of parents to give grace to their children. They may give them what they have of this world, but that's all. To have grace given to them is a thousand times better, far more desirable, than to have a portion of this world's goods. But this is more than they can give. They can't give them sanctifying grace; they can't give them true repentance, for that is the gift of God, not of their parents. They can't give them faith in Jesus Christ; no, that

none but God can give. A godly man can no more make his children godly than he can raise the dead out of their graves. None but God can do that, and He alone must have the praise and glory of it.

4. It is not safe for children to build upon having an Abraham for their father. Matthew 3:9: "Think not to say within yourselves, 'We have Abraham for our father.' " This is a foundation not to be built upon, for you may have for a father as good a man as Abraham and yet perish forever in your unbelief. How was it with one who died and went to hell, and when in torments there he cried out, "Father Abraham, have mercy on me!" This child of Abraham in torments added, "I have five brethren alive in the world. Oh, that one might go from the dead and tell them what a terrible place hell is, so that they may not come into this place of torment." Why? Is there any charity in hell? No, but they know that if their brethren come there it will be worse for them, an aggravation of their misery! Therefore he begged, "Oh, let them not come here!"

Then you who are the children of godly parents, here is a solemn word to you. If you live and die in your impenitency, you shall have the most terrible witnesses against you. Your father, and your mother who loved you so dearly, who has wept and prayed for you so many times, your father and your mother will condemn you; they will justify God in condemning a sentence of eternal condemnation upon you at the last day, and will say to God, like the angel in Revelation, "Thou art righteous in that Thou hast so judged." Thus it will be said at the last day: your father and your mother will say, "Lord, I concur with Thee. Thou art righteous in passing a sentence of eternal condemnation upon this child of mine. I warned him many a time to repent and turn to God, but he would not; so that Thou art righteous in all that has come upon him."

5. The children of godly men should be careful that they themselves are godly. Now the children of New England are (or, once were), for the most part, the children of godly men. What did our fathers come into this wilderness for? Not to gain estates, as men do now, but for religion, and that they might leave their children in a hopeful way of being truly religious. There was a famous man who preached before one of the greatest assemblies that ever was preached unto, seventy years ago, and he told them, "I have lived in a country seven years, and all that time I never heard one profane oath, and all the time I never did see a man drunk in that land." Where was that country? It was New England! New England! But, oh, degenerate New England, what are you come to at this day? How have those sins become common in you that once were not so much as heard of in this land? A sad thing it is! Well, then, turn to God, you who are children of godly parents. Remember that God calls you to it. Now He calls you to it in a solemn way by a grievous disease which He has sent into this town, and how far it may proceed we do not know. Is not God speaking to you now? It will be a wonder if the slain of the Lord are not very many before this disease is over. Children, be concerned to turn to God, to make sure of Christ. Then you shall be happy; nothing else can make you happy. You cannot be sure of your lives, but you may make sure of Christ. If you make sure of Him, you will be happy whatever befalls you.

And so I leave you with these charges:

First, seek God early. You read in Proverbs 8:17: "They that seek Me early shall find me." Oh, that there may be many early seekers of God, many who set themselves in good earnest to seek Him. When you seek God, plead with Him the relation wherewith you are advantaged, as sometimes Jacob did, "O God of my father Abraham, O God of my father Isaac." It is as if he were saying, "My father and my grandfather sought Thy face; they were Thy servants. Oh, let me be so too." And remember the solemn exhortation that David gave to his son Solomon in 1 Chronicles 28:9: "Thou Solomon, my son, know thou the God of thy father, and serve Him with a perfect heart, and a willing mind; if thou seek Him He will be found of thee, but if thou forsake Him He will cast thee off forever."

Do not say, "We cannot convert ourselves." Yes, but then don't do that which will hinder your conversion! Don't hearken to evil counsel. We read in the Scriptures of Ahaziah, after the death of his father, that the house of Ahab were his counselors to his destruction. Remember Proverbs 13:20: "He that walketh with wise men shall be wise, but a companion of fools shall be destroyed." Oh, do not let any of you be a companion of such! If you love your souls, beware of vain company, for there is nothing more destructive to the souls of men than that. If you choose to follow them, they will be your ruin, and will undo you forever.

Second, wait on God in the use of His own means, that He would be merciful to you. Therefore, give diligent attention and earnest heed unto the Word of God when it is preached unto you. Don't let yourselves sleep at sermons. I remember that a man died in this place many years ago, who died in doleful despair; this man, when dying, said to me, "Sometimes I set myself to sleep on purpose when you have been preaching, and do you think there is any mercy for me?" Yes, there was mercy for him if he repented; but he died in doleful despair. Take heed of setting yourselves to sleep when you should be hearing for your lives, for your souls. And then also, cry to God that He would have mercy on you. Do as Paul did. In the pangs of the new birth it was said of him, "Behold, before that he was a Pharisee." The Pharisees often prayed; but he did not pray in earnest. Now he prayed in good earnest, as if his soul was concerned, as indeed it was. Pray as for your life and soul, and God will hear and answer you.

Last, do not quench the Spirit of God. It is complained of the Jews in Acts 7:51 that they resisted the Spirit of God. It is a dangerous thing to vex and grieve the Spirit of God! God has said, "My Spirit shall not always strive." Dr. [John] Preston speaks of a man who had been guilty of a great sin, and was troubled very much that he had been guilty of such a sin. He went to a vile companion, who gave him this wicked advice, and Satan himself could not have given him worse, "Go your way; commit that sin again, and you shall be never more troubled about it." The poor wretch did so, and he was never troubled again. Why? Because God gave him up to a reprobate mind, to hardness of heart. Remember that it is said of Saul, "The Spirit of the Lord departed from him." And, "Woe to them if I depart from them," said the Lord. If you sin against the strivings of God's Spirit, you may provoke Him utterly to depart from you; but, then, woe unto you! Think on this frightful Scripture which I shall leave with you, for I knew a man many years ago whose conversion to God

was promoted by serious meditations on it. That
Scripture is Ezekiel 24:13: "Because I would have purged
thee, and thou wast not purged, thou shalt not be
purged . . . any more till I have caused My fury to rest
upon thee."

Now, may the God of our fathers mercifully preserve
the children of New England from that apostasy which
may provoke Him to cast them off forever. May He be
with them as He was with their fathers, and in that faith
and order of the gospel which they walked in; and may
He neither leave them nor forsake them.

Counsels to the Young

by William Burkitt

(Taken from *A Help and Guide to Christian Families*)

"Remember now thy Creator in the days of thy youth,
while the evil days come not, nor the years draw nigh
when thou shalt say, 'I have no pleasure in them.' "
Ecclesiastes 12:1

This timely counsel is from the lips of a man who
became pious when young and was eminently favored
by God. But in the high day of human life, and while
the bright sun of human grandeur shone upon him,
his spiritual horizon was obscured. As he advanced in
years, the clouds were scattered and his prospects grew
brighter.

The text, from the lips of such a man as Solomon, is
the language of touching tenderness. He thought of
the young as aged Christians are very apt to do. He foresaw their responsibilities and was desirous that they
should meet them manfully. He foresaw the snares that
would beset them and was desirous that they should escape them. He had just told them that human life is not
all sunshine, and that, amid its dazzling joys, it may not
be forgotten that there would be days of darkness. And
when, as he anticipated, this chilling thought was
laughed to scorn, he addressed the disdainful youth in
that keen and scorching irony: "Rejoice, O young man,
in thy youth, and let thy heart cheer thee in the days of

thy youth. Drain the goblet of earthly pleasure to its dregs. Youth is the time for gaiety and joy. Walk in the ways of thine heart and in the sight of thine eyes."

Let this one thought go along with you in your ardent and reckless career: Youth vanishes, and that bounding heart will soon beat sluggishly with age and become still in death, and after death is retribution. "Know thou that for all these things God will bring thee into judgment!" And then, by a reaction by no means unnatural, his own mind becomes tenderly affected with this all-subduing thought. He drops his sarcasm, and his tone of feeling is changed to the affectionate expostulation: "Remember *now* thy Creator in the days of thy youth, while the evil days come not, nor the years draw nigh in which thou shalt say, 'I have no pleasure in them.' "

It is melancholy to see how universally, and to what extent, men have become alienated from God. In every age and place, throughout all the borders of the earth, and in every individual of the human family, from the loveliest and most accomplished to the most abandoned and abject, the uniform characteristic of our race is its indifference to God and its forgetfulness of God. Its great moral delinquency, its great master sin, is its neglect of God. Men may not be immoral, but honest, truthful and pure; yet are they unmindful of God. They may be neither unkind, ungenerous, nor unobservant of any of the decencies which give order and beauty to the social relations; but they are without God in the world. They may hold forth to their fellow men not a little that is amiable and praiseworthy, and be among the respected and honored of the earth; yet there may be no fear of God before their eyes and no love of God in their hearts. They are lovers of pleasure rather than lovers of God. God is not in all their thoughts. They have forgotten the God who made them, and have lightly esteemed the Rock of their salvation.

There is force and emphasis, therefore, in the precept, "*Remember* thy Creator," because the initial step in the process of reform is the sinner's return to that God from whom he has so wickedly revolted. Nothing is done until the axe is laid at the root of this prolific source of evil, and the salt of divine grace cast into this polluted fountain. The instructions and counsels of the Bible all proceed upon this recognized principle; and therefore the message has gone forth and sounds in the ears of young and old, and even of those who are the farthest off in this exile and alienation, a blessed message of recall and welcome from the mercy-seat: "Remember thy Creator." This precept bids every thoughtless, prayerless man to enter into the business of meditating upon God, holding conversation with God, and acquainting himself with God. It says to him, "No longer suffer other things so to interest you that the thoughts of God shall be distasteful, and the language of your heart be, 'Depart from us, for we desire not the knowledge of Thy ways.' " God cannot be remembered where He is not thought of, nor where, when He is thought of, these thoughts are eagerly banished. A devout mind cherishes its thoughts of God. They are absorbing thoughts by their sovereign influence. To the man who truly remembers God, all things are but the dust of the balance compared with Him.

Nor is this all. There is the tenderness of love in these thoughts of God. They are affectionate remembrances. When the foul tempter stole the heart of man from God, and thankless man became an exile from his heavenly Father's house, rather than abandon him to his exile and his woe, the God of love so set His heart upon him that He commanded His own Son to the agonies of the cross in order to restore the fallen and save the lost. And now, as though all the affections of the renewed nature were thrown into this act of hallowed memory, He says, "Remember thy Creator. My son, give me thy heart." That great and glorious Being, who is our God over all and blessed forever, would be remembered not in the "cold thoughts of a steady contemplation only," but in the delights of a complacent affection, the gratitude of a heart warm with love toward Him for His thoughts of love to us.

Nor is it a powerless and sentimental remembrance of the heart any more than it is a cold remembrance of the thoughts. Where God has the thoughts and the heart, He has all the rest. These are the principles of all moral action. The whole man obeys them. It is a practical remembrance. It restrains from sin and urges to sensitivity of conscience, to watchfulness, prayer, and honest, earnest, self-denying, and persevering efforts in works of obedience. To forget God in our conduct is not to remember Him at all. That remembrance is of little worth which in works denies Him.

Such is the duty: "Remember thy Creator."

There are considerations urging this remembrance upon different classes of men. The middle-aged are appealed to by the precariousness of the strength on which they rely, the wisdom in which they trust, the exposures of their elevated position, and the illusive prospects by which they are ensnared. The aged are appealed to by considerations drawn from the debility and cheerlessness of the days of darkness, the gloom of the grave, the solemn reckoning which is just before them, and the sovereignty of that grace which is sometimes extended to the eleventh hour of human life. The considerations addressed to the young are in some respects peculiar. They are in every view attractive, full of beauty and of hope. They are some of the noblest and most disinterested that can be addressed to the human mind. They appeal to its ingenuousness, its truthfulness, its purity, its honor, its finest sensibilities, and to all that is lovely and of good report. It is with this class of considerations that we are now concerned.

It is an interesting truth that the great Creator Himself has special claims upon the young. His eye and his heart are upon them. Whether He will be honored or dishonored in the world which He has made, and whether or not His kingdom will be here advanced, depends not so much upon the risen as the rising generation. In this, as well as other particulars, the arrangements of nature and providence do but herald the higher methods of redeeming mercy. One of the marked features of the economy of grace is that its provisions and its claims meet the children of men at the very threshold of their existence, and that infant apostasy finds its counterpart in infant redemption. The first promise was to an embryo race. The first prefiguration, by purely material things, of the promised Deliverer was set forth in the memorable words: "Come thou, *and all thy house,* into the ark." The first visible seal of God's covenant faithfulness gave the Church the welcome assurance that He would be a God to them, and to their seed after them. Every instance of circumcision under the old dispensation, and of holy baptism under the new, proclaims that His mercy is coeval with man's want and woe, and with unutterable tenderness urges the divine claims upon the love, the confidence, and the hopes of the young.

When the God of Israel entered into covenant with the assembled tribes, He was careful not to exclude their children and little ones. They were the children of those whose carcasses fell in the wilderness, which He engaged to bring to the land forfeited by their fathers. It was because they caused their children to pass through the fire unto Moloch that He drove out and extirpated the ancient nations of Palestine. "Lo," says He, "children are the heritage of the Lord, and the fruit of the womb is His reward"—the heritage He gives and the heritage that He claims. And it is in enforcing this claim that the Savior now says, "Suffer the little children to come unto Me, and forbid them not; for of such is the kingdom of heaven." What a joyous day was that when the children in the Temple sang, "Hosanna to the Son of David; blessed is He that cometh in the name of the Lord!" The temple above is rich in the fruits of early piety. Praise is perfected from the mouths of babes and sucklings.

God urges His claims upon the young with great frequency and tenderness. He would "give subtlety to the simple, and to the young man knowledge and discretion." He tells him how he may cleanse his way. His parental language over and anon is, "My son, receive My words, and hide My commandments with thee. My son, forget not My law, but let thine heart keep My commandments. My son, attend unto My wisdom, and bow thine ear to My understanding." The great mass of

the young, more especially if they have been religiously
educated, are not so thoughtless as they appear. There
is a deep sea of troubled feeling in the youthful mind
which is often stirred up, and which, if not cared for, is
apt to subside in the imperturbable stupidity of sin and
death. There are few, if any, in Christian lands with
whom God's Spirit does not strive, and to whose awakened sensibilities He has no access. In the midst of all
their joy and buoyancy, earthly pleasures pall upon
their taste. They lose their interests in the concerns of
time, and in the multitude of their thoughts within
them they would fain be looking toward the things that
are not seen and eternal. This solicitude may be lost,
and this sobriety of thought chased away. Temptations
are everywhere, and everywhere snares beset them. They
may take their swing in the world; they may slumber
on, and awaken only to learn that the harvest is past,
the summer has ended, and they are not saved. But the
God of Zion has other thoughts toward them, and
other claims upon them. They were born under the
mediatorial reign of His redeeming Son, and to the
sweet hopes and winning expostulations of heavenly
wisdom. He has no pleasure in the death of the wicked,
even when the blow falls upon "the hairy scalp of him
that goeth on still in his trespasses," much less in the
overthrow of the child of prayer, and the desolated
hopes of the youth in whose character and destiny He
feels such an interest, and on whom His love has such
and so many rightful and gracious claims.

Youthful piety is also specially beloved of God.
Wherever it is found, true piety receives no equivocal
tokens of His love. Yet is there emphasis in the
promise: "I love them that love Me, and they that seek

Me *early* shall find Me." Most emphatically is piety
beloved and cherished by Him when it takes root in the
young heart, and combines the unsophisticated impulses of nature with the purer impulses of heavenly
truth and grace. It is a beautiful view when the graces of
the Spirit are thus engrafted on the green, fresh stock
before it has been scorched by the summer's sun, or
riven or withered by the blasts of winter. It is as when
the "fig tree putteth forth her green figs, and the vines,
with the tender grapes, give a good smell." It is bud-
ding, blossoming, fragrant piety. It was of the Church,
espoused to her heavenly Head and Husband in the
days of her *youth,* that the inspired poet exclaims, "Who
is this that cometh out of the wilderness like pillars of
smoke, perfumed with myrrh and frankincense, with
all the powders of the merchant?" In describing the
triumphs of the gospel in the last days, the Psalmist utters the beautiful prediction, "Thy people shall be willing in the day of Thy power. In the beauties of holiness,
from the womb of the morning thou hast the dew of *thy
youth."* Just as the opening morning discloses to the de-
lighted eye the spangles of the early dew, so does youthful piety sparkle in all brightness and purity. They may
not be the richest, but they are the most unsullied by
contact with the world, and the least saddened by subsequent and, it may be, bitter experience. There may be
more of the appendages of a self-righteous spirit in the
wearer, but there is a sweeter consciousness of moral
transformation, and a more gladdened confession of
the change, as men exclaim, "Behold, what hath God
wrought!"

   The God of Israel is not unmindful of this early at-
tachment to Him, even in the subsequent years of a

tardy and more doubtful pilgrimage. It was of His back-sliding people of other times that He said, "Behold, I will allure her, and bring her into the wilderness, and speak comfortably to her. And I will give her vineyards from thence, and the valley of Achor for a door of hope, and she shall sing there *as in the days of her youth.*" How often have I seen this sweet promise verified when at the bedside of God's dying people, who, though they became pious early, wandered from Him in later life, and who I feared would be called to the last struggle in darkness. These fears were groundless. God's ways are not as our ways. He remembered that early consecration to Him which they themselves had almost forgotten.

There are sacrifices made by the young in turning to God that are not made by the old. It is at some cost that they relinquish the joys of earth and youthful companionships, and take up the cross. They are sacrifices which, while they have no claim of merit, God takes notice of. "Go," says He, "go, cry in the ears of Jerusalem, 'Thus saith the Lord, "I remember thee; the kindness of thy *youth,* the love of thine espousals, when thou wentest after Me in the wilderness, in a land that was not sown." ' " Israel was holiness to the Lord, and the first fruits of His increase. He never forgot that youthful generation. He took it kindly that they loved Him. Long afterward He mentioned it to their praise, and never ceased to be their Guardian and Guide, and to defend them in all their course through the desert, over the Jordan, and to the promised land. And what He thus remembered in them and did for them, He remembers and virtually does for all who seek Him early.

A pious youth has the all-sufficient God for his permanent and everlasting Friend. Whom He loves, He loves to the end. Promises He once makes He never alters. "The gifts and calling of God are without repentance." God hides the youthful Christian in the secret of His presence, and keeps him safely in His pavilion. He would not be half so safe, were his tabernacle guarded by a legion of angels, as he now is, guarded on every side by the everlasting arms. Amid all his inexperience and exposures, in all his conflicts, in all his conscious infirmities, follies, and sins, that God whom his young heart chose as his Portion and Refuge keeps him as the apple of His eye. He "shall cover thee with His feathers, and under His wings shalt thou trust; His truth shall be thy shield and buckler." There is no safety to the youthful mind like this, and no repose so sweet. The Shepherd of Israel makes him lie down in green pastures, and leads him beside the still waters. His journey may be prolonged in this desert land, and it may not always be the straightforward and rectilinear course, but his divine Shepherd restores his soul, and leads him in paths of righteousness for His name's sake. Wanderer he may have been, but he shall come to his end in peace. Jesus shall meet him on the banks of the cold river; he shall pass over unhurt and, as from Jordan's farther verge he looks back on all the way the Lord has led him, shall give Him praise that he was enabled to remember his Creator in the days of his youth.

In addition to this, early piety is the most useful piety.

Every youth lives to be a blessing or a curse to his fellow men. He exerts an influence that makes them better or worse, more happy or more miserable forever.

He may become a Christian in middle life and have much to weep over, and much to undo of evils which an earlier consecration to God would have prevented. There is a vast difference between the growing brightness of that Christian career which is early entered upon and the flickering light which is kindled in a dusky old age. Among the reasons why most persons who become pious at all become so in their youth is the fact that youthful piety has time to grow and bear fruit. Its light shines brighter and brighter to the last. It is true that God sometimes arrests the youth in his thoughtless career for no purpose so ostensible as to fit him for an early grave, and it is a beautiful expression of His love when He thus calls the pious young from the conflicts and storms of earth to their heavenly home. These flowers of hope bloom sweetly in the heavenly paradise. Death is the messenger of heavenly love, sent down by the great Husbandman to His garden below to gather these young fruits of righteousness, and transplant them to purer skies. It is but another lily gathered when the youthful Christian dies.

Yet we are to remember that this is not the ordinary procedure of a wise providence. God more usually spares the pious young as living exemplifications of the truth and grace on which He has caused them to hope. They occupy spheres of responsibility and usefulness which cannot be occupied by the ungodly. God had His eye upon them from the first for this end. He watched over them for this purpose, trained them up for it, and early introduced them into His kingdom so that they might become the guardians and promoters of these high and sacred interests.

The thought is not always present to the mind (even

of the most attentive observers of the work of God's Spirit) that comparatively few become the disciples of Christ beyond the period of youth. He does not ordinarily wait to convert men until their habits of sinning and processes of thought have become matured by time, until their religious sensibilities are palsied, their heart as hard as a millstone, and the world, the flesh, and the devil have made them captives. It would be a melancholy table of statistics that should exhibit the conversion only of those who were brought to the saving knowledge of Christ after they had become forty years of age. If we would see a richer and brighter record, we must turn to an earlier page of man's history. I was induced several years ago to examine the biography of nearly sixty Christian men and women who were greatly distinguished for their piety and usefulness, and I find the following notice at the close of this inspection: "With four exceptions, all these became the subjects of divine grace between ten and five-and-twenty years of age." This remark is emphatically true of almost all the ministers of the gospel I have ever known or read of. Is it not also true of pious mothers? We do not say that piety is matured at this early age; nor do all the subjects of it at this early age express the strongest hopes; nor at this early period do they all become professed Christians. In some instances these early impressions gradually wear away, and are apparently lost amid the follies of childhood and youth. There is, indeed, not a little in their history that has the semblance of backsliding, if not of an apostasy; but in God's own time the light comes out full and clear and, with now and then a brief eclipse, sweeps its bright course to the western sky.

If there is no force in this consideration in favor of early piety, it is because the selfish heart of man is dead to the noblest of motives. It is not the most worthy incentive to godliness when we seek to obtain religion early enough simply to save us from hell. Nor do we mean by this remark to utter a thought that is discouraging to the aged; the eleventh hour forbids despair, but are there not brighter hopes for the young? Is it so that God our Maker asks only for the poor remnant of a life jaded with pleasure and worn out with sin? Have you no honest desires to serve God? Or is it only that He may serve you that you would fain delay seeking Him as long as you can? Away with this base thought, and "remember *now* thy Creator in the days of thy *youth!*" Think of the privilege, the honor, and the blessedness of serving Him. Think more of Him, and of His goodness and long-suffering mercy. You can never pay the debt of love you owe Him, were you to serve Him faithfully from your cradle to your grave. You may honor Him who bore shame for you. You may honor Him who died so that you might not die, but live to Him. Glory, honor, immortality—these are the prizes of your high calling. Worm and sinner as you are, you can yet honor Him, and in no way so effectively as in loving, reverencing, and obeying Him in these days of your youth.

Nor may we suppress the thought that early piety is the happiest piety.

The lessons which true piety teaches are not learned in a day. Those just and clear perceptions of God's truth which are so essential to the tranquility and vigor of Christian hope demand early and long-continued teaching. It is no marvel that those who enter the school of Christ at a late period of life understand and apply them so imperfectly. If now and then you find a strong and vigorous Christian whose conversion was delayed until late in life, he forms an exception and not the rule of Christian experience. Rich and varied experience of the divine mercy and goodness, of the way in which God leads His people, of the discipline by which they are weaned from the world and fitted for heaven, of the unchanging faithfulness of His promises, and of the consolations of His everlasting covenant, in order to be fully enjoyed, must be enjoyed early. They cannot be crowded into a short compass. The mind can not at once grasp them. Nor can they be so vividly felt as when they grow with its growth and strengthen with its strength.

Youthful piety alone gives full proof of the declaration, "The ways of wisdom are ways of pleasantness, and all her paths are peace." It is the only piety which truly credits a declaration which is so generally discredited by the gay and giddy world. Youthful piety not only credits, but prizes and exemplifies it, and at an early age, when, of all others, it is least likely to be so exemplified and prized. When the sons and daughters of pleasure look upon religion as beneath their notice and treat it with contempt, or stigmatize it as a morose and gloomy thing, the youthful Christian rescues it from this reproach, and makes it his joy. It is his relaxation from toil, his comfort in trial; amid storms it is his tranquility, his refuge in temptation, and in joy it is his song. He is gloomy and depressed only when he does not enjoy it. There are wayward hours when he forgets God, but he has no peace until he returns to his first love. There may also be seasons when his pleasures become forbidden pleasures, and are followed by the stings of remorse, and then none is so restive as he; nor can he find rest until, like the wearied dove sent forth by Noah, who found no rest for the sole of her foot, he goes back to the ark.

There is one thought in relation to the blessedness of early piety which may not be duly appreciated. The dispensations of grace are, with few exceptions, in perfect keeping with the laws of the human mind; they do not contradict, but honor the work of God in man's intellectual constitution. When we look at men as they are, we shall find this observable peculiarity in the piety that begins beyond the midday of human life: it has few of "the pleasures of memory." Men are formed to look backward as well as to look forward, to remember as well as to anticipate. No small part of their enjoyments arises from the visions of the past. Hence it is that the piety that dates from the later periods of life almost always wears a somber aspect. All experience and observation teach us that the events and scenes most distinctly remembered by the aged are those of bygone and far-distant years. The proximate past is forgotten; the events of the past year and the past day are lost sight of in earlier memories. Their thoughts are with them in their good old age. There is, indeed, enough in the retrospect of those who remembered their Creator in the days of their youth to fill them with self-abasement and humiliation. But there is something else to look back upon. There are solemn Sabbaths and the awakening power of God's truth. There are deep convictions and the work of the Holy Spirit which is begun. There is the life-giving influence of His unsearchable grace. There is the dawn of light and hope, and the joys of the new-born soul, when she first put on her garments of gladness and salvation. There are "songs in the night," and there are the frequently recurring and well-remembered scenes of cheered fellowship with God and His youthful people, of concerted effort, prayer, and praise. And these are precious memories when, in the more advanced periods of their history, as their heart becomes heavy and cold, the seared leaves of autumn begin to fall, and the winter of life sets in, memory throws her thoughts backward and is cheered. The immediate past may be dark, but it is almost a chasm; the mind looks over and beyond it, and takes little interest in it compared with those earlier days and more vivid scenes that were made glad by the light of God's countenance. They are balmy breezes, sweet sounds, and the lingering echo of early songs. This is one of the rewards of early piety. Not only does it relieve the natural imperfections of age, but comforts its despondency and sorrows, and cheers its loneliness. It is a precious truth that the man who becomes pious in advanced life is safe. His hope is in the Rock, Christ. His "hoary head is a crown of glory," because, though late, "it is found in the way of righteousness." Yet it is not the piety that blossoms, like Aaron's rod, from the hither to the outer verge of the wilderness.

The young are slow to learn that the winter of life is coming on. Age has evils enough of its own without adding to them the burden and bitterness of youthful wickedness. The very strength of the years of an old man is "labor and sorrow." When "the strong men bow themselves," and those "that look out of the windows are darkened," there is need of other lights than the waning light of time. An old man without piety is a miserable man. Oh, it is wisdom to sow in the spring, and gather in summer, and while "the sun, or the moon, or the stars be not darkened, nor the clouds return after the rain!"

This is the affecting lesson so impressively enforced in the text. "Remember *now* thy Creator in the days of thy youth, while the evil days come not, and the years draw nigh in which thou shalt say, 'I have no pleasure in them.'" When "the almond flourishes, and the grasshopper is a burden"; when "the silver cord is loosed, and the golden bowl is broken, and the pitcher is broken at the fountain, and the wheel is broken at the cistern"; when "the dust returns to the earth as it was, and the spirit to the God who gave it," it will be no grief of heart to you that you remembered your Creator in the days of your youth. You will not regret it when God shall bring you into judgment. No son nor daughter of Adam will on that day be heard to say, "I wish I had taken my swing in the world a little longer. I was pious too early. God loved me too soon!"

If I know anything of my own heart, I have prepared this discourse from an earnest desire to influence the beloved youth of my pastoral charge. I have reached the outer verge of life's wilderness, and if there is any one blessing I have more reason to be thankful for than another, it is that I was led by God's infinite and sovereign mercy to give my heart to Him in the days of my youth. With the strong impulsiveness of my nature, it seems to me that I should have been among the most daring of the presumptuous, and long ago in the bottomless pit, had not his matchless grace snatched me as a brand out of the fire while I was young. I am anxious for you, my beloved young friends, and "jealous

over you with a godly jealousy." I wish to see you a chosen generation, protected from the contagion of the
world you are just entering, and early acknowledging
your father's God to be your God. Oh, be not followers
of the multitude to do evil! It is not the world that is to
guide you; it is God's will and law. Search His Word;
frequent His sanctuary; and wherever else, and in whatever else you may be wanting, see to it that you have a
name and a nail in His holy place. Never forsake the
house of God. Most sacred are the duties which the
pulpit owes to the young. It is the pledge of better
things when you heed its counsels. Do not carry to your
dying bed the painful thought that you have been the
despiser of the Sabbath. It is the presage of ruin. Would
you remember Him? Ask Him to remember you. "In all
thy ways acknowledge Him, and He shall direct thy
paths." Be reconciled to Him through faith in His Son,
and delay not that reconciliation to a more convenient
season. Your time may be another day, but His time is
now. Your time may be when your heart is hardened,
and His Spirit grieved away. It may be the time He has
appointed for you to contend with the king of terrors,
to die without God and without hope. I look around
upon this assembly and do not see a young person present who was not born to die. The next Sabbath may
not dawn upon you. Oh, how many of the young who
have attended upon these ministrations now slumber
with the dead! You know not what it is to die. None of
us know. The scene will be new, the reality new, and,
when you meet them, you will feel as you never felt before. What a scene would this house present were a single youth it contains now in the agonies of death! What
a sermon would the grim messenger preach should he

look in at your window this night, and steal behind the curtain where you slumber! Oh, thoughtless and profane youth! The world does not record greater folly than yours. I may not say that the voice has not already gone forth, "Thou fool! *This night* thy soul shall be required of thee!" Before the night of death shall shut in, therefore, when this bloom and vigor will decay, when these eyes shall be suffused with tears, before that evil day comes, and while yet the morning of life is bright upon you, *remember your Creator.* Delay not, for the hours are short and few. Raise an earnest look to heaven, and remember your Creator in the days of your youth!

The Best Ornaments of Youth

by Cotton Mather

(A short essay on the good things which are found in some, and should be found in all young people, and which, wherever they are found, heaven will take a favorable notice of them)

"In him there is found some good thing toward the Lord God of Israel." 1 Kings 14:13

This is a good character, and it is given of a young person. But in a son of such disadvantages (and such discouragements, as far as every good thing), who would have expected such a character! Oh, the sovereign grace of our God! Samuel has a wicked son, and Jeroboam has a godly one. A child of an idolater proves to be a gracious child, while the child of one who had made himself an alien from the common-wealth of Israel has in him a gracious disposition to-wards the Lord God of Israel. O ye children of parents who have the grace and fear of God conspicuous in them, if you should have in you no good thing toward the Lord God of Israel, how inexcusable are you!

Jeroboam has a son who is taken sick. He sends his wife to inquire of an aged prophet of the Lord as to what should be the result of the sickness. He would not send to one of his own ministers. No, when wicked men come into distress, they often have a conscience telling them who are the true ministers of God, what ministers are most likely to declare the mind and the truth of God unto them.

The reverend man of God faithfully sets before the queen the sin and fate of her idolatrous family; he foretells that, because it had been an idolatrous family, it would also be a miserable one. One thing is foretold as a misery to the family which yet would be a mercy to the person whom it should more immediately fall upon, and that is the death of the son, whose mother was now making her inquiry concerning him.

The early death of the lad is foretold, but it is a death which would be much lamented by all the nation, and a death which would not be attended with such tragic circumstances as were to befall the rest of the family—yea, and a death which would happily transplant the spirit of the lad into the garden of God, happily translate him from the bosom of Jeroboam to the bosom of Abraham. It is plain that this young man was to have some special marks of the divine favor upon him, above the rest of the family to which he belonged. Behold now the reason for it: because in him "there is found some good thing toward the Lord God of Israel."

Some have proceeded so far as to tell us most particularly what good thing it was. The Jews tell us that Jeroboam set guards of soldiers to hinder the more devout Israelites from repairing to the worship of God at His temple. But this excellent young man hindered the soldiers from offering that violence which his father would have had them to have offered unto the sincere worshippers of God. We have no sure authority for this confinement of the matter. The good thing may import some observable discovery of goodness and virtue in him. In general, it is agreed that piety is the good thing which this young man was adorned with.

I call him a young man, and I will tell you why. He was not an infant, for there was notice taken of what was in him. He was not of full age, for he is called a child. He must then be a young man. He was a good young man. He fared the better for his goodness. The good doctrine which now calls for the attention of my young people is this:

DOCTRINE: When young persons come to have some good thing discernible in them, the good God will take a favorable notice of it. He will favorably observe it and reward it.

If there is any notable good in young people, God will take a kind notice of it. No good thing in any people shall go unobserved and unrewarded by God. But if a good thing is in young people, it will come under a more special observation of God.

Come, you children, hearken unto me, and I will teach you what good thing we would have to be found in you, what good thing you may expect from God if it is found in you, and why the good God will do such good unto the young people who have a good thing found in them. Give a good attention to these three things. I think that you cannot but count them worthy of a great attention. Oh, that good things might be produced among our young people by our discourses on them!

1. There should be some good thing found in our young people. But what is that good thing? Truly we can, in our wishes, abate you nothing of what you find expressed in Romans 15:14: "I am persuaded of you, my

brethren, that ye are full of goodness." We will so express it. I am desirous for you, my children, that you may be full of goodness. However, let us begin with some good thing toward the Lord God of Israel. And we will hope that, though the beginnings are but small, the latter end will greatly increase. It is a glorious Christ who is the Lord God of Israel. It is God in Him who is the Lord Jehovah, the God who chose Israel for His peculiar people, the God chosen for their God by all the genuine people of Israel. Well, then, a good inclination to serve the great God and His glorious Christ, and to have Him for your God—if this inclination is in you, O young people, then there is found in you some good thing toward the Lord God of Israel. At the hearing of His Word, let the wishes of your souls be fired to cry out, "Lord, incline me! Lord, incline me to undertake Thy service! Lord, incline me to take Thee for my Portion."

But let us be more particular. First, there are some things which are called in Hebrews 6:9 the "better things," even the things which accompany salvation. These are good things indeed. If salvation from all evil, and if the rest that remains for the people of God, are good, then these things must be so also. Faith is one of those good things. We read that the end of your faith is the salvation of the soul. Repentance is one of those good things. We read that repentance is unto salvation. Holiness is one of those good things. We read that he who orders his conversation aright shall see the salvation of God. When these things are found in young people, then there are some good things found in them. Children, at this intimation fall down before the Lord, and cry unto Him, "Oh, that faith and repentance and holiness might be found in me! Lord, from Thee let these good fruits be found in me!"

Second, the knowledge of the only true God, and of Jesus Christ whom He has sent, is a good thing. Is not life eternal so? We read in 2 Chronicles 30:22 of the good knowledge of the Lord. Young people who know the God who made them and the Christ who bought them, and who, by consequence, know their own state before God, and the duty which they owe to God and man, these have some good thing in them. We read of some young people in 2 Timothy 3:15 that they are "made wise unto salvation." Oh, good thing indeed! The soul without knowledge cannot be good or see good. But how good is it for a young soul to be made wise unto salvation!

But suppose that young people are yet very destitute of knowledge, very defective in their knowledge! Can there be no good thing in them? Yes, there can be a desire; a hungry, thirsty desire after knowledge would be a good thing. We read in Proverbs 2:3–5: "My son, if thou criest after knowledge, if thou seekest her as silver, then shalt thou find the knowledge of God." I will say, my child, if you have an insatiable desire to know the things of your everlasting peace, if you do use all proper means so that you may know what would be for your good, then there is a good thing found in you, and you shall also find the knowledge of the Lord.

Third, a principle of abhorrence of sin and obedience to God is a good thing. We read in Psalm 73:28: "It is good for me to draw near unto God." Young people have some good thing found in them when they abhor that which is evil. A sorrow for sin, and a hatred of sin as the worst evil in the world—when this is found in young people there is then some good thing found in them. We read of one who could say, "I fear the Lord from my youth" (1 Kings 18:12). A fear of sinning against God, a fear of incurring the wrath of God by sinning against Him, is a very good thing. It is the beginning of wisdom, and all good is entailed upon it. A young person should repel temptation to sin as the young Joseph did, who said, "How shall I do this wickedness and sin against God?" Such a one has most certainly some good thing found in him. And young people have some good thing found in them when they strive to obey God, and count it good for them so to do. It is commanded of young people in Ecclesiastes 12:1: "Remember now thy Creator in the days of thy youth." That remembrance includes obedience. It is a good thing, we have been told of old: "It is a good thing for a man to bear the yoke in his youth." Young people who cheerfully put their necks under the golden yoke of the Lord-Redeemer, who cheerfully say, O Lord, truly I am Thy servant. I am Thy servant!"—these have some good thing found in them.

Fourth, even the desire of good is to be counted as "some good thing." The young persons who desire that which is good have some desirable good thing found in them. We read in Proverbs 11:23: "The desire of the righteous is only good." All good begins as the desire of good. Those young people have some good thing found in them who desire to be good and to do good. There are young people who may say, with Nehemiah 1:11, "O Lord, we are Thy servants, who desire to fear Thy name." And Isaiah 26:8: "The desire of our soul is to Thy name and to the remembrance of Thee." There is found some good thing in these persons, and there

toward the Lord God of Israel" some translators render
as "some good thought toward the Lord God of Israel."
Young Abijah could not have a good thought come
into his mind but the God of heaven was pleased with
it. If young people begin to think (oh, do it, my children!) of turning to God, closing with Christ, and becoming seriously religious, even this is a good thing,
and pleasing to God. Much more is it so when the desire for good grows more flaming and active in them,
and their hands do not refuse to labor for it. There are
young people who heartily desire, "Oh, that my steps
were ordered in the way of God, and that no iniquity
may have dominion over me! Oh, that I had an interest
in the only Savior of men, and in His great salvation."
There is found some good thing in the young people
who desire this good. We desire it and fervently desire
it, for you, O our children!

2. And now, let us hear what good thing shall be
done for such young people. The good God will favorably observe and reward the good thing that shall be
found in them. The Almighty God will show a respect
unto good young people, a special respect unto them
that shall make it evident that they are, as John, the
youngest of all the disciples, even the disciples who are
beloved of the Lord.

More particularly, first, the young people who have
some good thing in them are oftentimes highly favored
of the most high God while they live in this world.
There is a remarkable providence of God often at work
for the young people who have some good thing in
them. They are the darlings of providence, the peculiar
care of heaven. The providence of God remarkably provides for them. Yes, though they are left orphans in a

wide and a hard world, yet the young people who have some good thing in them are strangely provided for, so that indeed they lack no good thing. They sing that song found in Psalm 27:10: "When my father and my mother forsake me, then the Lord will take me up."

In the providence of God, they often meet with remarkable deliverances. Young David had some good thing in him, and then God remarkably delivered him from the lion, from the bear, and from the Philistine. Such young people as have some good thing in them are oftentimes kept by God from evil so that it shall not grieve them. They are the subjects of remarkable preservations. And, as a token of his favor to them, God usually grants unto such young people to find favor among His people. We read in Proverbs 3:4: "My son, so thou shalt find favor and good understanding in the sight of God and man." Some good thing in young people procures for them a good name in the neighborhood. A good name is better than precious ointment; a good name is to be chosen rather than riches.

Young men, you be the judge in this matter. Which is the better of these two? To be thus described among the neighbors—"That young man is a foolish, profane, extravagant fellow"—or to be thus described: "That young man is a sober, discreet, virtuous person. He will never do a base or an ill thing; you may depend upon him."

You young women, which is the better of these two? To have this description among the neighbors—"That young woman is a vain, giddy, trifling fool. She knows nothing but the mysteries of the dress and the dance. And she is given so to lying and mischief; it is a dangerous thing to talk with her"—or to have this description: "That young woman is virtuous, modest, prudent, and in everything well accomplished; but especially for the fear of God." It is by some good thing found in them that young people come to have many a good thing spoken of them.

In short, young people who have some good thing in them are such as present their prayers to God continually; and the prayers of such find acceptance with God. Young Solomon found it so; the blessed Hearer of prayer said unto him in 1 Kings 3:12, "Behold, I have done according to thy words."

Young people who have some good thing in them are those who seek first the kingdom of God. Thus they secure the blessings of the kingdom; they see all the good of the chosen of God, and there is added unto them everything else that shall be good for them—and this while they live!

But, second, much more at their death, when they leave the world. When young Abijah came to die, then it was that he found the recompense of what good thing was found in him. There is no promise that such young people shall always outlive their youth. Sometimes they who have some good thing in them die early. They whom God loves may do so; yes, and it may be *from* His love unto them. Nevertheless, it is no rare thing for them who have some good thing in them while they are young people to live to be old people. The fear of God is such that this good thing tends to life; this prolongs days. I know no such likely way to stand a good while in the garden of God as to bring forth good fruit there. Some good fruit on young people will be some good thing in them. This, if anything, will prevent their being cut down. But whenever they die, they may have this for their satisfaction: "To me to die is gain" (Philippians 1:21).

Young people who have some good thing found in them often die joyfully. Their deathbed consolations are no small consolations. How comfortably could the servant of God say in Isaiah 38:3, "Remember now, O Lord, I beseech Thee, how I have walked before Thee in truth, and with a perfect heart, and have done that which is good in Thy sight." A young person who has had the good thing in him, when he comes to die, may make this comfortable appeal unto God: "Remember now, O Lord, I beseech Thee, how early I began to walk before Thee; how early Thou didst form and see some good thing in me. How heartily I have resigned myself unto the conduct of a glorious Christ, and made it my business to glorify Him!" Oh, the comforts; oh, the raptures wherewith such a young person may rejoice in the hope of the glory of God!

Or, if not joyfully, yet such young people at length die happily, and by death are carried into eternal joy. The young soul that has in it some good thing shall never lose that good thing; and, by consequence, the soul itself shall never be lost. We read in Philippians 1:6: "He which hath begun a good work in you will perform it." The good thing found in such a soul will be a token for good. By this token, the soul at its departure hence will be taken into the paradise of God. It will be a tree of life to the soul in the paradise of God. The soul will delightfully feed upon it, with its reflections, and be comforted. At the resurrection of the dead, the young people who have had some good thing in them shall renew their youth, and they shall mount up like eagles. With the raised and glorious bodies bestowed

upon them, they will be able to soar up with them; they
will be able to soar up with them as with the wings of
eagles. They shall flourish in a perpetual youth. The
almighty Redeemer, unto whom they devoted and resigned themselves, will redeem them from the power of
the grave. He will receive them into His holy city. He
who wrought in them the good thing, which prepared
them for the inheritance of the saints in light, will now
do for them all the good that can possibly be done for
the objects of His dearest love. And, oh, how great is the
good which God has laid up for those who fear Him in
their youth, and who have some good thing in them
while they are yet but children before Him!

Now, shall I say it? I see my children taking their
mansions in the heavenly Jerusalem! I hear their acknowledgments, their astonishments. "This I have, because in my youth I kept the precepts of God. All this
good from the Lord God of Israel follows upon my having in me some good thing toward the Lord God of
Israel! Oh! Why did I serve Him no better, who does all
this good unto those who serve Him?"

And I hear their Lord, with astonishing smiles for
them, wiping away tears from their eyes, and saying
unto them, "Come, ye blessed, inherit the harvest of every good thing which you ever had or did for the Lord
God of Israel. You are no losers by becoming Israelites
indeed while you were in your youth, and you did not,
you could not, bind yourselves too soon unto the service of the Lord God of Israel!" Such notice will the
good thing in you, young people, have taken of by God.

3. Why will the Lord so favorably take notice of the
good thing in young people, who are good early in life?

Why, it is engaged that it shall be so. We have an

engagement from the faithful God for it in Psalm 124:4: He will "do good unto them that are good." If young people have some good thing found in them, the engagement of God is that they shall find what is good.

Again, the good thing that is in any young people is the workmanship of God. We read in 2 Corinthians 5:5: "He that hath wrought us for the self-same thing is God." So, He who has wrought this self-same to us is God. God will take notice of His own workmanship; since it is His, it is very good. If there is a good thing in any young people, we may say that it is a workmanship of God, created for good works. But, then, we may not take it for granted. The Lord will not forsake or cast off the work of His own hands. It is the image of God which they have upon them in that good thing. The Lord loves His own image. He likes it wherever He sees His own likeness. Young people, you are the sheep of His hand. It is God who has made you what you are, if today you hear His voice. Therefore it is that His hand will do wondrous things for you!

Once more, the good thing in any young people will put them upon doing good. We read in 2 Timothy 2:21–22: "A vessel unto honor, sanctified and made meet for the Master's use, prepared unto every good work; flee also youthful lusts." One who flees youthful lusts is a young person who has a good thing found in him. Such a one is a vessel of honor for the Lord, and prepared for every good work. Young people who have some good thing in them will do an abundance of good. They will counsel others, reprove others, and awaken others to look after the same good thing. They will shame others in whom the good thing is wanting. They will find in their hearts to pray for the good of

others. They are profitable ones and God will not leave
all this good unrecompensed! But now for application.

Application

1. How can we do anything other than take up a
lamentation over many young people in our nation?
For, alas, there is no good thing in them toward the
Lord God of Israel. We read of one person in 2 Chronicles 36:8: "The abominations which he did, and that
which was found in him, behold, they are written. . . ."
Jerome thinks that this means the marks and brands of
idolatry which were found on his body after he was
dead (which were forbidden in Leviticus 19:28). Truly,
what abominations will be found in some young people! What abominable things are done by them! Oh, do
not do them! The Lord sees them and hates them; and
they render you hateful unto the Lord.

There are some young people of whom you can tell
there is no good thing found in them. They are altogether flesh, altogether filthy, and governed by that
flesh, in which there dwells no good thing. Is there any
good thing found in them? No. There is found in some
young people a gross disobedience to their parents.
Rebellion against family government? Why, these children of Belial have almost rendered it impracticable.
This cannot be a good thing, for there comes a heavy
curse on those who set light by their parents. In some
there is found vileness. Their fornications, their adulteries make a cry to heaven; they either frequent harlots
or are such. This cannot be a good thing, for whore-
mongers and adulterers God will judge. In some there
is found vile society. They keep company with those

who have drinking bouts, or gaming and reveling; perhaps they wickedly wrong their masters. This cannot be a good thing, for "a companion of fools shall be destroyed."

There are young people who, instead of having any good thing found in them, will scoff and flout at those in whom it is found. Woeful Ishmaelites! And there is no coming at them to advise them either. They slight good advice. They have no good thing in them, nor will they hear of any good thing. They have most antipathy and malignity to those who are most likely to do them good. If a good book is put into their hands, they will not so much as give it a reading; perhaps they will even brag of the contempt which they have cast upon it. We will mourn over you, O sleepy and secure sinners, whose damnation slumbers not; we will mourn over you, whether you will mourn over yourselves or not. Yes, we will therefore do it because you will not mourn over yourselves. Ah, Lord, have we brought forth these children for the murderer? Children, we will behold your condition like Rachel weeping for her children. Our voice must be heard, lamentation, weeping, and great mourning. We will weep for our children, and we will not be comforted, because they are not what they ought to be.

2. It would be a good thing for parents to take a proper notice of whatever good thing they may find in their children. It would be an imitation of God, and it would greatly edify the children.

Can you find any good thing in your little folks? If they are dutiful to you, that is a good thing. Are they mannerly in their carriage? That is good. Can you perceive that they love to read the Word of God and learn

their catechisms; that they shun idleness and all
wickedness, and are afraid of sinning against God; that
they conscientiously sabbatize on the day which the
Lord has made; that they take delight in serious discourses; and, above all, that they go alone to seek the
face of God in secret? These are *very* good things.

Well, take a proper notice of these things. But what
is a proper notice, you ask? Not to be proud of them,
not to boast of your children. That is a ridiculous vanity, nauseous and loathsome to solid people. In all
companies, to be crying up one's own children as
matchless and none-such things is one of the wonders
of this age! The geese are swans, and the crow is telling
what a fair, white bird she has! Away with this folly. No,
the proper notice to be taken is, first, to be sure to be
humbly thankful to God for every good thing in our
children! The servant of God could say in 3 John 4, "I
have no greater joy than to hear that my children walk
in truth." Oh, let this joy be raised into praise, and let
God and His grace have all the praise! Think, "It is the
mere grace of God that prevents it; else my children
would be all so many devils. My corrupt nature in them
is enough to make them so." And then commend,
cherish, and encourage every good thing in them. Let
them see that you like all that is good in them. Study
methods to gratify them. A good look and a good word
will go a long way to encourage that good thing. Make
them sensible that your sentiments of them are those
found in Proverbs 23:15: "My son, if thine heart be wise,
my heart shall rejoice, even mine." This will create new
matter of joy continually!

3. But when will all our young people make sure that
some good thing is found in them, yea, that every good

thing shall be found in them? When shall it be? Young people have solemn and awful warnings dispensed unto them, such as Ecclesiastes 11:9: "Know thou that God shall bring thee into judgment." In that judgment shall then, upon examination, be found, O young people, what good thing is to be found in you. And woe to you if there is then found none. Will you now therefore bring yourselves under examination? Oh, consider and examine whether you have that good thing, the fear of God, in you. Consider it in the fear of God!

Children, is there some good thing found in you? It may be that the world will take little notice of you. And some who do take notice of you will do it with malignity, like that of Cain against his righteous brother Abel. But, oh, "rejoice in the Lord, and again I say, rejoice." Rejoice in the favorable notice that God will take of you.

Though you may have only some good thing, only a little grace, only a hearty and settled purpose to cleave unto God, even this, if it is real and sincere, is of great account with God. We read in Matthew 12:20 that the smoking flax He will not quench. But if you have some good thing really in you, as it will certainly grow, so you will mightily labor for the growth of it. Oh, do not rest until you have become exemplary for every good thing; yea, never think you have enough, but still hunger and thirst after righteousness.

When, when shall we see our young people so improved in all goodness that they shall adorn the doctrine of God their Savior in all things; that they shall come up to communion with the Lord, His people, and His table in the highest form of Christianity; that they shall shine like breathing stars, be shining and flaming witnesses for a glorious Christ, and be examples of a sober, righteous and godly life unto an ungodly world? Oh, that the God of all grace would bring about such a thing!

My young people, I leave these counsels with you.

First, esteem it not enough that you have no bad thing found in you. No, nor esteem it enough that you have no more than some good thing found in you. Some young people seem to count it enough that they are not openly vicious and scandalous. Oh, let these words of the Lord Jesus Christ make a deep impression upon you. Matthew 7:19: "Every tree that bringeth not forth good fruit is hewn down and cast into the fire." You must get some good thing above and beyond mere morality. A fine, civil, hopeful, young man was lost for having no more than that. You may go a great way and yet perish if you lack one thing, even that good thing, a heart so renewed as to prize Christ above this world. And when you have attained unto that good thing that will save your souls, yet press after higher and higher attainments in it. Let the light shine more and more until the perfect day. Briefly, it is the uttermost conformity to a glorious Christ, the uttermost imitation of a glorious Christ, that is to be proposed unto your laudable ambition. He is the good One. Who can do anything other than bless you if you are the followers of the good One! This is the good thing in the best form of it. In the church at Mentz, there is a crucifix, an image of our crucified Savior, whereof the eyes are massy and matchless carbuncles, and that weighs six hundred pounds of gold. I will say this to you, a young person who has arrived unto the good thing, which is to be and walk like a glorious Christ, and to have His image in holiness and righteousness upon him—this is a vastly more valuable and admirable thing than a crucifix that weighs six hundred pounds of gold!

Second, remorse for every bad thing, and a hatred of every bad thing, a boiling zeal against it, must be ingredients of the good thing expected from you. You are called upon in Romans 12:9 to "abhor that which is evil, cleave to that which is good." The Greek expression used for that abhorrence is very emphatic; it literally means, "abhor it like hell itself." Children, you have had bad things in you. Oh, confess them all; bewail them; forsake them. You have had your original sin, whereof some understand Psalm 25:7 to read: "Remember not the sins of my youth." It has regard to all the sins which we all have in us from our youth. Abase yourselves before the Lord, in the sense of that fountain of sin, and cry out, "O wretched one that I am! One born a leper! Lord, unclean, unclean! From my very infancy I have been overrun with a cursed and a horrid leprosy! Who will deliver me?"

You have also had your actual sin, upon which you should look back with regret. Job 13:26: "Thou makest me to possess the iniquities of my youth." Take the exposition of the Ten Commandments; take a view of yourselves in that glass, a glass of more use than that which many of you so much converse with. See your omissions of what is required, your commissions of what is forbidden, in the holy Law of the Ten Commandments, which, because you have been enslaved by sin, you have thought of as a law of slavery. Upon all of them, judge yourselves. Know that they who do such things are worthy of death! So judge yourselves so that you may not be judged by the Lord. Come to

some agreeable resolutions. Resolve this: "I have done
iniquity; but I will do so no more!" And reclaim other
young people too, as far as you can, from their iniquity.

Third, esteem it no reproach to have a good thing
found in you. Esteem yourselves to be enriched by every
reproach that shall, for that good thing, be cast upon
you. Many young people seem willing to go without
some good thing in them rather than to bear the cruel
mockings of a few fools to which it will expose them.
Children, tremble before those words of the Lord Jesus
Christ from Mark 8:38: "Whosoever shall be ashamed of
Me, and of My words, of him also shall the Son of Man
be ashamed." Abijah was the son of a king. It is an
honor unto a young person of the best quality to have
some good thing found in him. A young gentleman
cannot consult his honor more than, by such a good
thing in him, as to loathe all sin, reject the familiarity
of wicked men, unite himself with the churches of God,
and espouse the right ways of the Lord. A young Moses
was a person of quality; yet this great Moses thought
himself no way lessened, but rather enriched and advanced by being reproached for his adherence to the
people of God. Oh, come to this persuasion: "If a bad
thing will make the vile more vile, and a good thing
will make the good person better, then I am resolved
that the better I shall be!"

Fourth, there are good things whereof you find examples in the memorable young people whom the Holy
Scriptures have kept in everlasting remembrance.
Follow these examples, children, and you shall see the
good thing exemplified.

Was it a good thing in young Joseph to resist and
repel temptations to sin with his resolve: "How shall I

do this wickedness, and sin against God?" O tempted child, let this be your conduct! Say, "Sin, oh, that monstrous evil sin. I will by no means be brought over to it!"

Was it a good thing in young Josiah that, while he was yet young, he began to seek after God? Then come to this resolution: "I will seek after God with daily supplications. I will call upon the Lord as long as I live."

Was it a good thing in young Isaac that he retired to meditate? Then come to this resolution: "I will have my frequent meditations on God and Christ, on the state of my own soul, and on the things which are not seen and are eternal!"

Was it a good thing in young Solomon that he preferred wisdom above riches and honor? Then come to this resolution: "I will prefer spiritual blessings before temporal ones, and will be more concerned for my inward man than for my outward."

Was it a good thing in young Timothy that from a child he acquainted himself with the Holy Scriptures? Then come to this resolution: "I will mightily value an acquaintance with the Holy Oracles. I will mightily delight in reading and hearing the Word of God."

Finally, was it a good thing in young David that he could say, in Psalm 119:63, "I am a companion of all them that fear Thee, and of them that keep Thy precepts"? It cannot then *but* be a good resolution for you to say, "I will shun the company of the vicious, and will not sit with vain persons. I will choose those for my companions now whom I would hope to have so for eternity."

Oh, that our young people would come to such resolutions (but not in your own strength, my child)! No, but say, "Lord, I depend on Thy strength to perform the good thing which I resolve before Thee."

Fifth, would a young person have some good thing found in him? Let him ask it of God, who gives liberally. Ah, child, there is no good thing found in you until it may be said of you what is said in Acts 9:11: "Behold, he prayeth!" But, then, every good thing will follow upon that. Pray immediately; pray continually. And let your prayer to the good God be this: "Lord, let me have such a good thing as by grace created in me, I pray Thee!"

Yes, let me tell my hearers: there is an offer of the good thing unto our young people. Oh, let them embrace the offer. Is the Christ of God a good thing? Yes, of Him we read in Hosea 3:5: "They shall fear the Lord, and His goodness." You have this day an offer of Him. Is the Spirit of God a good thing? Yes, of Him we read in Psalm 143:10: "Thy Spirit is good." You have this day an offer of Him. Is a work of grace on the mind a good thing? Yes, it is called in Philippians 1:6 "a good work." It is this day offered unto you. Oh, what acceptance do these marvelous offers find with you? Then with surprised, conquered souls reply, "Oh, glorious God, I thankfully accept Thy wonderful offer. May Thy Christ be my Savior and Ruler. May Thy Spirit be my leader and my strength. May Thy grace fit me to be a vessel of Thy glory!" Young people, if you have embraced these good things, you are made good forever.

I must deal honestly with you, though. If these good things are not obtained in your youth, it is much to be feared that they will never be obtained at all. If you go on hardening your hearts and resisting the Holy Spirit of God until your youth is past, it may be feared whether you will not be given over to eternal hardness and blindness. The Word of God speaks dreadfully of those who are accustomed to doing evil. Indeed, there are no limits to be set unto sovereign grace. But I must warn you, it is a dangerous thing to dally with it. I hope you will be afraid of doing so.

I must carry on my expostulations with you. Young people are pleased with ornaments, and many of you are set off with very agreeable ornaments. But, children, the good thing in you will be the best of ornaments. I am commissioned to say that it will give to your head an ornament of grace; a crown of glory it shall deliver to you. Yes, you have no true ornaments upon you till you are adorned with some good thing in you, by conversion to God. There is a humbling statement made in Exodus 33:5–6: " 'Ye are a stiff-necked people; therefore now put off thy ornaments from thee.' And the children of Israel stripped themselves of their ornaments." From that I take it to mean that they who are on ill terms with heaven by being yet in their sins ought to apprehend themselves as being destitute of any real ornaments.

Ah, child in whom the good thing is wanting, your sin spoils all your real ornaments. Is your wisdom one of your ornaments? But your sin renders you a fool. Are you adorned with a good nature, a good humor? Your sin renders you a base creature, an ungrateful enemy to God, who is your Creator, Preserver, and wondrous Benefactor. Is your strength one of your ornaments? You are a feeble wretch; by sin you are feeble and sorely broken. Are you adorned with beauty? Your sin makes you blind, lame and ugly. Oh, you are under a universal deformity. Would it not be a doleful spectacle to see one so crooked and stooping that he could not look up; his eyes closed and running with putrid matter; his lips black and swollen and poisoned; his breath stinking to the offense of all who came near him; his feet stumbling every step; from head to foot, all wounds, bruises, and putrefying sores! Ah, sinner, you are that very spectacle. Rueful and loathsome spectacle! Are you adorned with riches? No, your sin plunges you into the worst poverty; it pillages you of all durable riches. Are your good relatives your ornaments? What, when the devil is your father? Have you the ornaments of splendid apparel upon you? Alas, your sin clothes your soul in rags. Oh, let shame cover you! What confusion of face belongs to you, O sinner, while yet in your sins, while yet without any good thing! But your conversion to God, which would introduce a good thing into you, what a lovely alteration would it bring upon you! Verily, it would set heaven rejoicing. The holy angels of heaven would fly to the windows of heaven, joyfully to look down upon you. The acclamations of joyful angels over your renewed soul would be, "Arise, and shine, O heaven-born soul; your light has come, and the glory of the Lord is arisen upon you."

And, oh, what good things God has reserved for the young people who have the good thing in them! Good and great things. The promises which tell you of those good things are very great and precious promises. Heaven is full of good things. There, there are you going! There you shall be satisfied with the goodness of the house of God, and of the holy temple.

I will say no more. I will break off by quoting 1 Corinthians 15:2: "Ye are saved if ye keep in memory what I have preached unto you," and by that I mean in a memory that shall bring on obedience.

How and Why Young People Should Cleanse their Ways

by William Cooper

"Wherewith shall a young man cleanse his way?
By taking heed thereto according to Thy Word."
Psalm 119:9

Never were the devout affections of a sanctified soul more copious or various than David's in composing this psalm. By it one may see what is the life of godliness in the soul of man and what are the exercises of true and unfeigned devotion. The composure of it is not so singular as the matter of it is sweet. Many a saint has singled it out as a part of Scripture which he would especially recreate himself in, saying, "For by it Thou hast quickened me, in both the way of duty and the exercise of devotion."

David's affection for his God may here be learned from his affection for His Word. It is the general scope and design of this psalm to magnify God's Word and make it honorable, and to set forth its excellency and usefulness, to commend it to everyone's constant study and diligent practice. Every verse in this psalm but one contains either some special commendation of the Word of God, some expression of love for it, or else a prayer for grace to conform to it. In our text, the Word of God is commended to us from the purifying influence it has on the souls and lives of men. In these words David asks a question of importance, and answers it in the best manner that can be.

First, David here asks a weighty question, which it concerns all young people to ask for themselves: "Wherewith shall a young man cleanse his way?" For young people (says one commentator upon this passage) themselves inquire by what means they may recover and preserve their purity; and therefore David asks the question for them. David was a king, and it is an inquiry worthy of him as such: "By what means may the next generation be made better than this?" Nothing can be more worthy of the care of the fathers of a people than this, how the virtue of the youth among them may be best preserved.

David was a father, and we may take this inquiry as an expression of his personal care and affection. He knew that his children, as they came from him, were defiled, and from that filthiness, which they derived from him, he was concerned that they might be cleansed. It may be that he, with grief of heart, saw some of them walking in the way which is not good; and for all of them he had a holy concern that they might be made clean, and keep clean from the corruption which is in the world through lust. He does not inquire as to how the young men shall be put in the right way? He does not inquire as to what the likeliest method is for them to take to raise their fortunes (as we speak) and advance themselves. But his question is: how they shall cleanse their way or keep their path clean? How shall they be directed to order their course so as to be right and blameless?

Second, he here answers this question in the best manner that can be: "By taking heed thereto according to Thy Word." Let them not walk heedlessly or carelessly, but circumspectly and by rule; and for their rule, let them take the Word of God, acquaint themselves with it, and conform to it. Let them take it for a light to their feet, and a lamp to their path; and then they will keep in the clean way and not be in such a danger of contracting pollution. And the Word of God too—if they will yield themselves up to it, and suffer it to have its proper influence over them—will help them to recover their purity, to make them clean from what defilement they have already contracted and now cleaves to them, for it is of a purifying, cleansing nature. "Sanctify them through Thy truth. Thy Word is truth." The doctrine is this:

DOCTRINE: It concerns young people to cleanse their way, which they may do by taking heed thereto according to God's Word.

The doctrine may be spoken to under these two propositions:

Proposition 1. It concerns young people to cleanse their way. David asks it as a thing of importance and concern: "Wherewith shall a young man cleanse his way?"

Proposition 2. They are to cleanse their way by taking heed to God's Word. "Wherewith shall a young man cleanse his way? By taking heed thereto according to Thy Word."

Proposition 1. It concerns young people to cleanse their way. First I will show what it is to cleanse our way, and then, second, I will show how much it concerns young people to cleanse their way.

This text shows that our way is defiled. To speak of cleansing it supposes and implies that it is polluted and defiled. And it is defiled, first, with respect to that original corruption which we all bring into the world with us. The nature of man has miserably lost its primitive purity, and has a permanent viciousness and corruption brought upon it; it is tainted with an evil disease which cleaves fast to it and is hereditary, so that none can be clean who is born of a woman (Job 25:4). From this corruption and pollution, we are not cleansed even to this day. It extends and diffuses itself though the whole man and through the whole life; so it may be said of us that we are defiled in all our ways, and that all our ways are defiled. Some degree of impurity is from hence communicated to all that we do. The impurity of our life and way necessarily arises from the impurity of our nature. Who can bring a clean thing out of an unclean one? Do men gather grapes from thorns or figs from thistles? Or does a corrupt fountain cast forth pure streams? The action or performance must be such as is the principle from whence it proceeds. So that if we say we have no sin and think our way is not polluted, we deceive ourselves. It must be otherwise with respect to our original corruption, from which we are not wholly cleansed while in this world. Proverbs 20:9: "Who can say, 'I have made my heart clean'? " And if they can't say that their heart is clean, be sure that they can't say their way is.

Second, our way is defiled by many particular sins which all of us—but more especially young people—are subject to. From this fountain, our original corruption, proceed many streams which affect us with pollution and defilement, and render our way unclean before God. Matthew 15:18–19: "Those things which come forth out of the heart, they defile the man; for out of the heart proceed evil thoughts, murders, adulteries; these are the things which defile a man." But Mark gives us a larger catalogue, adding seven particulars to these which have been named. Mark 7:21–23: "From within, out of the heart of men, proceed evil thoughts, adulteries, fornications, murders, thefts, covetousness, wickedness, deceit, lasciviousness, an evil eye, blasphemy, pride, foolishness. All these things come from within, and defile man."

I shall particularly mention some of these, which young people are more especially subject to, by which their way is defiled, and from which they are concerned to have it cleansed.

Things Which Defile a Man

1. Evil thoughts. These are the firstborn of the corrupt nature, the beginning of its strength, and most resemble it. Our thoughts, however light some may make of them, are rarely not sinful and hurtful. And sinful thoughts more especially lodge within the minds of young people. By "evil thoughts" we may understand corrupt reasonings, carnal fancies and imaginations, wicked contrivances and purposes, and thoughts which are vain, idle, and unprofitable.

The minds of young people are very apt to entertain corrupt reasonings concerning the blessed God, His holy Word and ways, sin, their own souls, this world and the other.

They sometimes too kindly entertain, and do not reject with enough abhorrence, some cursed suggestions which are from the wicked one, tending to shake their belief in the being and perfections of God, and of the truth of His holy Word; they are apt to conceive and entertain prejudices against the ways of God and religion, and to think that they are not ways of pleasantness, nor paths of peace; they sometimes persuade themselves that there is not such evil in sin as ministers make out, and that it is not so offensive to God or of such dreadful consequence; they are sometimes apt to entertain mean and low thoughts of their own souls, to argue corruptly concerning their nature, and to set their best and immortal parts at too low a rate in their own esteem and opinion; they are apt to think that the world and the things of it can make them happy, and that the things of eternity are not of such certainty, nearness, and vast importance to them. So vain and corrupt are the imaginations of the thought of the hearts of us all, but especially those of young people are apt to be concerning these things. Psalm 14:1: "The fool hath said in his heart, 'There is no God'; they are corrupt." Psalm 50:21: "Thou thoughtest that I was altogether such a one as thyself." Psalm 73:11: "And they say, 'How doth God know?' "

Moreover, carnal fancies and imaginations are evil thoughts, and these are often entertained in the minds of young people. A vicious fancy will make filthy thoughts and imaginations its entertainment when they don't proceed to the gross act, and will make a sport of reflecting upon what is past. But such ideas are polluting, and proceed from unclean lusts reigning within.

Again, wicked contrivances and purposes are evil

thoughts, which lodge especially in the minds of young people. They often devise mischief, and plot upon the thing which is no good; they contrive such an ill thing now, and purpose to prosecute it at a later time. So Simeon and Levi contrived a bloody fact, and accomplished it to gratify their wrath, which was cursed and cruel (Genesis 34:24). Many young people set their wits to work, devising ways and means by which to gratify their vile affections and sensual desires. Micah 2:1: "Woe to them that devise iniquity, and work evil upon their beds! When the morning is light they practice sin." Job 24:15: "The eye also of the adulterer waiteth for the twilight, saying, 'No eye shall see me.' "

Once more, vain, idle, unprofitable thoughts are to be accounted as evil ones. Useless, trifling, impertinent thoughts, which have nothing in them to make us call them good, must be called evil; they divert the mind from that which is good, keeping out good thoughts and making room for evil ones. Proverbs 24:9: "The thought of foolishness is sin." Swarms of these vain and idle thoughts crowd into the minds of young people. David hated such thoughts. Psalm 119:113: "I hate vain thoughts." These God would have us cast out and keep out. Jeremiah 4:14: "How long shall vain thoughts lodge within you?"

2. Evil words. These also come out of the heart, and defile the man and his way. False witness and blasphemies were mentioned before, along with speaking evil of God, and of our neighbor. But by evil words I mean all atheistic, profane speech which casts contempt upon the blessed God, or anything whereby He has made Himself known, and is an affront and indignity to His glorious and fearful name; all malicious,

slandering, back-biting, false or reproachful words which hurt or injure our neighbor, and are a breach upon the royal law of charity; all haughty boasting, vain-glorious words whereby we vaunt and exalt ourselves above what is fitting, and which are contrary to that most excellent Christian virtue or grace of humility; all filthy communication, foolish talking and jesting, which are not convenient; and also all vain, idle, impertinent talk, which is not good for the use of edifying.

These are all evil words, the natural, genuine product of our evil hearts; and none are so apt to offend in this kind as young people, to the dishonor of God, and to the hurt of others and of themselves.

Few young people set a watch before the door of their lips, and so take heed to their ways as not to sin with their tongues; but out of the abundance of that foolishness which is naturally bound up in their hearts, their mouth pours out foolishness (Proverbs 15:2). They are apt to think that words are but wind, and like it pass away and are gone; but they are much mistaken, for there is not one of those words in their tongue now but God knows it altogether; and for every idle word which they speak, much more for every profane one, they must give account in the day of judgment. "For by thy words thou shalt be justified, and by thy words thou shalt be condemned" (Matthew 12:36–37). When Christ shall come to judgment, He will reckon with men not only "for all their ungodly deeds, which they have ungodly committed, but for all the hard speeches, which ungodly sinners have spoken against Him" (Jude 15).

3. Pride is a sin which easily besets young people. There is no corruption that reveals itself in us more

early than pride; and some have made the observation that more young people are ruined by it than perhaps by any one lust whatsoever.

Young people are very apt to think of themselves as being above what they ought to think, to be puffed up in their own minds, and to carry it unseemly towards those who are above them. If they are handsome, they are apt to pride themselves in their beauty; if ingenious, in their wit; if strong, to glory too vainly in their strength; if rich, or likely to be so, to value themselves too much upon that. They often think themselves too wise to be taught and too good to be reproved, to be above their business and above restraint, and are often blind to their own faults, defects, and blemishes. Now, he who thus walks in pride makes his way unclean before God. For as a meek and humble spirit is in the sight of God of great price, so a proud and haughty one is just the contrary. The pride of life is put with the lusts of the flesh in 1 John 2:16, and is reckoned as defiling.

4. Sins against the seventh commandment very often (and especially) render the way of young people unclean before God. Adulteries, fornications, lasciviousness, filthy communications, chambering and wantonness, those fleshly lusts, are especially youthful lusts, and make the sin of many young men, like Eli's sons, to be very great before the Lord, and their life to be among the unclean (Job 36:14).

5. I will name no more but that which Mark puts the last in his catalogue, and that is foolishness, rashness, and imprudence in consideration. Ill thinking was put first, and unthinking is put last; for both are the spring and cause of much evil. The way of young people is defiled because they don't act cautiously, prudently, or

discreetly; they don't walk circumspectly, or behave themselves wisely in a perfect way; they don't ponder well the path of their feet, or take diligent heed to their steps. And therefore they so often stumble and fall, or contract defilement. If they think amiss at first, they don't think again, and admit second thoughts to correct the errors of the first.

This foolishness we find is put with adultery, pride, and such like heinous iniquities, and is said to defile the man as well as the others. We may be apt to call this behavior weakness and childishness; but truly the Word of God calls this foolishness sin. For it is a transgression of the command of God, who has bidden us to walk circumspectly, to take heed to our ways, to consider things, and therein show ourselves men. And He has given us reason to direct us, that candle of God within us as well as His Word without, which, if we don't duly and rightly use, we wickedly set aside and put out. Upon the account of these, and many other particular sins, as well as upon the account of their original corruption, the way of young people may be said to be defiled.

I have shown why our way needs cleansing; let me now show more specifically what it is to cleanse our way.

First, it is to get our hearts and natures renewed and sanctified by the grace of God. Our way will never be clean till our hearts are. We must first make the tree good before we can expect that the fruit will be good. The salt of grace must first be cast into the corrupt fountain before the streams will be pure. While the inward part is very wicked, all that is without will be unholy. If our natures are corrupt, vicious, and unsanctified, the stream and bent of our ways and practice will be according to it. If therefore we would have our way clean, we must get our hearts and natures renewed and sanctified. "Create in me a clean heart, O God; and renew a right spirit within me" (Psalm 51:10).

Second, it is to get our souls cleansed and purified in the blood of Christ, from that defilement which we have already contracted. How shall one cleanse his way? How shall he be made clean from that filth which he has already contracted in his way? Much guilt, and many stains, are upon us; our mind and conscience are defiled; there is none of us who has lived any time in the world who has kept our garments unspotted from it, and escaped the pollution which is in the world through lust. But how shall we be made clean? The blood of Christ applied to us will make us clean; if washed in this, we shall be whiter than snow. Under the law there was a brazen laver, and a brazen sea to wash in; but all the ceremonial washings could not make anyone's conscience clean. But now the blood of Jesus Christ, God's Son, cleanses us from all sin (1 John 1:7). How much more shall the blood of Christ, who through the eternal Spirit offered Himself without spot to God, purge our consciences from dead works to serve the living God (Hebrew 9:14)! Some of you, wrote the apostle in 1 Corinthians 6:11, were fornicators, adulterers, and the like, but you were washed, but you were sanctified, but you were justified in the name of the Lord Jesus, and by the Spirit of our God. Revelation 1:5: "Unto Him that hath loved us, and hath washed us from our sins in His own blood."

Third, we are to cleanse our way by the daily-renewed exercise of true repentance. Repentance, like the expulsive faculty in the body, is to separate and discharge all that is noxious or defiling. If the filth of sin has been at any time swallowed down, we must by repentance immediately cast it out again; if our feet have contracted any defilement in our way, through infirmity and inadvertence, the tears of repentance, together with a believing application of the virtue of Christ's blood, are to make them clean again. Even "he that is washed needeth thus to wash his feet" (John 13:10).

Fourth, to reform our lives and amend our ways is to cleanse them. "Wherewith shall one cleanse his way?" In other words, how can one not only make it clean but keep it clean? The beginning of Psalm 119 tells us who the undefiled in the way are: they are such as do no iniquity. Isaiah 1:16: "Wash you, make you clean, put away the evil of your doings from before Mine eyes; cease to do evil."

To cleanse our way is to flee youthful lusts, to deny all ungodliness and every worldly lust, to suffer no iniquity to have dominion over us, and to keep ourselves especially from our own iniquity, and the sin which easily besets us. It is to cleanse ourselves from all filthiness of flesh and spirit, and to perfect holiness in the fear of God; it is to watch and keep our garments unspotted. 1 Timothy 5:22: "Keep thyself pure."

In the first part of this first proposition, I showed what it is to cleanse our way. Now, in the second part of that same proposition, I hope to show that it greatly concerns young people to cleanse their way. David asks it as a thing of great importance and concern: "Wherewith shall a young man cleanse his way?" It concerns them to cleanse their way for these reasons:

1. The holy God looks upon and takes notice of their way. The Lord is in His holy temple, and from thence His eyes behold the children of men and all their ways. It is a most certain truth we find in Proverbs 5:21: "The ways of a man are before the eyes of the Lord, and He pondereth all his goings." "Doth not He see my ways, and count all my steps>" (Job 31:4). This God is of purer eyes than to behold iniquity, and cannot endure anything that is evil; if our way is not found clean before Him, it is abominable and offensive to Him. Young people have many eyes upon them, which should make them take heed to themselves and endeavor to keep their way clean; but above all, the awful apprehension of the eyes of the holy and jealous God being upon them should influence them to this. Can you think any longer that it does not greatly concern you to cleanse your way when your way is always before the Lord, and when His eye is upon you when all other eyes are off?

2. The gospel of Christ, under which you live, obliges you to this. The gospel is a doctrine according to godliness. It teaches and obliges us to deny those lusts and sins whereby our way is defiled, if we would have any benefit by it and share in any of the privileges of it. The manifest design of the gospel is to purify us to be a peculiar people. That which it teaches and enjoins is pure religion and undefiled before God and the Father; so it concerns us to cleanse our way if we would not thwart and contradict that which is the manifest design of the gospel we live under and hope to be saved by.

3. You are concerned to cleanse your way if you would not defeat and contradict the end, intent, and

obligation of your baptism. Most of us have been baptized; and as we cannot but value the privileges of our
baptism, so surely we cannot but have an awful regard
to the sacred obligation of it. By our baptism we are
obliged to deny the world, the flesh, and the devil; to
walk not after the flesh, not to be conformed to this evil
world. But while we live in any worldly or fleshly lust,
which makes our way unclean before God, the intention of such our baptism is defeated and the sacred
obligation of it broken. "Know you not that as many of
you as were baptized into Jesus Christ were baptized
into His death, that the old man might be crucified
with Him, that the body of sin might be destroyed, that
henceforth you should not serve sin? Wherefore reckon
ye yourselves [by the obligation of your baptism] to be
indeed dead unto sin, but alive unto God through Jesus
Christ our Lord" (Romans 6:3, 6, 11).

4. If our way is not clean before God, we cannot have
any confidence towards God or enjoy any communion
with Him. Psalm 24:3: "Who shall ascend into the hill
of the Lord? Who shall stand in His holy place? He that
hath clean hands, and a pure heart." None who were
ceremonially unclean might ascend the hill of Zion,
on which the temple was built; this was to signify that
cleanness of heart and life which is required in all
these who draw near to God or have any fellowship with
Him. The hands which at any time we lift up to Him in
prayer must be clean hands; they can have no blot
cleaving to them. The hearts with which we draw near
to Him must be pure hearts, purified by faith and
cleansed from their wickedness. This is necessary in
order to have a gracious assurance in coming before
Him and expecting blessings from Him. Job 22:23, 26:

"If thou put iniquity far from thee, then thou shalt have thy delight in the Almighty, and shalt lift up thy face toward God; thou shalt make thy prayer to Him, and He shall bear thee, and thou shalt pay thy vows." There can be no comfortable communion or correspondence between God and us if there is not this cleanness of heart and life. An unclean conduct, proceeding from an unsanctified heart, naturally tends to alienate the mind from God, and necessarily obstructs all intercourse with Him. "For what fellowship has righteousness with unrighteousness? And what concord has Christ with Belial? Wherefore, 'Be ye separate,' saith the Lord, 'and touch not the unclean thing; and I will receive you, and will be a Father to you, and ye shall be my sons and daughters,' saith the Lord Almighty" (2 Corinthians 6:15, 17–18).

5. It concerns us to cleanse our way so that we may keep a good conscience and get a good name. A good conscience is our best friend; it will always be a continual feast to us. A defiled way must make a defiled conscience, and there is nothing worse. But if our hearts do not reproach us, if our own consciences witness for us that in simplicity, and godly sincerity—not with fleshly wisdom, but by the grace of God—we have our conversation in the world, this may be our rejoicing in the day of evil and our comfort in the day of death.

And by this also we shall get a good name, which is a blessing to be sought for, to be valued by all, especially by those who are young; good names are often made by the good opinion others have of them and the fair character gained in youth. And such as are really careful to keep their way clean, to order their course so as to be right and blameless, commonly find favor and good understanding in the sight of God and man.

6. It concerns us to cleanse our way before God so that His way may be clean towards us. From what he had himself experienced, David laid this down as the rule of God's proceeding: God deals with men accordingly as their character stands with Him, and as their way is found before Him. Psalm 18:20–26: "The Lord rewarded me according to my righteousness; according to the cleanness of my hands hath He recompensed me. For I have kept the ways of the Lord, and have not wickedly departed from my God. For all His judgments were before me, and I did not put away His statutes from me. I was also upright before Him, and I kept myself from mine iniquity. Therefore hath the Lord recompensed me according to my righteousness, according to the cleanness of my hands in His eyesight. With an upright man Thou wilt show Thyself pure."

Let us cleanse our way, and, behold, all things will be clean to us. Then the paths of the Lord towards us will be mercy and truth. We shall then have a sanctified use of outward things. They'll be given to us in love, and clean from the dregs of the curse. Titus 1:15: "Unto the pure, all things are pure; but unto them that are defiled and unbelieving is nothing pure."

7. It concerns us to cleanse our way now because we must give a strict account of it in the great day. All of us must ere long stand before the judgment seat of Christ to give an account of everything done in the body, and to receive according to it. And every work must then be brought into judgment with every secret thing, whether it is good or evil. Oh, what a concern this should fill us with now! How careful should this make us to consider our ways, and to cleanse ourselves from all heart impu-

rities, which must then be laid open, and from all secret sins which must then be made manifest! For the day shall declare them. In that day all our youthful follies and extravagances will be called to account, all those particular sins by which our youth has been defiled. The royal preacher would have young people know and consider this, so that the thought of it might give check to them in their sinful ways. Ecclesiastes 11:9: "Rejoice, O young man, in thy youth, and let thy heart cheer thee in the days of thy youth, and walk in the ways of thine heart, and in the sight of thine eyes. But know thou that for all these things God will bring thee into judgment."

8. It concerns us to cleanse our way, for such as our way is now will our life be after this. If we continue in sin, and don't get our souls purified and our lives reformed, our life after this must be among the unclean, as Job speaks of some who die in youth (Job 36:14). We shall then be utterly unfit for the Jerusalem which is above, into which shall in no wise enter anything that defiles, neither whatsoever works abomination, or makes a lie (Revelation 21:27). We must then be made to take our part with the unbelieving and abominable, with the angels, those foul spirits of darkness, "which kept not their first estate, and who, giving themselves over to uncleanness, are set forth for an example, suffering the vengeance of eternal fire" (Jude 6–7). These things which I have just named show you why you should cleanse your way. How you are to do it will be said under the second proposition.

Proposition 2. Young people are to cleanse their way by taking heed thereto, according to God's Word. "Wherewith shall a young man cleanse his way? By taking heed thereto according to Thy Word."

If we would cleanse our way, we must take heed to it. If we would have our way kept clean, and order our course so as to be right and blameless, we must not walk heedlessly or carelessly, but with care, caution, and circumspection. Ephesians 5:16: "See then that you walk circumspectly." It is the fault of us all, but especially of young people, that we don't act with more care and caution, that we don't live more under the great law of consideration. It's no wonder if he who shuts his eyes as he walks, or is staring wildly up and down, stumbles and falls, and is then defiled.

If we would cleanse our way we must take heed, first, to our way in general and see that it is right and good. We must see to it that we walk in the way which is called holy, that our path is that of the just, the path which all good men walk in, which has in it the footsteps of the flock, by which we may know we are not of them who turn aside onto bypaths. We must be sure that we are in the good old way, the narrow way, the way to Zion, the way that leads to life, that leads to the Jerusalem which is above, the city of the Living God. He who walks in this way surely walks in the clean way.

We must take heed to the constant course and tenor of our life and conversation, and see that the stream and bent of that are not such as argue us to be under the prevailing power of a carnal, sensual mind. By the general course and tenor of our life, it should appear that we have a habitual care to please God, and a fear lest we offend Him; that we have a respect to all God's commandments, and hate every false way; that we exercise ourselves to keep a conscience void of offense, both towards God and towards man. And here I would say that, in taking heed to the course and tenor of our life, we should be particularly careful to know what the duties of our way are as well as where the dangers are, so that we may act accordingly.

We should be careful to know what the duties of our way are so that we may do them. There are the duties of our Christian life in general, and the particular duties of our respective callings and relations; these we should be careful to know and do so that our work may be found filled up before God. If we are careful to do what is good, and what the Lord our God requires of us, what is incumbent on us in our places and stations wherein we are called, this is so to take heed to our way so as to render it clean, i.e., pleasant and acceptable to God, and beautiful before men.

We should be careful to know where the dangers of our way are so that we may guard against them. There are many sloughs in our way which we are in danger of tumbling into, many stones which we are liable to stumble at, and therefore need to be well apprised of. There are snakes in the grass, serpents in the way, and adders in the path; and we therefore need to look before we step. Psalm 40:12: "Innumerable evils have compassed me about." We have sins which easily beset us, which we are most liable to from our calling, company, and the like; by these our way is in the most danger of being defiled, and therefore against these we should take the more diligent heed.

But, second, we are to take heed of any particular way which is before us, or to every step which we take in our way. Proverbs 4:27: "Let thine eyes look right on, and let thine eyelids look straight before thee. Ponder the path of thy feet, and let all thy ways be established.

Turn not to the right hand, nor to the left. Remove thy
foot from evil." Not only are we to take heed to our way
in general, but to the particular steps which we take
therein. "Is the thing which I am now about to do right
and good? Will not my conscience hereafter reproach
me for it? Does not the Word of God now forbid it? Can
I with any confidence ask God's blessing upon me in it,
or with any comfort think that His eye is upon me in
the doing of it? Shall I not hereafter think it would be
better not to have been done, and will I not wish I never
had?"

And here remember that "There is a way which
seemeth right unto a man, but the end thereof are the
ways of death" (Proverbs 14:12). There is often some
particular way which we would fain please ourselves
with in the notion that it is right and good, or at least
not very bad, because we desire to walk in it; but we
need to beware lest we flatter ourselves in that which
will prove to be our ruin.

Third, we are to take heed to our way by carefully
and seriously reflecting upon and reviewing our past
ways. Psalm 119:59: "I thought on my ways, and turned
my feet unto Thy testimonies." We should reflect upon
our past life, reviewing the paths we have walked in and
the steps we have taken. Haggai 1:5: "Now therefore
thus saith the Lord, 'Consider thy way.' " Lamentations
3:40: "Let us search and try our ways." It is our honor
that we have the power of reflection, and are capable of
reviewing our ways—and it highly concerns us to do
this. Without it we cannot be said to take heed to our
ways, but must be charged with the fault and folly of despising our ways. We should often, with much exact-
ness, consider what has been the temper of our souls

and the tenor of our conversation before God. We should give ourselves frequent leave and liberty to think what our management has been, wherein we have failed and done amiss, what are the blots and stains which cleave unto us. It was good advice which Pythagoras gave his pupil, that he should every night before he slept go over the actions of the day, asking himself seriously these questions: "What have I done? Wherein have I transgressed? What duty has been omitted?" If young people could be persuaded to be thus frequent and serious in reviewing their ways, it would be an excellent means to help them to order their course aright. How else shall we come to know what we need to be made clean from or to keep clean from? If we often compare our lives with the rule, we shall find out the errata that are to be corrected. If we frequently behold our faces in the glass, we shall see the spots we need to wipe off. In this way we may grow in an acquaintance with ourselves, and nothing is more necessary for us. Such as are not this particular and serious in reviewing their past ways cannot be said to take heed to them. Jeremiah 8:6: "I hearkened and heard (saith the Lord), but they spake not aright; none saying, 'What have I done?' "

In the fourth place, to take heed to our way is to carefully mind and observe the rule by which we should govern ourselves in the way. You are aware that this will bring me to say that the Word of God is the rule by which we are to be directed and governed in our way; therefore we should take heed to our way according to God's Word. But before I come to that, I would say that it is often the fault and folly of young people either to walk by no rule at all, or else to choose for themselves false rules.

It is often the fault and folly of young people that they walk by no rule at all. Because they are young, they think they may walk at random, and that the giddiness of youth will serve as an excuse for all they do amiss. They don't like to be kept within the hedge of any divine or moral precepts, but would play in a large pasture, or rather run wild in the wilderness like the ass's colt. They despise the Word, and do not fear the commandments, but burn the sacred bands of them asunder and cast the cords of those commandments from them. They condemn the counsel of their father and despise the advice of their mother; they will not obey the voice of their teachers, nor incline their ear to those who instruct them. They will not suffer either reason or conscience to check or control them, but will walk on in the way that seems right to their own eyes, and which they choose for themselves, let what will be said against it. Proverbs 1:7: "They are the fools that despise wisdom and instruction."

It is frequently their fault and folly to choose for themselves false rules, and to act according to them. They not only set aside the right rule, but are many times governed by such as are destructive and pernicious to them. The dictates of their own temperament and fancy are the rule they will act by. Solomon's ironic concession to the vanities and pleasures of youth they fix to themselves as a rule, to walk in the way of their heart and in the sight of their eyes. And sometimes they fix as a rule to do as others do, to follow the multitude though it is evil, to run with others though it is to an excess of riot. These and such like are the hurtful, pernicious rules which young people are often governed by and act from, while they set aside the good and the right rule.

The Word of God is the rule by which we should order our way, and according to which we should take heed if we would have it cleansed. "Wherewith shall a young man cleanse his way? By taking heed thereto according to thy Word." Let him walk by rule, and for his rule let him take the Word of God.

Here let it be said that the Word of God is so excellently well fitted to be the rule of life that if anyone takes heed to his way according to it, it must be kept clean, i.e., right and blameless. Some of the heathen philosophers have given excellent rules for the conduct of human life, but there are nowhere contained such perfect and sublime rules as in the sacred Scriptures. "The Law of the Lord is perfect," a perfect rule of life, for it is the work of Him whose works are all perfect. Psalm 119:98–100: "Thou, through Thy commandments, hast made me wiser than mine enemies; for they are ever with me. I have more understanding than all my teachers, for Thy testimonies are my meditation. I understand more than the ancients because I keep Thy precepts."

The Word of God directs us to everything that is wise and good, agreeable and fitting for us to do, and forbids us nothing but what is unreasonable, base, and unbecoming. The Word of God is exceedingly broad. It teaches to every circumstance and state of life, what to do in every relation and condition. It reaches the thoughts and motions of the soul as well as the outward actions. He has shown you, O man, in His Word what is good, and what the Lord your God requires of you. And "as many as walk according to this rule, peace shall be upon them" (Galatians 6:16). They who walk in this law of the Lord are the undefiled in the way, and are therefore blessed (Psalm 119:1).

The Word of God has such a purifying power that such as yield themselves up to it will be made clean; not only will it help them to preserve their purity, but to recover it. The Word is the instrument which the sanctifying Spirit uses in purifying souls. Ephesians 5:26: "That he might sanctify and cleanse us with the washing of water, by the Word." John 17:17: "Sanctify them through Thy truth; Thy Word is truth." The Word of God is pure, and has a purifying influence. Jeremiah 23:29: " 'Is not My Word like a fire?' saith the Lord." The Spirit of grace, by the Word, refines the soul and cleanses it from its corruptions, as fire cleanses the gold from its dross, and as medicine cleanses the body from its disease. John 15:3: "Now ye are clean through the Word which I have spoken to you." There is such a cleansing virtue in the Word that such as yield themselves up to it will be made clean by its working grace in them, and working corruption out of them. "The law of the Lord is perfect, converting [or restoring] the soul" (Psalm 19:7).

The Word of God is given to us for this very end and reason, so that by it we may be made clean and kept clean, so that we may get our souls renewed and our lives reformed. The Word of God is not only to amuse and entertain us, but to influence and govern us. It is not only to fill our heads with notions to talk of, but to enlighten our path to walk by. Psalm 119:105: "Thy Word is a lamp to my feet, and a light unto my path." Proverbs 6:23: "The commandment is a lamp, and the law is light." It is given to us for this end, and this is the use we should put it to, to direct us in the way wherein we should go, so that we may not be led into crooked paths nor wander on the mountains of desolation.

The Word of God is a doctrine according to godliness. Not only do the precepts of it oblige us, but the truths of it are designed and revealed to promote in us a sober, righteous, and godly life; they all conspire to bring us to that holiness of heart and life without which we cannot be accepted with God now, nor enjoy Him hereafter. The manifest design of God's Word is that by it we may be helped to escape the corruption which is in the world, and may be made partakers of God's holiness.

Wherefore we should take heed to our way according to God's Word. We should get acquainted with the Word of God; we should learn what it requires and what it forbids, what it would have us choose and what it would have us refuse; we must resolve to conform to it, to be ordered and governed by it, to give it its proper influence over us, and not to put it far from us as if it were a foreign thing to us. "I will meditate in Thy precepts, and have respect unto Thy ways. I will delight myself in Thy statutes. I will not forget Thy Word" (Psalm 119:15–16). "My hands also will I lift up unto Thy commandments which I have loved" (Psalm 119:148).

We should make God's statutes our counselors, as did David in Psalm 119:24: "Thy statutes also are my delight and my counselors." Young people especially need to ask for advice. Let them inquire, then, at the oracles of God; make God's Word their main counsel. There is more safety and satisfaction in consulting the Word than in a multitude of other counselors. The Word of the Lord is tried. The saints in all ages and in

all cases have tried it and taken counsel from it, and it
never failed them; but the closer they have adhered to it
the better.

We should take heed to God's Word as he who
writes looks to his copy, that he may write according to
it, and as the workman lays his model before him, that
he may do his work exactly. So did David in verse 30: "I
have chosen the way of truth. Thy judgments have I laid
before me." We should take heed to God's Word as the
traveler takes heed to anything that is to guide him in
his way, as the Israelites took heed to the pillar of cloud
and fire in their travel through the wilderness, as the
wise men of the east took heed to the star that directed
them to Christ, or as navigators take heed to the chart
and compass which they steer by. And, finally, we must
try and examine our ways by God's Word as metal is
tried and examined by the touchstone to see whether it
is right and good, and by the standard whether it is of
full weight. We should bring everything to the Law and
to the Testimony as the touchstone and standard; and
if anything does not agree hereunto, there is no truth
in it; it is not right and good, and it is not safe for us to
be concerned with it. These hints (some of which I
have borrowed) show how very exact and careful we
should be in ordering our way by God's Word if we
would have it kept clean. That it greatly concerns us to
do so has been said under the first proposition. We now
proceed to the application.

Application

USE 1. Let this teach us all, particularly those who
are young, to lay to heart the corruption and pollution

of our natures and lives, and to seek earnestly to God
for renewing and restraining grace. All flesh have corrupted their way; we are all gone aside; we are altogether become filthy. We are shapen in iniquity, and in
sin did our mothers conceive us. Our hearts are deceitful above all things, and desperately wicked; and as a
fountain casts forth her waters, so our hearts have cast
forth wickedness, and this has been our manner from
our youth. We may well cry, "Unclean, unclean, we are
unclean. We are polluted in heart and way before the
holy God, abominable in His sight, unfit for communion with Him and the enjoyment of Him." And should
not this affect us? Should not our corruption be our
lamentation? Should we not be earnestly seeking renewing grace? Should not we pray that the Lord
Himself would come into our souls, in the purifying influences of His Spirit, like a refiner's fire and fuller's
soap, and purge us from our filth, that we may be holy
to the Lord, and may offer Him an offering in righteousness? Should we not pray also that by His grace He
would restrain us from every evil thing, and preserve us
blameless and harmless, as the sons of God without rebuke in the midst of a crooked and perverse generation? We need to pray so that our hearts may not be inclined to any evil thing, to practice wicked works with
those who work iniquity; that God would turn away our
eyes from beholding vanity, and quicken us in His way;
that He would hide pride from us, remove from us the
way of lying, and grant us His law graciously; that He
would cleanse us from secret faults, and keep us back
from presumptuous sins, so that some may be upright
before Him, and innocent from the great transgression.

USE 2. Should young people be careful to cleanse their way? What shall be said then of such as are grown old, and are not yet cleansed from their filthiness? If these lines should fall under the eye of any such, let them consider that awful word from Isaiah 65:20: "The sinner being a hundred years old shall be accursed." Oh, how filthy must they be who have been defiling themselves throughout a long life! What a load of guilt must be upon those who have been every day adding to it for many years together! In what sorrow must they at last be! How cursed, how cursed shall the aged sinner be who goes down to the dead laden with guilt! Mountains of guilt upon him now, and mountains of wrath upon him then!

USE 3. Let us from hence call to remembrance the sins of our youth; let us be sensible of particular sins whereby our youth has been defiled before God. Who has not had youthful faults and follies? And these should be lamented and bewailed by those who have grown old. Call to remembrance then the former days, the days of your youth, which, it may be, are long since past; and bear upon your soul a penitential remembrance of the faults of it. Time has not worn out the guilt. The record of your youthful sins is not blotted out of the book of God's remembrance, nor should it be out of your own conscience. God sometimes makes His people smart in age for the sins of their youth. Job 13:26: "For Thou writeth bitter things against me, and maketh me to possess the iniquities of my youth." Ephraim is brought in reflecting upon his youth, and bewailing the sins of it. Jeremiah 31:18–19: "I have surely heard Ephraim bemoaning himself thus: 'I was turned, I repented; after that I was instructed, I smote upon my thigh. I was ashamed, yea even confounded, because I did bear the reproach of my youth.' " The sins of his youth he accounts as the reproach of his youth, and he now suffers his own conscience to reproach him for them. Such as are now past their youth should, in a penitential remembrance of the sins of it, pray with David in Psalm 25:7: "Remember not the sins of my youth, nor my transgressions. According to Thy mercy, remember Thou me, for Thy goodness' sake, O Lord."

USE 4. Does it so much concern young people to keep their way clean? Then such as have the care and oversight of youth should be concerned that they may do so. David acts like a wise and good father of both his people as well as his own family in the inquiry which he here makes. He knew that the happiness of communities lies much in the virtue of their youth. He knew that he would have but little comfort or credit in the children of his own family if they were not in some way concerned to keep their way clean; and therefore he asks this question and resolves it for them. And in this concern which he here manifests, he is a worthy pattern for all who have the care and inspection of youth. If young people are apt to be careless about their own way, and not to take heed to it, let parents and masters have more care concerning them. Charge them, warn them, advise them, require of them an account of their way, and endeavor by all means possible to restrain them. If you don't do this, whatever defilement they get in their way, you are not clean from it, and their sin lies in no inconsiderable degree at your door. Parents should be in great concern lest they incur Eli's guilt and curse, whose house God said He would judge forever for the iniquity of which Eli knew.

His sons made themselves vile, and he restrained them not (1 Samuel 3:13). Parents are commonly enough concerned how to put their children into a way to live in the world. Oh, that they were as much concerned how they might keep clean from the corruption which is in the world, and be made clean from that filthiness which they derive from them, and bring into the world with them.

USE 5. Learn hence the evil of sin which defiles our way and renders it unclean and abominable before God. Sin is the defilement of the soul, it is turpitude and corruption. The same then is true of our way, and renders it unacceptable and offensive to God, uncomfortable to ourselves, and base before men. Job took comfort in that God knew the way that he took (Job 23:10). In other words, God liked and approved of it. But if our way is defiled by sin, God is far from approving it. He knows it, but he abhors it. Psalm 14:2–3: "The Lord looked down from heaven upon the children of men, and they were all gone aside, they were altogether become filthy." Sin makes our way filthy, and hinders us from having God with us in our way. Let us then conceive a loathing of that, and keep at the greatest distance from it. That must be an odious, putrid, hateful thing in itself that makes our way so to God; and shall it not be accounted so by us?

USE 6. See the excellency of the Word of God in the purifying influence which it has on our way; and let this recommend it to us, to get acquainted with it, and to be governed and guided by it. There are many excellent properties and uses of the Word of God, which recommend it above any other word whatsoever. One, and not one of the least, is that it is the honor of God's

Word that as it is itself refined from all corrupt mixture, so if we receive it in the light and love of it, it will purify and refine us. And this excellent property of it should very much commend it to our affection and regard. Psalm 119:140: "Thy Word is very pure; therefore Thy servant loveth it." We should therefore be industrious to get acquainted with it, and learn the excellent precepts and wise instructions therein contained.

From our childhood we should know the Holy Scriptures. Young men should have the Word of God abiding in them. In the study of their Bibles they should incline their ears to wisdom and apply their hearts to understanding; by the rules and laws of it they should, at all times and in all cases, regulate and govern themselves. "So shall I keep Thy law continually, forever and ever. And I will walk at liberty, for I seek Thy precepts" (Psalm 119:44–45).

USE 7. Let this teach such whose way has not been defiled by any gross sin to be humbly thankful to God for it. If through the restraints of God's grace you have escaped the gross pollution which is in the world, and have not been left to get such a wound and dishonor and blot as shall never be wiped off, oh, be humbly thankful to God for it. Let every vain, self-exalting thought be far from you. Consider who has kept you and preserved you, and be not high-minded, but fear. Fear lest, as the apostle says in 2 Peter 2:20, "For if after that they have escaped the pollutions of the world, through the knowledge of the Lord and Savior Jesus Christ, they are again entangled and overcome, their latter end is worse with them than the beginning." Do not think that you are out of danger yet, or that you have escaped cleanly. But let humility, fear and prayerfulness preserve you in the future way.

USE 8. Let this teach all who are young to take heed to our way. Let us account it a thing of great concernment that our way be made and kept clean. I beseech you, my brethren, suffer this word of exhortation; cleanse your way by taking heed thereto according to God's Word.

In order hereunto, let me lay before you, and leave with you, a few considerations, and a few directions. First, a few considerations.

• Consider that, though you are reasonable creatures, you don't act as such if you do not take heed to your ways. God has dignified you above the beasts in your rational powers and faculties. You are capable of thought and reflection; and what can you so well employ those powers about as yourselves, your own ways and conduct now, as they stand related to your everlasting interests? It is in this way that you are to show yourselves men. If you don't act with reason and consideration, with care and caution, and for your interest, you act like babes, yea, like brutes. Remember this and show yourselves to be men (Isaiah 46:8).

• Consider whether the honor God has done you in giving you His Word to be the rule of your way doesn't strongly oblige you to take heed to your way according to it. Great is the honor God does us in giving us divine revelation, His written Word to guide us in our way. This shows us of what concern God counts it to be to us that we walk in the right and clean way. And shall we be careless about that which God has shown so much care about? O foolish and unwise!

• Consider that the best excuse those who are careless and heedless of themselves and their way can now

make is that they don't mind; for their part, they mind
nothing at all about it. But consider that a little, I pray
you. Will it suffice to say, "I was careless and did not
mind," after you have been so solemnly called upon to
take heed to your ways? God Himself calls upon you to
do so. Haggai 1:5: "Now therefore, thus saith the Lord
of Hosts, 'Consider your ways.' " And again in verse 7:
"Thus saith the Lord of Hosts, 'Consider your ways.' "
And since He has taken pains to give you His holy
Word, according to which you may take heed, can you
then with any confidence offer this now, or will it serve
you in the great day of account?

• Consider how much defilement you have already
contracted, how much guilt and how many stains are
already upon you. From that filthiness which you
brought into the world with you, you are not cleansed
to this day. And how much have you contracted since
you have been in the world? You will not be able to
keep yourselves quite pure after you have done your
best. You need then to take great heed to save yourselves as much as possible, since so much defilement
will cleave to you, do what you can.

• Consider that you do not know how soon God may
call you to give an account of your way, and to guide you
in your way. If you don't reform and cleanse your way
while you are young, you may not have any other season
for it. We see many die in youth. Solomon bids the
young man to know that he must be brought into
judgment. And this Word, which you now despise and
refuse to be guided and governed by, is that Word by
which you must be judged. This will be your condemnation: you refused to walk by it because your deeds were
evil.

Now let me leave you a few directions.

• If you would have your way kept clean, be sure to keep your heart with all diligence. This is the advice of the wise man found in Proverbs 4:23. There he gives the reason for it: "because out of it are the issues of life." Our lives will be as our hearts are. There is the fountain, and the issues will be according to it. Our great work then lies with our own hearts, as from them is our greatest danger. Let us then carefully watch over the motions of our hearts, and endeavor to mortify the corruptions of it; seek to get that well cleansed and well principled. This we must keep with all keeping, or above all keeping, if we would keep our way clean.

• Beware of evil company. Nothing more endangers young people than this. If you have any fellowship with the unfruitful works of darkness, you cannot well keep clean. The evil communications of others will corrupt you. "He that walketh with wise men shall be wise. But a companion of fools shall be destroyed" (Proverbs 13:20). Therefore, do not go in the way of sinners; do not enter into the path of the ungodly; contract no intimacy with them; avoid them; pass away from them. Take the advice of wise Solomon in Proverbs 1:10, 14–15: "My son, if sinners entice thee, consent thou not. If they say, 'Cast in thy lot among us,' my son, walk not that in the way with them; refrain thy foot from their path." Say as David did in Psalm 119:115: "Depart from me, ye evil doers. For I will keep the commandments of my God."

• Mind and value faithful, friendly reprovers. Be willing that others should watch over your ways and tell you when you are in the wrong path. Be not offended with those who deal plainly and faithfully with you.

Account the smiting of your fathers and brethren to be kindness, and their wounds faithful.

• Take heed of all appearances of evil, and all approaches to it. In matters of a disputable nature, count it best to keep on the safer side. And in things lawful be sure to keep within due bounds. Don't boldly venture to the utmost limits of lawful liberty. One of the ancients said, "Lawful things undo us." And the apostle enters this caveat in Galatians 5:13: "Ye have been called unto liberty, only use not your liberty for an occasion to the flesh." From the utmost bounds of lawful things to sinful things, the transition is easy; therefore he who is concerned to keep himself pure will take heed how far he advances. Ecclesiastes 5:1: "Keep thy foot."

• Observe the ways of others; take pattern and warning from them. Follow others, wherein they follow after the things that are good. We see, through the grace of God (as loose as the times are), many young people walking in the ways of godliness, who are examples of the things which are holy and good, who are the hope and joy of the people of God. Well, whatsoever things we see in others that are lovely and of good report, in which there is any praise and virtue, let us think on those things. And let us observe the faults and miscarriages of others, not to censure and reproach them, but to take warning by them. We may see in some many things which may shame and quicken us, and in others those things that may make us be very jealous over ourselves, and take the most diligent heed to ourselves. For these reasons we should keep our eye upon their way.

• Lastly, if you would have your ways kept clean, commit them unto the Lord. The way of man is not in himself. Let us be much in prayer to God, then, to order our steps in His Word, to hold up our goings in His paths, so that we never wander out of the ways of His commandments. If we seriously and solemnly commit our ways to the Lord, He will take the oversight of them. He is the good Shepherd, and will not only restore our souls, but lead us in the paths of righteousness for His name's sake. We know whom we trust, and He is able to keep that which we commit to Him. To God then, and to the Word of His grace, let us commit ourselves and our ways, who is able to keep us from falling, and to present us faultless before the presence of His glory with exceeding glory.

Young People Warned

by Jonathan Todd

(A sermon preached to young people August 5, 1740)

"I made their streets waste. I said, 'Surely thou wilt fear
Me, thou wilt receive instruction, so their dwelling
should not be cut off, howsoever I punished them.' "
Zephaniah 3:6–7

"Shall a trumpet be blown in the city, and the people
not be afraid? Shall there be evil in a city, and the Lord
hath not done it?" Amos 3:6

So great is the corruption and depravty of human
nature that a spirit of vanity and sin, and an inclination
to depart from the living God, have become natural to
men. Hence, perhaps there has not been found any nation or people of any long standing upon the face of
the earth who have not run to such a length in sin and
wickedness, and so increased their iniquities, as to
render it necessary for the vindication of the divine
providence and perfections that awful judgments are
sent upon them to be testimonies from heaven for God
and against impious, blaspheming mortals.

Indeed, God is abundantly, yea, infinitely good. He
is kind to the rebellious nations, and does not at once
stir up all His wrath. Yet, if He spares them for the present, and, being full of compassion, does not speedily
raise up Himself to destroy them, He does not forget

their wickedness and sins, but writes them down in His book. And when their iniquities are ripe, He will visit their sin upon them (Exodus 32:34).

So the prophet Amos, in the name of the Lord, assures the great and populous kingdoms, which then were famous in the world, that they had iniquities remembered by God that must, when they had filled up their measure, be punished upon them (see Amos 1–2).

Judah and Israel, though they were the peculiar people of God, the singularly favored of heaven, have their sins remembered before God as well as the other nations, and so might expect that a woeful day would sooner or later come upon them (Amos 2:4–8). Yes, the sins of these especially needed to be punished upon them. For God had done more for them than others, which laid them under stronger obligations. So that their sins were attended with very aggravating circumstances, in that they showed more ingratitude, more unkindness and stubbornness, which were the greatest affronts to an indulgent heaven (Amos 2:9–13).

The prophet Amos, in the name of the Lord, here declares the necessity and certainty of God's judgments against His own backslidden and greatly provoking people of Israel. Amos tells them that as God has been especially good to them, so their sins especially call for punishments; as He had peculiarly undertaken the care and government of them, and made them in a peculiar manner His own family, so it was but congruous and fitting that He should see the laws of His family executed upon them, correct them for their offenses, and punish them for their iniquities (3:2). It is indeed necessary that they be forsaken and left to God, and given up to misery and evil, when their ways are contrary and provoking to God, when they despise His laws and give Him no becoming reverence and glory. Verse 3: "Can two walk together except they be agreed?" Can any two walk together, and so have communion and fellowship one with the other, when they are not enough of one mind to walk the same way or take the same course? The similitude is easily applied: when God and His people are contrary one to the other, there is no communion between them. In this case, as they walk contrary to God, so He to them—and that implies His forsaking and punishing them.

And as it is necessary that they be punished for their iniquities, so it is certain that the Lord is offended and about to punish them; and therefore they may be sure that there are sins found with them rendering this necessary. We have proverbs that speak to this: a lion will not roar in the forest, nor a young lion cry out of his den, for nothing; a bird is not caught without some snare; and no man will think it worth his while to take up a snare that has taken nothing. In every one of these instances, whether it is a lion's roaring, a young lion's crying, a bird's being caught, or a snare taken from the earth, there is some reason and occasion for the same. See verses 4–5, in which the prophet seems to lead us to consider that there is nothing done by the design of any agent without some reason or moving occasion. And his intention doubtless is to convince us that God does not threaten or send His judgments for nothing, or without any cause. So that if God utter His voice and brings any judgments upon a people, they may know that there is some reason therefor. God is offended, and is about to punish them for their iniquities; and therefore it becomes them to prepare to meet God.

This same thing the prophet in a most convincing way further insists upon in our text. "Shall a trumpet be blown in the city, and the people not be afraid? Shall there be evil in the city, and the Lord has not done it?"

"Shall a trumpet be blown in the city, and the people not be afraid?" Shall there be an alarm given, and the people take no notice or be concerned? When a trumpet is sounded for such an end, men conclude that there is danger; their hearts are presently filled with fear; they conclude that this warning is not for nothing. The design and application of this is easily seen: if God has sounded His trumpet, has given an alarm, there is good reason to conclude that it is not for nothing; but He warns us that He is coming forth in the way of His judgments, and it concerns us to be ready to meet Him.

But perhaps this would not be convincing to some except they better understood what alarm was given by God, or what trumpet of the Lord had been blown among them. Perhaps they would say that they had heard no voice from heaven; they knew of no warning God had given them that might be compared to a trumpet sounding an alarm.

To inform the minds of such, and to fasten the conviction, there is added, "Shall there be evil in a city, and the Lord hath not done it?" Shall there be any judgment in the city, any calamities, and the Lord not have a hand in the same? If there are evils, any sore afflictions, or any terrible providences, are not these the goings of the Lord? By these God utters His voice, warning and threatening you.

From the words thus opened, we may gather these things as plainly implied and insinuated in our text:

1. God has a holy hand in all the judgments brought upon us or our friends. "Shall there be evil in a city, and the Lord hath not done it?"

2. One end of God's judgments is to be a warning to the people. They are compared to a trumpet sounded for an alarm.

3. It is the duty of all, when God warns them in the way of His providence, to take the warning, hear the voice, fear the danger, and endeavor to escape it. The simile made use of and improved upon this occasion plainly teaches us that as a people who hear the trumpet sounding an alarm, fearing the danger, take themselves to their arms or forts, so people should take warning by the trumpet of the Lord, be afraid of the approaching danger, and prepare to meet Him.

These things I purpose at this time to consider as so many doctrinal propositions.

1. God has a holy hand in all the judgments brought upon us or our friends. Nothing is more evident than that the same almighty Being who at first commanded the universal world to exist exercises a providence over the world He has made. This may be proven from the perfections of the Deity, from the necessary dependence of the creature upon the Creator, from the continued harmony and order in the visible world, and from tokens of the presence and overruling power of God in providences that happen. But at this time it is not our design to offer proofs for a divine providence, but to consider the extensiveness of God's providence.

Many allow that God exercises a providence in the world, who yet have but stingy thoughts of His providence. They allow that He beholds the children of men from the habitation of His throne, that He takes notice how things are managed in the world, that He does good to His friends, yes, is kind to His enemies, to the evil and unthankful, and that sometimes He frowns upon the workers of iniquity. They look for a time also when He will gloriously reward His friends with immortal blessings, and spurn His enemies from His presence into outer darkness and everlasting horrors. Yet there are a thousand things happening in providence that they don't consider the Almighty as having anything to do with, other than as a spectator.

But if we well consider things, we shall find the providence of God to be more extensive than such imagine; yes, that it extends to all things, and all the accidents and circumstances attending them. What we call natural or second causes are conducted and influenced by God's providence. It is by His providence that the regular returns of day and night, and the successions of summer and winter, are made. It is by His providence that the sun shines upon the good and bad (Matthew 5:45). It is by His providence that the heavens are covered with clouds, and the rain prepared for the earth (Psalm 147:8). And even those events that to us may seem casual and fortuitous are ordered and ruled by His providence. So we are informed in Proverbs 16:33 that "The lot is cast into the lap; but the whole disposing thereof is of the Lord." And although it is true that there are some events which happen by the design of rational, created agents, yet these also are ruled by divine providence. If any such agents do us good, we should consider them as instruments which God uses; and if we suffer evil from them, they are the rods wherewith the Almighty is pleased to correct us. Thus the Assyrian, who had it in his heart to destroy and grievously wound Israel, is called "the rod of God's anger"; and the staff in their hand is said to be His indignation (Isaiah 10:5). The destroying Assyrian is again compared to the ax in the hand of him who hews therewith, and to a saw shaken or lifted up by him who makes use of the same (Isaiah 10:15). Again, he is compared to a razor that is hired in the hand of him who shaves (Isaiah 7:20).

Upon the whole, then, let us meet with whatever things in the world, and from whatever cause, the hand of God is to be acknowledged in all of these; whether good or evil things befall us, God's providence is still concerned in the same. "I form the light," says the Lord, "and create darkness. I make peace, and create evil. I the Lord do all these things" (Isaiah 45:7).

Not only then are we to acknowledge the hand of God in all our blessings, but if there is any evil in the city, we are to acknowledge that God has done it; if there is any sore affliction, heavy calamity, and sickness or death among us, there is the hand of the Lord in the same. So, doubtless, Eliphaz understood the matter when he said in Job 5:6, "Affliction cometh out of the ground." And therefore, as for himself, he says that if at any time he should be brought into affliction, he would seek God, and unto God he would commit his cause (Job 5:8).

2. But we proceed to consider that one end of God's judgments is to be a warning to the people. The judgments of God may be considered as His awakening voice to a stupid world. They are signs or effects and fruits of His anger against sin, tokens from God that sin shall not go unpunished.

The apostles make the judgments of God brought upon any, even in distant ages, that come to our ears to be our examples, and which are designed for our admonition (1 Corinthians 10:6–7). So the Apostle Jude makes the fall and misery of the angels to be warnings to us (Jude 5–6). And he tells us that Sodom and Gomorrah, and the cities around them, were set forth for an example, suffering the vengeance of eternal fire (verse 7). So the Apostle Peter represents God's bringing the flood upon the world to be a warning to all who hear of it (2 Peter 2:5–6).

And if the judgments of God that we hear of in such distant ages have such a speaking voice, how much more do the judgments of God that are just at hand and fall within our sight? Moses seemed to think that the judgments of God that fall out within the sight and knowledge of any have a clearer voice than those we hear to have been in distant ages. Deuteronomy 11:2–7: "Know ye this day; for I speak not with your children which have not known and which have not seen the chastisement of the Lord your God. . . . But your eyes have seen all the great acts of the Lord, which He did."

God's judgments, then, that overtake us in our persons, families or friends are a loud warning to us of the danger of abiding in sin, and of the necessity of hiding ourselves under the wings of the Almighty before the floods of divine indignation come upon us. Thus God's judgments are called His voice crying unto the city in Micah 6:9. Thus the prophet represents the Most High as uttering a mighty voice, and speaking very loudly to men in the way of His judgments. Jeremiah 25:29–31: "Lo, I begin to bring evil on the city which is called by My name, and should ye be utterly unpunished? Ye shall not be unpunished. Therefore prophesy, and say unto them, 'The Lord shall roar from on high, and utter His voice from His holy habitation.' "

3. We come now to consider that it is the duty of all, when God warns them in the way of His providence, to take the warning, hear the voice, fear the danger, and endeavor to escape it.

When God's judgments are in the earth, the inhabitants of the world should see, and learn righteousness (Isaiah 26:9–11). When the Lord's voice cries to the city, the man of wisdom will hear (Micah 6:9). If God sends His judgments for this end, namely, to be a warning to a careless world, it is evident that sin will lie at the door of those who do not receive the warning. For we only comply with the design of God in His judgments when we consider His hand, hearken to His voice, and do our best to be ready to meet Him, so that we may escape the severe judgments of heaven and be hidden in the day of the Lord's anger.

Indeed, this proposition is so evident from what has been offered under the foregoing, and from the end and design of God's judgments, that I need not offer anything more to confirm it. For shall God Himself give us warning, and we not think ourselves obliged to receive it? Shall God Himself blow his trumpet, and we not be afraid? When the Almighty gives notice, that is beset with wrath for His enemies, as the day of the Lord has, shall we not think it reasonable to be moved with fear, and, if it is possible, to prepare an ark and secure ourselves under the covenant of the Almighty's wings?

Application

What is yet before us is the application of these truths which we have been considering. And so I proceed to various uses of these doctrines.

USE OF INFORMATION. Is it as we have heard, that God has a holy hand in all the judgments brought upon us or our friends? Are all the sorrows and evils in the world directed and ruled by Him? Then we may infer that those who have God engaged for them, and are secure of His favor, are safe in the saddest times; and therefore we may, with hope and security, commend ourselves and our circumstances to God in well-doing in the most difficult times. The face of providence is some times overspread with clouds and darkness; the eyes of many mourn by reason of affliction. Terrors and pestilential arrows fly by night, and destruction waits at noonday. There seems to be distress on every hand; there is desolation within doors and fear without; abroad one calamity prevails, and another just as dreadful at home.

But in such dark times, there is this for the people of God to live upon, and comfort their weeping hearts in the consideration of: the Lord reigns, who rides upon the heavens to the help of His people, and in His excellency of the sky. He rules over all; justice and judgment are the habitation of His throne. He is good, a stronghold in the day of trouble, and He knows those who trust in Him.

We may therefore—in all such sad and doleful days, when, were it not for this, it would not be strange if our hearts should sink and fail in such sad times—put our trust in God; we make the Most High our refuge, and

unto His wings take ourselves for shelter. And we may
be confident that nothing shall hurt us without His
permission; none of the destroying arrows that fly
about shall light upon us without His permission. So
that, if we can but be sure of an interest in His favor, we
need not fear, "though a host should encamp against
me" (Psalm 27:3). Nor, "though the earth be removed,
and though the mountains be carried into the midst of
the sea. Though the waters thereof roar, and be troubled; though mountains shake with the swelling
thereof" (Psalm 46:2–3). We need not be afraid of the
snare of the fowler, nor the noisome pestilence. We
need not be afraid of the terror that comes at night, the
arrow that flies by day, the pestilence that walks in
darkness, nor the destruction that waits at noonday. We
need not be afraid of any evil that shall beset us, nor of
any plague that can come nigh our dwelling (Psalm
91). Yea, though we walk through the valley of the
shadow of death, we need not fear any evil (Psalm 23:4),
for God will cover us with His feathers, and His truth
shall be our shield and buckler. With life He will satisfy
us, and show us His salvation (Psalm 91:4, 16).

Is it as we have heard, that one end of God's judgments is to be a warning to people? Then if there are
judgments among us, or round about us, we learn what
interpretation to make of the same. By them God gives
us notice what He will do unto us if we are found in the
ways of sin and do not return to Him. And because He
will do this unto us, He hereby designs to excite us to
prepare to meet our God, to seek righteousness and
meekness before the decree brings forth, before the
fierce anger of the Lord comes upon us.

God, being infinitely good and delighting in mercy,

most frequently sends His awakening judgments before
He proceeds to the utmost against men. He warns them
and gives them a space for repentance. He sometimes
visits with awful and distressing sickness. He sends the
destroying angel, and takes away some as a warning to
the rest. And, if some of the best are taken away, the
warning is not less; only there is more of God's love to
souls discovered while those who are ready are taken
away to peace and the enjoyment of heavenly love, and
others are warned to be ready.

If then any awful sickness, any sore judgment, is
sent among us, we may reasonably conclude that God is
giving us warning to prepare for all events and be ready
to meet Him, in whatever way He shall be pleased to
come unto us.

And particularly, we may so interpret the dispensation of providence whereby an awful distemper has
been sent into a family in this place, and one of your
contemporaries, by a sudden stroke, has been removed.
God hereby calls upon us to be also ready. He wants us
to think with ourselves, and put ourselves into a ready
posture to stand before Him.

And it may be justly considered as being more especially a warning to you who are in your youth. To you,
the Lord's voice cries, "You also must be ready; make
haste, and get all things in readiness for a solemn
meeting with God." For against the young people especially has the frightening and desolating distemper
been commissioned.

We of this place may still have in remembrance our
affliction and our misery, the wormwood and the gall,
when some years ago we felt some strokes of the distemper, and some of your contemporaries were re-

moved. And yet the heavy stroke on us was light compared with what many other places felt. Ah, what desolation it has made in some places! How terrible has God been in His doings! Numerous families have been emptied! A great number of the children are cut off from without and the young men from the streets. Many once happy parents, whose hearts have rejoiced in the blessing of children, are bemoaning themselves as in Jeremiah 10:19–20: "Woe is me for my hurt! My wound is grievous . . . my tabernacle is spoiled, and all my cords are broken. My children are not." Where but a little while ago an abundance of youthful songs of mirth might be heard, now mournful ditties, elegant songs and lamentations are chiefly in use. And, ah, how few are left to join the mournful song! Here and there a youth escaped, a monument of sparing mercy, wondering that he was not consumed with the sweeping contagion!

And is the fatal distemper sent among us again? How loud is the voice to prepare to meet a holy God, who threatens us of coming forth in His indignation? For if it prevails, and we do not prevent it by earnest prayer, humiliation, and amendment, how many of this present company will likely, in a little while, be in the immovable state? It affects my heart to behold such a number of youth together, and think of the sweeping distemper's coming among them! Think what desolation, if God should give permission, it would make! Oh, may a merciful God prevent so sad a calamity and spare us, and by gentler methods of grace bring us to amends!

Is it as we have heard? Then all should be carefully considering God's works, taking notice of the operation of His hands. They should observe the judgments and doings of the Lord, and behold His works. Sometimes God speaks once, yea twice, and men do not perceive it. He speaks by His Word and in His providence, and is not heard. Men's eyes are blinded, and they do not see; their ears are dull of hearing, and they do not give attention to the voice of God. Yea, it is to be feared that many do not hear His voice until the decree goes forth, till the day passes as the chaff, and the fierce anger of the Lord comes upon them; till their fear comes as desolation, and their destruction as a whirlwind. Ah, miserable souls! Unhappy man! They do not perceive God speaking to them till it is too late to cry for mercy, or to hope to avoid the floods of divine indignation! Poor creatures! How they must feel when death has snatched them away, and all their opportunities of grace are over!

Doesn't it make all our hearts sigh to think of that sad eternity before them! Oh, how much more comfortable will a due consideration and improvement of God's judgments make us at last, when the good design of a merciful God shall be happily obtained by awakening us to repentance, and driving us to the feathers of the Almighty's wings for protection!

But how can we hope that the instructive voice of divine providence in those sensible things done in righteousness should have this happy effect upon us if we take no notice of the works and doings of the Lord? If we will not yield attention, what means of instruction are likely to avail? We know that while unobserving, learning never makes proficiency, but loses many means of instruction. And so while we fail to observe the providences of God, we shall likely lose the benefit we might otherwise have from many instructive dispensations of providence. God may speak often, and we not perceive it, and so the gracious end of divine warnings may be frustrated.

If it is as has been shown, then we may infer that great thoughtfulness and seriousness become us when God's judgments are among us. Shall a trumpet be blown, an alarm given, and the people not be afraid? Shall warning be given us to prepare to meet our God, and we remain as senseless, thoughtless, and inconsiderate as ever? How unsuitable would this be! And shall the Almighty Himself awfully speak, and utter His voice in the way of His providence, and we yet indulge ourselves in levity and mirth, and let our heart cheer us as though we had no warning to look out for an evil day, and were not at all concerned in the afflictions of our friends and the judgments of God? Can we but abhor such a spirit? To me, nothing seems more indecent than a jolly, careless, merry humor indulged when God, in the way of His judgments, is calling aloud to prepare for a solemn meeting with His dreadful majesty. God's judgments are serious, and it is a serious thing to meet Him when he comes forth in those judgments.

And I can't but be pleased (and I hope it is a token for God) that the young people of my charge are inclined to be serious, and to consider the voice of God in the alarm that seemed to be given them. Oh, that your goodness may not prove as the morning cloud, and as the early dew go away.

USE OF AWAKENING. This use is for those who, though unready to meet God in the way of His judgments, yet live at ease and are seemingly secure.

Is it as we have heard, that God's judgments are for

warning people to prepare to meet Him? Then seeing
judgments from God have been sent among us, awake,
you careless souls, who lie open to the judgments of
God, and have nothing to defend you from the arrows
of His vengeance. Shall a trumpet be blown, and the
people not be afraid? Shall the omnipotent Jehovah utter His voice, and His creatures not tremble? Shall God,
by awful judgments, warn us to be ready to meet Him,
and we not fear? And may we not apply this and say, as
in Amos 3:8, "The lion hath roared; who will not fear?
The Lord God hath spoken; who can but prophesy?"
Has not the Lord warned the youth of this place, and
called to them to secure an interest in His favor before
the flood of His indignation overtakes them? Has He
not uttered a loud voice in this part of His Zion, and
called the rising generation to attend and be ready for
sickness, death, judgment, and eternity? I hope that we
have not as yet forgotten the sound. I think the voice
plainly cried, "All flesh is grass, and all the goodliness
thereof is as the flower of the field. The grass withers,
the flower fades . . ." because the Spirit of the Lord
blows upon it. I think that it especially cries to us who
are young, "Be ready to be next; be ready quickly to depart."

And, alas, what shall the unprepared soul do if it is
quickly called away? If the fatal distemper foils, dis-
patches, and makes short work, ah, my dear friends,
how sad, how dreadful it would be! How reluctantly
must that poor, unhappy soul depart. And what becomes of that sad soul in the eternal state? How fearful
a thing will it be to go into the presence of a holy God,
and fall into His hands with an unsanctified heart and
unprepared spirit! Alas, what can such expect but to be

spurned from God's presence, cast out of His favor, and hurled down to hell in His wrath? What can they expect but everlasting destruction and the horrors and deaths that the enemies of God are destined to! And, oh, who knows the power of God's anger, or can conceive the inexpressible dreadfulness of being purified with His indignation? His power is infinite, and as His power is, so is His wrath. How miserable, then, is that soul that must always endure the same! Would it not be dreadful if it should be one of us? Could our poor hearts endure, or could our arms be strong enough? If any of us should this day, or tomorrow, or the day following that, or at any time be seized with the devouring distempers, hastened away before our Judge, doomed as His implacable enemies, and bound in fetters of wrath and chains of despair, would it not be unspeakably sad, beyond all the notions of horror that we can now entertain in our minds? Don't our very souls tremble and our hearts almost move out of their places at the thought of this? Are we not afraid, then, to remain in such a condition that we cannot stand in the judgment or safely meet the Lord, if He comes forth to punish the inhabitants of our land?

Awaken, then, awaken! You stupid and careless souls, who are now void of grace and have no interest in the favor of God, who so are unready for an evil day, awaken speedily, lest, before you are aware, you are called away. The warning has been given; do not add incorrigibleness to your other sins; for thereby your danger will be but the greater.

Nor is there any safety or reason in referring the warning and danger to another, as though God means only to warn others, and they were likelier to be taken away than you. Oh, remember that, for all you know, you may be the next to be summoned away. That very person, who hopes and flatters himself that whoever dies, he shall not, may perhaps be the next. And what will you do if it should prove to be so? Are you willing to run such a hazard of being lost forever, and having an eternity to spend in extreme anguish and woe? Are you willing to run the chance of meeting God clothed in vengeance, and you destitute of everything to shelter you from His wrath? Oh, remember that the day of the Lord, when it comes, will have such darkness and no light, very dark and no brightness in it! Consider how dreadful it will be when the incensed justice of the powerful God shall make an utter end, and affliction shall not rise up the second time. Have you thought how dreadful is the presence of an angry God, how the very mountains tremble at His presence, and the pillars of heaven shake at His rebuke; how much like fire His fury is poured out? And are you willing to meet such a God in the fierceness of His wrath? Oh, for your soul's sake, consider these things! Awaken from carnal security lest terrible storms of vengeance awaken you when it will be too late to find any advantage therein.

USE OF EXHORTATION. This use is so that all will take notice of the judgments of God, consider His ways, hearken to His providential warnings, and prepare to meet Him.

God has warned us. His voice seems near unto us, to seek the Lord and His favor and be ready to meet Him before wailing shall be in all streets, and men in all houses and highways are saying, "Alas, alas." God calls us to be afraid of a day of trouble coming on, to be afraid lest, if we do not immediately turn unto the Lord, we are emptied and utterly spoiled, our joy is darkened and our gates are smitten with destruction.

The voice has cried; the trumpet has sounded; let us take alarm, hasten our escape, and fly to the mountain. Oh, who knows how soon a fatal day may come on, and a great part of you who hope to escape are taken. Make haste, then, and be ready for all events; fly to Christ the Savior. Do not delay, and do not look back.

To enforce this exhortation:

1. Consider that the voice cries for early repentance and speedy preparation to meet God. Sometimes, when God has been warning a people, they are ready to say, "The vision is for many days to come. Where is the word of the Lord? Let it come now" (Jeremiah 17:15). "They say, 'Let Him make speed, and hasten His work, that we may see it; and let the counsel of the Holy One of Israel draw nigh that we may know it' " (Isaiah 5:19).

But, I think, the voice of God now earnestly urges speedy repentance so that we are presently ready for the woeful day. It not only cries that all flesh is grass, and the goodliness thereof as the flower of the field, but that the Lord of the same is preparing and whetting His scythe to cut it down. I think it calls us to be teaching our young men to wail, and the daughters of God's people to lament, because the pestilence has come among us.

Fly, then, you youths, unto the wings of the Almighty before the evil befalls you. It is dangerous delaying for even a day. There is no staying safe in all the plain. The best, if not the only, opportunity for this in a little time may be over. Death may be doing its work. And, oh, what an unhappy time will that be for the work of repentance, when the soul, if sensible of its condition, will be full of anguish and consternation, and the oppressed heart sick and tremble, and almost die with him! What distracting fears will likely fill the soul, and disable it from consideration! In what disorder will the distracted soul likely be! How unfitted for a due preparation to come before God will it be!

Besides, the pains and languishings of the body render it an unhappy time for so great a work. Men generally find it enough then to bear the pains of the body and grapple under the load of their disease. Their girding pains so possess the mind, or fainting turns interrupt the thoughts, as to render a fixed attention to soul-work an impossible thing; and groans and terror of the sinning and expiring nature very often call away the mind from everything else. Alas, if this shall ever be the unhappy case of any one of us, to be brought on a dying bed and our work not done, how bitter will our complaint be! How much heavier will our stroke be than our groaning! How will the unprepared soul then wish it had been sooner and more earnest in seeking God, and making its peace with Him! It is enough to startle one, only to offer to his thoughts the miserable case of such.

Their hearts sink and their souls tremble; their looks call for pity from bystanders, and are affecting enough to beget tender motions of pity even in cruel-hearted men. Poor creatures, how earnestly they look to their unable friends to do something for them. And yet they do not know to which of the saints to turn for help. How earnestly they beg the physicians' best endeavors; with flowing tears and affecting motions they beg the minister to look to heaven with earnest cries, and use all his interest there so that they may be spared.

And when they endeavor to improve a remaining moment in doing something for their souls, the distressed body diverts the thoughts and forces away the mind.

Moreover, the overwhelming fear that will likely attend persons at such a time may deprive them of that prudence that at other times they may have, and lead them to take unlikely courses to save their souls.

At such a sad time, poor creatures, frightened and amazed, full of perplexity and their whole souls in a tumult, oftentimes lay hold of what will never save, as a drowning person will lay hold of anything for safety, though he is at the bottom, which is a sure way to make his ruin certain.

There is no doubt but that many in their dying anguish fly to courses that will prove altogether fruitless, and will not help their souls at all. They lean upon that which will sink under their weight. They turn to the saints, and hope for mercy for their sakes. They depend on the prayers of their friends. They trust a dying prayer for mercy. They trust their forced sorrow and concern, their forced desires of religion, and their low esteem of the world, because they can no longer enjoy it. They comfort themselves in the mercies of God when their hearts are as dead in sin as ever.

So there is the utmost danger lest the miserable soul, at this unhappy time, lay hold on some foolish ground of hope, but miscarry and perish forever. Oh, then, now, while health lasts, in the calm of our lives, even now, while we have so good a time, let us prepare to meet God.

2. The Lord now waits to be gracious. In wrath He remembers mercy. Though He has warned, threatened, and lifted up His hand, yet He seems to stop and give us

an opportunity for repentance. He hearkens and hears, if we will speak aright. Then let us repent us of our wickedness and say, "What have we done?"

As He has warned us, so He invites us to seek the Lord before the decree brings forth judgment, before the fierce anger of the Lord comes upon us (Zephaniah 2:2–3). He lets us know that He is not inexorable; that He does not retain His anger forever, but delights in mercy; that He is willing to turn again and be reconciled to us if we will turn to Him (Micah 7:18–19). A scepter of mercy is yet held forth, a door of mercy is open. Oh, let us come in while we may. Let us take with us words, and turn to the Lord, and sincerely say unto Him, 'Take away all iniquity, and receive us graciously." And so shall we live in His sight (Hosea 14:2 and 6:2).

It would be sad if, after God had warned us of being exposed to His judgments, and in His abundant goodness allowed us an opportunity to hide ourselves from the approaching evil, we yet should make light of His warnings, despise His goodness, abide in our sins, and be overtaken with the heavy storms of wrath we had noticed were gathering.

3. Why should we delay? There will never be a better time for repentance and making our peace with God than now. We must turn to the Lord by true repentance or iniquity will be our ruin. Repentance is a work that must be done or we are undone forever. Either our sin or our souls must die. We cannot always abide in our sins, estranged and alienated from God, at any cheaper rate than the blood of our precious, immortal souls. Christ has once and again assured us that, unless we repent, we shall all likewise perish. As surely, then, as we are now here, we shall perish if we are not con-

verted. If we remain unsanctified, we shall be cast off with the unholy, who shall never enter into the kingdom of God. So it concerns us to repent and be converted unto God, as much as our souls are worth.

And since it must be done, why shall we not endeavor to do it now—especially considering that we shall never have a better time? For suppose that God in mercy prevents the prevailing of sickness and mortality among us, and our space in the world is lengthened out. Yet it will never be a better time for repentance and seeking a reconciliation with God than now. Yea, never will there be again so good a time for this work as now.

Young people are strangely apt to imagine a more convenient season before them; but it is a delusion, an ungrounded imagination. The time of youth is really the best time for this work.

God directs His offers of mercy particularly to young persons. He calls to them in a particular manner to come and partake of His love. Psalm 34:11: "Come, ye children, hearken unto Me." Ecclesiastes 12:1: "Remember now thy Creator in the days of thy youth."

There is a special encouragement given to youth that, if they apply themselves to seek the Lord, they shall succeed. Proverbs 8:17: "Those that seek Me early shall find me."

Moreover, God has manifested how pleased He is when persons in earnest seek Him in their youth. Remember the examples of Samuel and Josiah, who sought the Lord when they were young, and what gracious respects God showed to them. He blessed them, and made them blessings in the world.

Besides, there is not so much contracted obstinacy in the hearts of youth as in those of more advanced years. It is true that they have natural corruption and principles of sin in them as well as others, and hearts so hard as to need an omnipotent power to soften the same. But there is an increasing obstinacy in the hearts of men; and young persons have not made such advances in it as they will arrive to by longer continuance in sin. But then, by a daily continuance in sin, this will increase upon them; the heart will grow more hardened against the counsels of grace, more set against religion, and averse to a compliance with the terms of peace; repentance will become more difficult and hazardous. Jeremiah 13:23: "Can the Ethiopian change his skin, or the leopard his spots? Then may ye also do good, that are accustomed to do evil."

Again, the encumbrance of life increases upon persons as the increase in years. Yet there will likely be more worldly cares and concerns to call off your minds from the care of your souls afterwards, if your day in this world is long honed out, than you have now; the time of youth is the freest from worldly cares and troubles of any. And therefore the wise man calls upon youth to remember their Creator in the days of their youth, "while the evil days come not" (Ecclesiastes 12:1).

Nor may we expect to be freer from temptations to delay, and put off this work of repentance to hereafter rather than now. There will be as many temptations hereafter still to put off, without any doubt, as now. Delaying will not make it better, but worse upon this account. Have not some of you had thoughts of setting about the work of repentance years ago, but through one temptation or another have neglected it till now? And is it any better upon that account now than before?

Are there not as strong temptations to defer as ever? And so you may expect there will be if you delay longer. Delay no longer, then, but seek the Lord while He may be found; and call upon Him while He is near. Improve this good time while you have it.

4. If you will not hearken to the counsels of God, nor take warning by His judgments, who knows but that God will say in righteous judgment, "Why should you be stricken any more?" and leave you in the congregation of dead souls? It would be but a righteous retribution—if we resolve to delay the work of repentance any longer, and harden our hearts against the warnings of God—if God should leave us to a hard and impenitent heart, to treasure up unto ourselves wrath against the day of wrath, and the revelation of the righteous judgments of God.

And how sad a judgment would this be! Then we might hear, indeed, and understand not; see but perceive not. Then, if we remained longer in the world, we would be like the barren fig tree upon which no fruit grew, or like the dejected earth which bears thorns and briars, whose end is to be burned.

Some have thus been left to God. So when God had counseled and warned Israel, and it proved to no purpose, He righteously gave them up to their own hearts' lusts and said, "Why should ye be stricken any more? Ye will revolt more and more" (Isaiah 1:5). So sometimes He lets persons go on in their own ways. He takes away His Holy Spirit and strives no move with them.

And it has been sometimes observed that when God begins early to warn persons, and to strive with them by His Spirit, if His warnings be slighted, and the strivings of His Spirit resisted, God early leaves them, and takes away His Holy Spirit from them.

Thus many who have had awakening means and the strivings of God's Spirit in their youth have been left when they advanced in years, and suffered to walk in their own counsels all their days. Oh, then, while God warns, while His Spirit strives, while we have a special season of grace, let us hear His voice.

5. If hereafter God should give you saving repentance, delaying to repent will be a matter of bitter sorrow to you then. If there are some instances of such as have long delayed repentance and found mercy with the Lord at last, yet they mourn at the last, and bitterly bewail their former times. They find that they have been wronging their own souls, and with tears lament it before the Lord. It fills their hearts with sorrow that they have lost such precious opportunities, miserably wasted away their days, and misspent a season of grace. It afflicts their very souls to remember how much they have dishonored God, and lived in vain, or, what is worse, lived to the evil purposes of sin, full of misery and death. Now the sins of their youth cause their hearts to ache, and fill their bones with sorrow. So that, if we find mercy at last, it will cost us abundance of sorrow if we delay the necessary work of repentance.

And what a pity it is to lay in for after-repentance and sorrows. We have sin enough already to cause an abundance of sorrow, and to make the very inmost parts of our hearts ache when they shall be brought to a sense of the same. What a pity it is that we should lay in any more for repenting tears and heart-depressing sorrows.

In a word, what a pity it is that we should indulge ourselves any longer in that of which, we may be sure, there will be no good fruit, and of which there is danger that the end will prove to be the death of our souls. Let us suppose the best, that we obtain forgiveness from God. We shall be ashamed; we shall mourn and be in bitterness for it, and our souls will be humbled within us.

6. If you remain unconverted and impenitent, all your lifetime, through fear of death, you will be subject unto bondage. Your hearts will reproach and condemn you; and an unpeaceful witness will reside in your breast which, if it is stifled, will at some time or other awake and give it testimony to God against you.

There is a principle of spiritual horror in unconverted souls, if they seem at any times to be at ease, and to live in security. Conscience may sleep a little while, but terror stands ready to seize the soul as soon as it wakes.

And, in general, impenitent souls are prone to take pains to lull their consciences to sleep which will be often reminding them of a day of reckoning. So there is no quiet in their minds, but their consciences cry out against them, or they are doing violence to themselves to suppress their uneasy and accusing thoughts.

And, for the most part, after all their industrious and painful labors to drown the noise and clamor, their consciences rise within them, so that they have many terrors in the night and tedious reflections by day.

Whenever God brings His judgments upon them, and it looks as if God was coming forth in earnest to punish the inhabitants of the earth (except some few hardened wretches, whom God has given over to a reprobate mind; who are past feeling, having their consciences seared with a red-hot iron), their guilty breasts tremble as the leaves of the forest. If sickness lights upon them, or death presents itself before them, they presently howl upon their beds; their hands become faint, and their hearts fail them for fear, and for looking after those things which, they apprehend, are coming upon them.

7. Nothing is more unkind and unreasonable than to reserve for the service of God only the worst part of our lives. Thus to requite the Lord argues a vile and wretched heart. What! Can we think of devoting the best of our time and strength to the service of our own lusts to gratify the flesh and serve the devil, and of turning off God with the leavings of our lusts? What! Can we think of devoting our prime and strength to the service of sin, and when the evil days come, in which we cannot find pleasure in gratifying our lusts, devote that time to God? How vile is that thought, and worthy of hell!

Surely such cannot be thought less blameworthy than those of whom the prophet complains in Malachi 1, who offered polluted bread on God's altar, and the blind, the lame, and the sick for sacrifice. As that was, so this is such an offering as none would make to their governor; nor would they expect the acceptance of it if they did.

I think our language does not furnish us with words emphatic enough to represent the baseness, the execrable ingratitude and horrible wickedness, of purposing thus to treat the most high and glorious God, to whom we are indebted for being and every mercy, or the indignation and sacred rage with which our minds should rise against the detestable thought.

God is full of compassion, infinite in goodness and clemency, as well as His other perfections, or, we might conclude, the heavens would never bear such an indignity as this at the hands of impious mortals. It declares God to be unspeakably good if the heavens don't immediately gather blackness, angry storms arise, and devouring lightning blasts the impious wretch who thus presumes to treat his God.

And if God spares for a while the wretch who lives in sin, and presumes that God will accept the less of his life, that person may justly fear that ere long God's provoked wrath will break out upon him.

And if now there is one soul among us who entertains the base thought and purpose of thus requiting God, let him seriously consider the curse pronounced against the deceiver who has in his flock a male, and vows and sacrifices unto the Lord a corrupt thing (Malachi 1:14).

8. Our whole lifetime is not too much to be devoted to the service of God. Why should we not be willing to devote our best time, yes, our whole time to the service of God? We are His, and to Him we owe ourselves; and He may justly claim our best and constant service. We have been born and carried by Him from the womb. And even to our old age He is still God (Isaiah 46:3–4). It is God who upholds and provides for us all our lifetime, and therefore justly claims the whole.

Or do we think our life will be too long to be devoted to the honor of the infinite God? Why, can we ever utter the memory of all God's wonderful works, show forth all His praise, and declare all His greatness? Can we think that His service will be too little for our whole lives? Or can we do too much for Him who gave

us our beings and supports us every day, Him who is the
Author of all our mercies, and the foundation of all our
reasonable hopes of any future good? Surely an eternity
is not too long to serve and praise such a God in!

And can we then think the best life that such poor,
imperfect creatures as we can attain unto is too good an
offering for God? Can we think so small a space as that
of the life of man in this world is too much for the service of God? Surely, if we have any such thoughts, we
have no becoming apprehension of the infinite glories
of God and our obligations to Him.

And, indeed, had we but any suitable knowledge of
God and ourselves, we would see that it must be grace
in God that He will accept our service when we have
done our best; such service as we can yield unto God,
though it is of our whole lifetime, is but an imperfect
offering.

9. Consider how solicitous and importunate your
friends are for your early conversion. O you children
and youth, did you know how much your souls' salvation lay upon the hearts of your parents and friends;
did you know their concern for you, how they travail in
birth again until Christ is formed in you, how often
upon the bended knees of their souls they are wrestling
with God for you, I think you could not but be concerned for yourselves.

How much have our parents undergone and done
for us? And shall we not try to let them have some comfort and rejoicing in us? Now, nothing will more rejoice their hearts than to see us walking in the truth,
remembering our Creator in the days of our youth.

O children, your parents hope and fear for you; what
a burden you will ease their souls of if you would now

turn to the Lord in truth! If they could see you in earnest seeking the kingdom of heaven and its righteousness, their hearts would rejoice; and they will esteem themselves blessed of the Lord. Their souls will have comfort while they hope God means good to their house for a great while to come.

10. If we turn early to the Lord, and sincerely devote ourselves to His service, there will be grounds to hope for the continuance of God's presence when our fathers are gone, and the rising generation comes in their place.

Now in all generations, it is the blessing of the Lord, and His gracious presence, that makes a people happy. Our fathers have been blessed with the presence of God. He has dwelt with them and among them. They have seen His power and rejoiced in His grace. Ask them, and they will speak highly for God, and give large testimonies for Him. They have found Him to be a good God. By Him they have been often delivered in dangers, helped in weakness, and saved in troubles. God has often supported them when they have been ready to faint and to sink. This He has done for them at such dark times when vain was the help of man. They have trusted in God and He has delivered them. In a word, God has been their portion, their defense and glory; and great is His goodness which He has wrought for them.

How much is it to be desired and wished that those who are next coming upon the stage might also be accountable to the Lord for a generation! Then when the fathers have fallen asleep, you may still have God among you, a God near at hand to do for you, and to whom you may repair at all times.

Well, if you who are in your youth may be awakened
to repentance, and be persuaded in good earnest to set
yourselves to seek and to serve God, you may hope that
your fathers' God will be your God. So David encour-
ages us in that well-known exhortation to his son
found in 1 Chronicles 28:9: "My son, know thou the
God of thy father, and serve Him with a perfect heart,
and with a willing mind. If thou seek Him, He will be
found of thee."

But if our youth will not regard the works of the
Lord, not be awakened to repentance; if they will make
light of their fathers' God, slight His warnings and reject His counsels, what a generation! And what a sad
time will it be when the fathers are gone, when the
glory shall be departed, and God will have forsaken
those who may be left!

We can scarcely imagine the wretchedness of such a
generation. Forsaken of God! It is a kind of damnation
upon earth, an emblem of the punishment of the
damned, who are punished with everlasting destruction
from the presence of the Lord!

If God shall withdraw His Holy Spirit and forsake us,
we shall be left in the hands and power of Satan; we
shall be taken captive by him at his will, and be drawn
by him from sin to sin, from one degree of wickedness
to another, till we have filled up the measure of our iniquities. The god of this world, the spirit that now
works in the children of disobedience, will rule in us
and lord it over us, and drive us along the road of death
and misery. So we shall lay up amazing treasures of
wrath against the day of wrath. And in the meantime we
shall be wretched, while employed in the sordid service
of Satan. Our reason will be enslaved to passion and

lust. We shall eagerly pursue vanities that will deceive and disappoint us. Our minds will be disordered, restless, and unquiet. Evil passion will distress our thoughts, and prey upon our hearts like furies of hell. And such will be the pride of our abandoned hearts that a spirit of discontent will fill our souls with continual vexation. A guilty conscience also may likely often torture us with sad reflections.

Moreover, besides these inward miseries that attend unhappy souls who are forsaken by God, captive by Satan, and led along the paths of sin, we may expect, if God withdraws His Holy Spirit and leaves us to the counsels of our corrupt hearts, an abundance of outward evils to attend us in the world. Sin and wickedness will so prevail that men will likely be plagues and curses to each other. Violence, falsehood, and oppression will reign; mutual confidence and trust will be banished from among men; confusion and every evil work will prevail. Then, if there shall be some few not given up with the rest to the power of Satan, they may with good reason turn themselves to God for help, and complain as the Psalmist did in Psalm 12:1–2, "Help, Lord, for the godly man ceaseth; for the faithful fail from among the children of men! They speak vanity every one with his neighbor; with flattering lips, and with a double heart do they speak." Yes, doubtless, as the Psalmist, they would mourn in their complaint and say, "Oh, that I had wings like a dove! for then would I fly away, and be at rest. Lo, then would I wander far off, and remain in the wilderness" (Psalm 55:6–7).

Now would it not be sad if, when our fathers shall have left us, such times should follow, times in which God is withdrawn, in which faithfulness has departed

from among men, and in which religion and its
blessed fruits are retired and gone, and in place of
these, Satan lords, sin prevails, wickedness destroys,
and all evils abound?

Let us then by early repentance and religion secure
an interest in the favor of our fathers' God so that we
may hope that He will not forsake us, but dwell with us,
and carry out His own work in the midst of us after they
have been taken away.

If these considerations are weighed and laid to
heart by us, I cannot but hope the exhortation will
come with force upon us that we must turn early on to
the Lord by true repentance, and seek His favor by an
early choice of religion. Oh, that the Spirit of the Lord
then, who can effectually open the heart and make way
for His truths to enter into our souls, would impress
these considerations upon your minds, and cause them
to sink deep into your hearts, so that you may be effectually stirred up to seek the Lord and His favor in this
day, before the evil day comes.

Before I conclude this discourse, let me plead with
all the earnestness I possibly can. And, oh, that I could
do it in a more moving way, and in a deeper sense of
the worth of your souls! I say, let me plead with you, and
entreat you to consider what has been offered, and to
suffer yourselves to be prevailed with by such weighty
motives to receive the exhortation, take the warning
given, and speedily prepare to meet God. My dear children, for your own sake, for your friend's sake, for your
poor minister's sake, be entreated. Why will you not
hearken and consider? Why will you suffer the god of
this world to blind your eyes? Why will you so expose
your precious, immortal souls, and abide in the way of

God's indignation? Why will you run so dreadful a venture of meeting the Almighty clothed with vengeance, and armed with the instruments of His devouring wrath? Oh, consider the awful and amazing threats against the sinner; open your eyes and behold the preparing storm of wrath! See the gathering clouds, and who shall be able to abide the storm, or stand before the indignation? Whose heart can endure or hands be strong when He comes forth in the fierceness of His anger, with the mountains shaking, the hills moving, the earth trembling at His presence, yes, the world and all that dwell therein? I hope that none of you, the youth of my charge and love, will harden yourselves against the threatened vengeance and the terrors of God's wrath. For, alas, how soon, when the threatened storm shall come, will your countenances change, your courage fail, and you cry for mercy, and wish you had hearkened and prepared yourselves to meet the Lord! I hope you may never know by experience the dreadfulness of being pursued, overtaken, and borne down by the vengeance of an angry God, as His implacable and obstinate enemies must. It raises pity and is affecting only to think of the dreadfulness of the day of the Lord to such poor creatures! What will they do! What can they say! How confounded and amazed will they stand before their Judge! Oh, then, be entreated before that day comes to reconcile yourselves to God and make haste lest it be too late.

I don't think that I know how to conclude or leave off entreating till I may hope some are persuaded in earnest to seek the Lord. And yet there is this melancholy thought in laboring with you, namely, that if you will not be persuaded or hearken, the day of the Lord's wrath will be so much the more dreadful to you. The warning of God not considered or laid to heart will make the day more dreadful; and this discourse and exhortation, meant in love to your souls, will make it worse. For you will likely hear how you receive this very exhortation. If you hearken, you will likely, many a time, bless God for it; and if you refuse, alas, it will be a witness against you! Conscience will say, when your calamity comes, "Ah! You were warned and entreated, and yet you would not hear!" And your Judge will say, "I have called and you refused; you set at naught all My counsel, and would have none of My reproof."

Let me, then, with all the seriousness and solemnity I can, charge you, with the hope that you will so improve this exhortation that in the day of the Lord, when you and I must stand before my Lord and Master, who has sent me unto you, I need not be forced to give witness against you.

Would to God that when I must come before my Master at His judgment seat, to give an account of what I have done, with respect to the souls committed to my charge (my soul trembles in holy fear, remembering the solemn day)—would to God that I need not have to bring in testimony against them! And particularly, dear children of my care, I pray that I need not have to say against you that on this day, I warned you, entreated you, and pleaded with you, and yet you would not hear!

Be entreated, then, to take this warning, comply with this exhortation, and turn to the Lord. So shall my soul rejoice; and you will be so far from repenting of it that it will make your hearts glad forever.

It seems to me that nothing would seem too much that was in my power if I could but gain you for Christ.

How willingly would I spend all my strength in entreating if that would do! How willingly would I make myself your servant, and entreat upon my knees, if that would do! But, alas, what can a weak, insufficient creature do? Oh, that the almighty God would undertake and make you willing by His powerful grace!

I want to know whether there are none persuaded, and fain would hope that there are some whose hearts are overcome. And, for my encouragement, some of your countenances appear as if they were affected, concerned, and intend to hear. But then, I am afraid, in a little time they will forget themselves; their concern will vanish and their goodness will be as the morning cloud, and as the early dew that passes away. I am afraid that in a little while they will forget this exhortation, slight the warning, and return to carnal ease and their former carelessness. At this my heart trembles, and almost moves out of its place. Even when I remember, I am afraid, and trembling takes hold of my flesh! Oh, that it might not be so, but that the impressions may abide!

However sincerely, my friends, I desire and long for your soul's salvation; however willingly I would do what I may to promote the same, yet I can do no more than this. The success of my poor, weak endeavor I must leave with God, in whose hands are the hearts of men.

If God graciously inclines your hearts, and you are brought to be willing to receive His Word, God shall have the praise and the glory will be His. If you will not hearken, and find no mercy with God, my soul shall weep for you; and by reason of that relation I stand in to you, that charge divine providence has committed to me, and that love which I think I have for your souls, I must have continual grief and sorrow for you.

But whether you will hear, or whether you will forbear, I will offer these two directions to you, with which I purpose to conclude.

(1) Endeavor to know yourselves. It cannot be expected that any motives will prevail with us to turn to the Lord and make it our concern to secure His favor if we do not know what we are, or what our relation to God is.

Now, it is one part of the misery men are naturally fallen into that they do not know themselves; they do not know what manner of persons they are, nor what is their state with God. Destruction and misery are in their ways, and they do not know it.

Hence it is easily accounted for why the most weighty arguments used to persuade them to be reconciled unto God come but with little force. For they do not know their natural alienation from Him. For the same reason they are not filled with any great concern when the terrors of the Lord are mentioned and God's judgments are abroad in the earth. Not being acquainted with their own guilt, and the power of sin and death in their souls, they do not apprehend their danger and how exposed they are unto it. Nor is it much to be wondered at if men live in vain, and run into misery and ruin, so long as they do not know what they are, what they were made or live for, nor what is the state of their souls. Let everyone, then, be concerned and take pains to know himself: what he is, what is his last end, what is the state of his soul.

And seeing that all men are fallen into a state of death, that they have become depraved and corrupted, children of wrath, oblivious to all miseries, temporal and spiritual and eternal, let everyone endeavor to search the plague of his own heart, to become acquainted with the corruption of his nature and his exposure to the judgments of God.

A timely acquaintance with our own natural poverty, nakedness, and misery would lead us in earnest to tremble at God's judgments and inquire, "What must I do to be saved?"

(2) Acquaint yourselves with Christ, the Savior, the only name given under heaven among men whereby we must be saved. Endeavor to know who Christ is, what His purpose was in the world, what He has done, and what He offers to do for sinners. And, oh, that you would know Him as He is represented in the gospel! As our Savior said to the Samaritan woman, "If you knew the gift of God, you wouldest have asked of Him, and He would give you living water" (John 4:10).

We must not, however, think that everyone who has learned to tell something of the Scripture and speak of Christ knows Him as will infallibly let them ask for and receive the grace of Christ. There is a sort of knowledge that is fruitless and vain; it does not move the heart, nor influence the life. But there is a knowledge of Christ that is saving, that wins the heart and enters the soul. So to know Christ is life. Oh, let us then wait upon the Father of lights, and beg that He would shine in our hearts and give unto us to know the mystery of the kingdom of heaven, make us know the voice of Christ, give us such a discovery of Him that we may be enamored with His excellencies, esteem Him as chiefest among ten thousand, yield up our hearts with pleasure to Him, and choose Him for our Lord and righteousness, loving and resolving to worship Him.

Early Piety Recommended and Exemplified

by Charles Chauncy

(A sermon occasioned by the death of Elisabeth Price,
an eminently pious young woman, who departed
this life at the age of 17 on February 22, 1732)

"Wherewithal shall a young man cleanse his way?
By taking heed thereto according to Thy word."
Psalm 119:9

My text is the only passage of Scripture that mentions the young man by name, and calls upon him to keep himself pure from the defilements of this evil world. Perhaps the design of the Holy Spirit herein might be to place an emphasis upon this age of life, and recommend religion as a business peculiarly seasonable for persons in their young and tender years. It is certain that religion never appears more lovely than as exemplified in the well-ordered conversation of those who are in the bloom of life. Nor can such employ their time and pains more to the divine honor and acceptance, or their own truest advantage, than by an early care in governing their appetites, purifying their hearts, and forming within themselves the seeds and principles of virtue and a holy life.

And to engage our young people in a zealous application of themselves in the use of all proper means to such noble purposes is the design I have in view from the words which have been read to you.

They are found in that inspired psalm which is the longest, and (as some think) the most artfully composed of any in the whole book of Psalms. The general scope of it is to show forth the excellency of the written Word and laws of God. And it is justly admired for that variety of thought in which it recommends them to our practice.

It has been disputed who was the penman of the psalm; but so much of the royal prophet is apparent in every part that it is generally ascribed to David.

The verse I have chosen for my text is made up of two parts: a question and an answer to it.

The first part of my text contains a question: "wherewithal shall a young man cleanse his way?" By "a young man" we are here to understand all in their youthful days, both men and women. And from the express mention of persons of this age and character, we are naturally led to look upon those who are in the prime and vigor of life as under peculiar obligations to become seriously pious and sober. For this is the great thing meant by cleansing their way, which they would not with such particularity have had urged upon them if there had not been some special reasons binding them hereto as their inviolable duty.

I am sensible that there are several things of considerable importance obviously implied in the phrase of my text, under which the duty of early piety is recommended to us. And I might accordingly to good purpose employ your meditations on both the natural and contracted filth young persons are too commonly defiled with, as well as the particulars of that purity of heart and life wherein the sum of true religion consists. But as I'm obliged to confine myself to a single discourse, and it may be presumed we are fully instructed in these things, I shall pass over them and make it my only business from this part of my text to represent to you, in clear and strong a light as I am able, the special considerations that oblige young persons to be religious in their early days.

And here I would offer as follows:

1. This age of life is the best and most convenient in which to enter upon a religious course. I would charitably hope that there are a few who look upon a religious life as a matter of necessity, and who have accordingly determined to take themselves to it at some time or other since they will not give up all hope of future and eternal blessedness. And if religion is at all a matter of necessity, it is certainly wisdom to take that season to engage in it which is the fairest and best, the least entangled with difficulty, and attended with the most hopeful prospect of success. Now such a season is the age of youth. We may, at this time of life, begin and go on in a religious course with greater advantage than we shall be ever able to do afterwards.

There are indeed, it must be acknowledged, some difficulties that seem almost peculiar to this age of life. Some of these are a high relish of the pleasures of sense, the ungovernableness of carnal appetites and evil passions, an exceeding aptness to be seduced by bad example, an over-airiness and gaiety of temper, lack of judgment and experience, rashness, fickleness in consideration, and the like. But these inconveniences are vastly more than balanced by distinguishing advantages common to the days of youth.

We are now most free from a wrong bias, and lie most open to the impressions of religious principles, and the power of those gospel motives, by which the practice of true piety is recommended and enforced. For this age of life is easily wrought upon, and molded almost into any form. A young and tender plant readily takes the ply, which he who tends it thinks proper to give; and if by accident it becomes warped, and has received a wrong bent, by due and early care it is easily reduced. But if it is suffered to continue so a considerable time without suitable attendance and grow old, it becomes stubborn and inflexible.

Also, we are now most under the influence of conscience, and a natural sense of shame and modesty. There are scarcely any stronger restraints to keep us from doing evil than these. As corrupt as human nature is, persons can't at first commit sin without trouble and uneasiness from conscience; and they naturally have such a sense of the indecency and irregularity of most wicked actions that they ordinarily start back from their first approaches towards them. I doubt not but that most men have had their innocence preserved in many instances by the sole help of innate modesty and shame, which powerful principles can't at once be stifled and suppressed.

Besides, sin has not yet gotten so full a possession of us, nor have we contracted so many vicious habits, nor are they so deeply rooted as in those who have for a considerable length of time accustomed themselves to doing evil. For by repeating the acts of sin, the habit is strangely encouraged; and by degrees it will become so obstinate as to make it an impossibility to get recovered from it. The prophet therefore describes this matter in such strong language as this: "Can the Ethiopian change his skin, or the leopard his spots? Then may ye also do good, that are accustomed to do evil" (Jeremiah 13:23).

Moreover, fewer clogs and encumbrances now lie in the way of religion than there will be when we are settled in the world, and are entangled with business; the cares, temptations, difficulties, hurries, and disappointments of life are so many and great that there is the danger that we will not so much as think of our souls if a sense of religion has not before been impressed upon our minds. And under these circumstances we shall be far more likely to put off the business of salvation than ever before. Our inexperience of the world may keep us from feeling the force of this argument, but the further we get into the world, and become acquainted with the cares and distractions of it, the more weight shall we find to be in it.

Further, we shall certainly have more time for the work of religion if we engage in it now. For every moment we defer this work, the space allotted to us to accomplish it is in the same proportion lessened. This, perhaps, we may not be much concerned about, if we imagine religion to be a matter of ease, a business we may begin and finish at our leisure. But we are herein greatly mistaken. It is truly a hard and difficult matter to be sincerely pious, and will require a great deal of time and labor. And if ever we are made seriously concerned about our souls, we shall certainly find it to be so. It is therefore an advantage, the longer time we have for the work of getting ourselves prepared for heavenly happiness. And if we are wise for eternity, we can't but esteem it to be so. To be sure, the longer time we have, the greater progress we shall be able to make in holiness, and the more strengthened will the habits of virtue be likely to be in us, the more mature and perfect the graces of God's Holy Spirit. Nor is it possible that we should ever be eminent in piety, exemplarily proficient in grace and goodness, if we cut short the time to improve herein by not entering upon a life of religion till we have passed the prime of our days.

In summary, we have in this age of life the most hopeful prospect of being effectually assisted by the Holy Spirit of God in the great work of serving our Maker. For young persons may, at least ordinarily, be supposed to have least resisted the Holy Ghost, quenched His motions, stifled convictions, and opposed the methods of divine grace. And having given least provocation to the Holy Spirit, there is the least danger of His withdrawing and giving up on striving with us. And of all persons, we have the highest encouragement, upon suitable applications herefor, to expect those supernatural operations and assistances that are needful for us. It is found true in experience that the Holy Spirit usually strives more with young persons than others. They are more often brought under convictions, filled with concern about their souls, and made seriously inquisitive as to what they must do that they may inherit eternal life. In this age, we are most likely to be wrought upon and prevailed with, and therefore the Holy Spirit does not lose this best opportunity, but improves it by more abundant strivings and motions in us.

And, oh, how great is our advantage in being actually under the influences of God's Spirit, and the most hopeful prospect of all supernatural aids as we may

need them! There cannot be a stronger encouragement to us to enter upon a religious course in these our
first days. For of ourselves we can never turn to God or
serve Him acceptably. The assistances of divine grace
are absolutely necessary hereto. And in this time of life
these we do in some measure enjoy, and have the highest reason further to expect them in degrees proportionate to our wants. And is it prudent to make no use
of such an inestimable privilege? And shall we not, by
slighting and despising it, provoke God to resolve that
His Spirit shall not afterwards strive with us? Do we not
hereby provoke Him to say concerning us, "I am done
with him, and he shall bear no more of My despised offers, nor any more reject the motions of My Spirit. Let
him now take his own course; he shall for a while hear
no more from Me till I speak in quite another manner,
and rend the membranes of his heart and take away his
rebellious soul"?

2. Religion in this age of life is most pleasing and
acceptable to God. It is indeed of so commendable a
nature that the glorious God is pleased with it, and will
graciously accept it, whenever and in whomsoever He
beholds it. Though we should have spent the first of
our time and strength in the service of sin and Satan,
yet if we afterwards heartily devote ourselves to God, and
faithfully employ our powers to the purpose of a holy
life, He will not upbraid us with our former folly nor
deny us His favor. The repentance of a sinner is always
a matter of joy to the blessed God. He takes pleasure at
this in whatsoever age of life we come to ourselves and
return to our duty, and will readily receive us to mercy.
But early piety is *peculiarly* pleasing and acceptable to
God. He has the most endeared affection for young

converts. None are so welcome to Him, or meet with such distinguishing regards from Him. God says, "I love them that love Me. And those that seek Me early shall find Me" (Proverbs 8:17). Of all the apostles of our Lord, John was the youngest, and is frequently spoken of in this way: the disciple whom Jesus loved (John 13:21; 19:26; 20:2). Yes, the blessed Jesus is represented as having an uncommon love for the young man in the gospel, who was only in a thoughtful, serious frame of spirit, expressing itself in respectful desires of knowing what he must do to inherit eternal life (Mark 10:21 compared with Matthew 19:20). God is pleased with everything that looks like a tendency towards early piety. And when we read of the first born and first-fruits (Exodus 22:29) as appointed to be separated for the service of God, may it not symbolically represent our duty to devote the first of our time and strength to the honor of our Creator, as what He would most kindly accept at our hands?

And it is entirely compatible with reason to suppose that the blessed God will be most pleased with the service of our youthful days. For we are now most active and vigorous, our spirits brisk and lively, our resolutions animated, our strength firm, our health unbroken, and, in a word, the various powers of both our souls and our bodies are in their prime and glory. Upon these accounts, we are in our best capacity for the services of religion. And to exercise ourselves to godliness now, in this most valuable part of life, when we are best able, in the best manner, to do the duties and go through the difficulties of religion, is most valuable in itself, most conducive to the divine honor, and will never fail to receive the most distinguishing acceptance. If we should be so unhappy as to neglect God till afterwards, we might, it is true, of His abundant mercy, upon our thorough humiliation and sincere repentance, notwithstanding this most unworthy treatment of His divine majesty, be admitted to His favor. But it is not reasonable to think that we will meet with as easy and free a reception under these circumstances as if we had returned to Him in the flower of life. Our youthful capacities are as the male in our flock, with which God can't but be most of all pleased and readily accept.

3. Religion in this age of life is peculiarly seasonable, and will make those who practice it signally amiable and lovely. The wise man observes, "To everything there is a season, and a time to every purpose under the heaven" (Ecclesiastes 3:1). And when is the proper season in which to enter upon a religious course unless it is upon our first coming to the free exercise of our rational powers, while the blessing of life is now, the sense of it fresh upon our minds, and we are newly arrived at a capacity of knowing the Author of our beings, and rendering back to Him our most grateful acknowledgements? If there is at all a fit opportunity to begin to be seriously godly, it is now, upon the buddings of reason and understanding. It is at the first appearances of a capacity to distinguish between moral good and evil, so that the principles of virtue may, with our intellectual powers, gradually grow up to a state of maturity; and when our life comes to be in its highest perfection, we shall be in the most vigorous, lively, and perfect religious capacity to serve and honor our Creator and Father.

And what is a more lively sight than that of a young person, in his most early days, inquiring after the God who made him, in the language of holy Job, "Where is God my Maker, who teacheth me more than the beasts of the earth, and maketh me wiser than the fowls of heaven?" (Job 35:10–11). It adds a beauteous luster to religion to be practiced by those who have but lately come out of the hands of God and are in the pride and vigor of life. And none among the sons of men shine more brightly and gloriously than such instances of early piety. Their name is better than precious ointment; they are esteemed as the excellent in the earth, are universally well thought and spoken of, and the grace of God appearing in them is admired and acknowledged to their own honor, as well as the honor of God. They are beloved and treated with uncommon respect by all who have a regard to virtue and goodness, and even the wicked and profane, who are open enough to ridicule religion, will yet inwardly feel reverence and veneration for them.

4. There is a great hazard that we shall never be religious if we are not so in this age of life. For who of us knows whether our youthful days are not the only ones we have to live in the world, whether God has not designed us to be in the number of those millions who die in youth, in their full strength, being wholly at ease and quiet, having their breasts full of milk, and bones moistened with marrow? Or if we were secure of our lives, is there not danger, when we have vexed and grieved and quenched the Spirit, of His departing from us? Would it be any wonder if He should so resent our contempt of Him in resisting His motions and stifling convictions as to retire and withdraw forever? And would not this be fatal to our ever turning to God, since of ourselves we can do nothing, and must have our

chief dependence upon the assistance of divine grace? But besides this, what likelihood is there of our being recovered to God and duty after we are grown old in sin, when we could not be prevailed with in our young and tender years, while our young hearts are soft, our wills pliable and yielding, our consciences easily awakened, our affections moved, and our minds impressed with a sense of religion? And if when under these advantageous circumstances we are not restrained by the Word, nor providence, nor the Spirit of God, from walking in the way of the ungodly, what probable prospect is there of our being called back afterwards and converted to God? And the hope of this will be still less after we have long continued in our evil courses; for by this means we shall contract and render obstinate and inveterate innumerable, vicious habits. And these shall very much weaken, if not quite destroy, the influence and authority of conscience; they shall make our hearts like an adamant stone, hard and unrelenting; and in a word, we shall become stupid and entirely lost to all sense of virtue and religion. Under these circumstances, what hope is there of our repentance and conversion to God? It is indeed a possible thing; but there is little more than a naked possibility of it. Nicodemus's question is in this case very pertinent: "How can a man be born when he is old?" It is a most unlikely thing! One of the greatest rarities! And whenever it happens, it may be justly looked upon as even a miracle of superabundant grace in God!

5. In the last place, it will be much to our advantage to be seriously godly early. This is the best method we can take to secure the divine blessing in outward regards. For our Savior has encouraged us to hope, upon

our seeking first the kingdom of God and His righteousness, that all those things shall be added unto us (Matthew 6:33). Agreeable to this is what the apostle wrote: "But godliness is profitable unto all things, having promise of the life that now is, and of that which is to come" (1 Timothy 4:8). And by virtue of this promise, those who serve God, especially those who do so in the first of their days, may with the greatest confidence depend upon the divine power and goodness for the supply of their wants. They are, of all persons, the most likely to be smiled upon in providence, and so come to the enjoyment of temporal good things—at least so far as God shall see it to be best for them. But besides this advantage, there are vastly greater ones of a spiritual and eternal nature.

By our being pious early in life, we shall early obtain the pardon of our sins, the favor and friendship of our Maker, an adoption into the family of heaven, and with it an investiture in all the rights and privileges of the sons of God. We shall hereby escape innumerable sins and follies, which would wound our consciences, defile our souls, dishonor and provoke God, and make work for a most bitter after-repentance. We shall hereby have a longer opportunity for the work of serving God, and our generation according to the will of God; and so we shall be able to do more good and be greater blessings in our day. We shall hereby take the most certain and easy way to live and die as good men. For once the seeds of virtue have taken root in our young and tender minds, they will grow up into nature and make us fit to live in the world, setting us in a good measure free from the power of lust, preserving us from the infection of evil examples, and guarding us against the force of those numberless temptations we shall meet with.

We shall hereby be likely to enjoy, in the most uninterrupted course, that inward ease, peace, and religious satisfaction wherein consists the greatest happiness on this side of heaven. Those who have given way to youthful lusts, and were not seriously inclined until in their latter years, are often strangers to this. Or if their consciences are sometimes at ease, it is often interrupted with perplexing fears and doubts, whereby their lives are rendered very uncomfortable. But those who have, by the grace of God, been enabled to enter upon and walk in a religious course from their early days ordinarily, for the most part, enjoy a holy calm in their breast, that peace of God which passes all understanding. Persons, even in old age, have received more solid comfort from a reflection on their early piety than from all other considerations whatever. And when nothing else has been effectual in their melancholy hours to bring ease to their minds, it has at once scattered their fears and doubts to look back upon that grace of God whereby, in the pride and flower of youth, they were assisted to prefer a course of religion to the pleasures of sin, and to hold on in this course amidst all the temptations of this evil world.

Oh, the blessed peace and serenity of mind, the holy joy and triumph of soul, such will likely be filled with at the hour of death! Conscience shall then testify that they began to seek God while they were yet young, and that they have all along had their conversation in the world in simplicity and godly sincerity; not by fleshly wisdom, but by the grace of God. The reflection hereon will excite the lively acting out of faith and hope in the mercy of God through Christ, yield an unfailing spring of consolation to their hearts, and enable them in the midst of the throws and agonies of death to sing in that triumphant language: "O death, where is thy sting? O grave, where is thy victory? The sting of death is sin, and the strength of sin is the law. But thanks be to God, which giveth us the victory, through our Lord Jesus Christ" (1 Corinthians 15:55–57).

But the greatest advantage of all is that our future and eternal crown of glory will hereby be the greater. There will, no doubt, be degrees of glory in the coming world. The Scriptures plainly teach this by distinguishing between the reward of a prophet and an ordinary righteous man (Matthew 10:41), and by assuring us of both a sparing and bountiful future harvest, according as we have at present sown either sparingly or bountifully (2 Corinthians 9:6). But the most full declaration of this doctrine is in the parable of the ten servants (Luke 19:12 and following), who received from their lord, being about to go into a far country, one pound each to trade with till he should return. At the time when he called them to an account, he is represented as rewarding every man who had made a good use of the pound delivered to him; and the reward bears an exact proportion to the several improvements made by the servants. He who had gained ten pounds is made ruler over ten cities, and he who had gained five pounds is made ruler over five cities; which obviously and unavoidably leads us to conceive that the future glory will be proportioned to men differently, according to the different improvements they have made in grace and goodness. Nor does this inequality in the least argue their happiness to be imperfect who are admitted to the lowest degrees of future glory. For a star is as perfect in its order as the sun, yet they shine in a different luster, which is agreeable to what the apostle wrote in 1 Corinthians 15:41–42: "There is one glory of the sun, and another glory of the moon, and another glory of the stars; for one star differeth from another in glory. So also is the resurrection of the dead." Here he argues that the resurrection bodies of the saints will differ from each other in their several glories, as the moon and stars are perfect in their degree and order, though they shine with far less glory than the sun.

Now since we have reason to believe that God will reward men in the coming world with different degrees of glory, according to the different improvements they have made in holiness, who among men will shine with such distinguishing luster as early converts? As they have had the longest opportunity and best advantages for it, we may well suppose them to be most confirmed in goodness, to be most grown in grace, to have done most service in the world, and to have brought forth most of that fruit whereby our Father in heaven is glorified. They are therefore most fit for future glory, and will not only be admitted to it, but to the highest degrees of that glory. And, oh, how great will be their blessedness when they shall be made the most distinguished subjects of that happiness, the lowest degree whereof is so surpassing that "eye hath not seen, nor ear heard, nor has it ever entered into the heart of man to conceive of it!"

And having thus laid before you some of those many considerations, which can't be denied to come with peculiar force upon young persons, obliging them in the strongest manner to be religious early in life, I think I may with propriety now turn my discourse into an earnest exhortation to the duty of early piety. And, oh, that those of us who are in our youthful days would be prevailed with to engage in the great affair of religion and our souls' salvation. This is what the blessed God most heartily desires, and would be peculiarly well-pleased with. He therefore often, with the greatest particularity, bespeaks the service of our young and tender years. Holy David puts the question in my text, "Wherewithal shall a young man cleanse his way?" intimating the great stress that is laid upon the age of youth, and that now to cleanse ourselves from sin is emphatically our duty. Hence young persons are by name solemnly called upon in Ecclesiastes 12:1: "Remember now thy Creator in the days of thy youth." And so it is in 1 Chronicles 28:9: "And thou, Solomon my son, know thou the God of thy father, and serve Him with a perfect heart and a willing mind." And because young people are generally inclined to rejoice in their youth, to let their hearts cheer them in the days of their youth, and to walk in the way of their own hearts and in the sight of their own eyes, great care is taken to check and restrain this irregular inclination. Particularly in Ecclesiastes 11:9: "But know that for all these things God will bring thee into judgment." And why should God thus single out and particularly advise, caution, and direct young persons but that it is their distinguishing duty, and eminently His expectation from them, to yield up themselves to Him, cleansing their way from sin and employing their powers in His service?

Our obligations hereto are very solemn and particular. And I would fain hope that we are so far convinced of the reasonableness and necessity of complying with them that we are resolved upon loving and serving our

most merciful God and Father. But it may be that we
flatter ourselves with the thought of having a more
convenient season for the work of religion in the later
part of life, and so put it off till then. This I believe is
the vain imagination of most young persons, and an effectual bar in the way of their becoming seriously
godly. To this I would say, what if death should be between us and our hereafter-opportunity for the business
of our souls salvation? This is no improbable supposi-
tion. Multitudes of the same age and character as ourselves die within the reach of our observation. And who
can say that it won't be our own lot to die young? And if
this should be our case, how strange and unreasonable
will our conduct appear to be; reasonable creatures sent
into the world to seek and serve God, who are made capable of it and who had time for it, but went out into
the world and spent all their time in an utter disregard
and neglect of God, forgeting the principal end and
business of life! Besides, we shall certainly be as unfit
and indisposed for religion afterwards as we are at the
present; and we will look upon any later season, when
we come to it, as inconvenient as the one we now enjoy,
and be under the same temptation to adjourn this
business. For let us pitch on whatever part of life we
please, it will be encumbered with difficulties of one
sort or another; and innumerable pretenses for delay
will offer themselves, and be apt without the greatest
resolution to prevail with us. We shall be ready to say
with ourselves, "Tomorrow will we amend our ways."
And when that tomorrow comes we shall still say again,
"Tomorrow," and so our tomorrows will prove endless.
In short, the greatest objection we have against the present season is that it is present. And whenever our

imaginary hereafter-season comes to be present, we shall have the same objection against that, and find it just as hard then to leave our sins and return to God and our duty.

Or, if any should be discouraged from early piety, apprehending it to be a matter of such difficulty that it can't be accomplished without the greatest labor and pains, I would say that if it should be allowed to be a difficult thing to be truly religious, this ought not to be used as an objection against our endeavoring to be so. For it is an affair of absolute necessity that must be engaged in, if ever we would hope for admission into the eternal kingdom of God. And therefore, the proper use to be made of the difficulties of religion is not to discourage us from setting about it, but to put on so much more resolution to labor in it with the utmost speed and all possible diligence. And in so doing, we may upon good grounds expect aids of divine grace proportionate to the need we stand in of them, and the difficulties and temptations we may meet with.

But what is peculiarly matter of encouragement in this case is that, notwithstanding all the difficulties of a religious course, many young persons have been enabled to go through them, and to become illustrious patterns of an early and close walk with God. The Scripture examples of this sort we are all acquainted with. Nor have there been wanting even from among ourselves remarkable examples of the same kind. And this leads me to make mention of a young woman from this congregation, Elisabeth Price, who last week went to her grave; of her it may with good reason be said that she was an uncommon instance of that early piety of which we have been speaking. And as this is a case wherein I flatter myself that I should not be suspected of sinister views, I have been rather inclined to take public notice of it to the honor of free grace, and to recommend religion to our choice and practice in our youthful days.

From a child she was deeply impressed with an awe and reverence for God, which remarkably manifested itself, upon the first deliberate exercises of her reason and understanding, in a careful endeavor to abstain from those things that she apprehended to be evil. She was scrupulously fearful lest in anything she should offend God. Particularly, she discovered a great abhorrence of the sin of lying, and guarded against that vain, thoughtless temper and conduct which are so incidental to childhood and youth; she often expressed her displeasure thereat to those acquaintances in whom she perceived these faults to reign.

She was observed to be constant, even from her most early days, in retiring evening and morning to pour out her soul before God. She only now and then intermitted this duty, but never from a negligent, careless frame of spirit, as is too commonly the case. But whenever she was blamable in this matter, it proceeded from perplexing fears and temptations, uncommon to one of her age, for which omissions she was heartily sorry, and would bitterly complain of herself.

Her carriage towards her parents was full of love, tenderness, honor, and reverence. She cheerfully obeyed their commands, attended their instructions, hearkened to their advice, and followed their counsels. And as she did not allow the least unseemly, disobedient behavior towards them in herself, so neither could she bear to see it in her brothers and sisters. And

whenever she observed any discoveries of disrespect, ir-
reverence, or undutifulness, either in their words,
looks, or actions, it would sensibly affect and grieve
her, especially when they were grossly guilty. And she
would never fail to take an opportunity to present to
them the sin of undutifulness to parents, how offensive
it was to God, and how provoking it was in His sight.

She was favored with a peculiarly soft and tender
conscience, which made her watchful against sin, careful to avoid even the appearances of it, and to maintain
a close walk with God. And this was the case when,
many times, she was under great spiritual fears and
darkness. As far as I could observe, she was of a
thoughtful, pensive temper, and was, by her constitution, subject sometimes to the power of melancholy. To
this I attribute her not enjoying, at least not consis-
tently, the comforts of religion in so great a measure as
might be expected. I do not doubt that the hand of
Satan was evident in many of the temptations, discouragements, and perplexing fears that she passed
through, which were greater, and of a more extraordi-
nary nature, than is usual for persons of so few years.

I don't remember her being able to fix upon the
particular time in which she thought she might pass
under a work of sanctifying grace. Nor is it at all to be
wondered at, when it was never observed that the principles of corruption were habitually predominant in
her in any part of her life. From the first appearances of
reason, and all along till the time of her death, her
general temper and behavior were such as gave
grounds to hope that from a child she was savingly
converted to God, which is a most distinguishing privilege. Three times as happy are they who are the subjects

of it. The grace herein discovered can never be enough magnified and admired.

She was a great reader of her Bible, not suffering it to lie by as a neglected book. But as her delight was in the love of God, so she made it the main part of her counsel, repairing to it upon all emergent occasions, besides her more stated times for studying of it.

She was a strict observer of the Sabbath, behaving herself as one who had an awakened sense of the solemnity of the day; she constantly went up to the place of public worship where she appeared with a visible awe and reverence, and attended with such care and diligence that she was able to bring home, and from her memory repeat, more of the preached Word than is common for persons grown to years, who yet are persons of good understanding. And though, through a mistaken apprehension of the Lord's Supper, as if it was an ordinance designed only for Christians of more than ordinary attainments in holiness and satisfaction about their good state, she dared not venture to approach it, yet she would not willingly neglect being present at the administration of it, at which time she was often most sensibly affected, and her soul refreshed and comforted.

In her sickness, by which she was for a considerable time detained from the house of God, it was admirable to behold her breathings after God in His sanctuary. With holy David, her soul thirsted for God, the living God. And her complaint was, "Oh, when shall I come and appear before God!"

Her bodily pains were great and of long continuance, which gave opportunity for the illustration of divine grace in that uncommon degree of patience, meekness, contentedness, and subjection to the Father of spirits; she was an eminent pattern of never complaining or murmuring, but always acknowledged her own deserts, and justifying God in all that He laid upon her.

I hope that her brothers and sister will never forget her calling them to her bedside, when with a holy freedom of soul she gave her dying testimony in behalf of religion and took her farewell of them, with great earnestness beseeching and exhorting them to seek and serve God in their youthful days; she encouraged them to improve the perfect season of grace, and those in their youth to the purpose of a holy life. And, oh, with what fervor of soul did she repeat the words, "Oh, that we may die in peace and meet together in glory at the day of Christ." Nor did her concern for religion end here, but she advised, cautioned, and exhorted all who came to see her as she had opportunity and apprehended it to be proper and decent.

But what is still more wonderful, though she was but in her seventeenth year, is that she was enabled in the midst of tormenting pains, and the near views of approaching death, to correct the excessive sorrow of her distressed parents. She reminded them of the sovereignty of God and, from the consideration that all things are ordered by Him, recommended to them the duty of submission. And in various ways, she more than once endeavored to calm their grief, compose their spirits, and bring them to a willingness to resign her up to the God who had given her to them.

She was in the beginning of her sickness, and for some time under darkness and fear; and she expressed a desire, if it might be God's will, to live still longer in this world. But for many days before her death, she had a comfortable sense of her interest in Christ, a good hope through His merits of future glory and immortality, and was freely willing to depart hence to be here no more; and this she declared upon several occasions. Once, upon her mother's displaying her grief under the view of parting with her, and asking her whether she was willing to die and leave her, her answer was, "Yes, yes." And she added, "Though you have been a loving, tender mother to me, I can at God's call readily forsake all to go to Christ." At another time, recovering from a fainting fit, and overhearing somebody say they thought she was gone, she presently cried out, "Oh, that I *had* gone then! It would have been happy with me now." Some time later, being asked whether her faith and hope held out; she replied, "Yes, yes," doubling the word. And a little before her death, she was asked to allow her mouth to be moistened, which was almost scorched up with a canker; she said, "No, for I am going where I shall no more want drink." And not long afterwards, in a holy calm and blessed serenity of soul, she fell asleep in Jesus.

How happy the parents of such a child are! You have infinite reason to magnify and adore this distinguishing, rich grace of God. Nor should you think harshly of God for taking from you one so dearly loved when He first did so much for her in making her meet for heavenly happiness. In the enjoyment of heaven, we trust, she is now solacing herself. Comfort yourselves with this thought. Oh, be excited to the greatest diligence in working out your own salvation so that you may hereafter come to be where she is, to behold her face in glory, and never be again parted from each other!

In closing this point, my heart's desire and prayer to God now is that there may be in this church many such instances of an early conversion to God! We trust there are some such. Alas, they are so rare! May the good Lord increase their number. O young people, you are the hope of this church of our Lord Jesus. Its increase, its glory, its very continuance in being is in a measure dependent on you. If you should rise up in your fathers' stead to be a generation that does not know God, what is likely to become of the gospel worship and ordinances in this place? I want to believe that the breasts of many of you are warmed with a generous concern for the honor of God and perpetuating religion when your fathers are dead and gone.

Let us then give our hearts to God, seek first His kingdom and righteousness, repent of our sins, believe in Christ, and yield up ourselves absolutely and entirely to Him in an everlasting covenant. And, oh, let us this day choose our fathers' God for our God; let us know and serve Him with a perfect heart and a willing mind. So shall we rejoice the hearts of God's people; yes, we shall cause joy all over heaven, making glad not only the holy angels, but God Himself and the Lord Jesus Christ too. But so much for the question in my text.

The second thing observable in my text is the answer to this question: "by taking heed thereto according to Thy Word." And here are two things which the time will allow me to give you only a few hints upon.

1. If we should become truly religious, we must take heed to our way. We must not live without care or caution. Rather we must consult with our reason and conscience, taking pause before we act, and not entering

upon any course heedlessly, without thought or consideration.

This fault is too common, especially among young
persons who are therefore particularly here directed to
guard against it. And this is not only because it is in itself a gross inconsistency—for what sounds more in-
congruous than a rational and intelligent, yet thoughtless and inconsiderate creature?—but because it is a
means necessary to our being preserved from the pollutions of sin. It is very much owing to that giddy
thoughtlessness, which is so exceedingly apt to prevail
among young people, that they are so often led astray
in the path of wickedness that terminates in destruction. And unless we take care to rectify this temper, and
recover a seriously thoughtful, cautious, and considerate disposition, there will be great hazard of our never
becoming truly religious. Consideration is the first step
mentioned in David's return to God and his duty. And
if with him we would turn our feet unto God's testimonies, we must, as he did, first think of our ways.

Let us realize the necessity of becoming seriously
considerate. Let us not allow ourselves to live without
thought, as though we were not endowed with the noble powers of reason and understanding. But let us deliberate before we act. And let us review our past actions, and often bring them under strict examination.
So there will be a hopeful prospect of our being kept
within the line of duty, or otherwise we shall soon see
our mistake, be likely to repent of it, and alter our
course, before we get into a habit of doing evil.

2. We must take heed to our way according to God's
Word. This also is a proper and wise direction in order
for us to become truly religious, for these reasons:

(1) The Word of God is the best and most suitable rule by which to govern ourselves in the business of religion. One great reason why young persons especially are so often found walking in a wrong way is that they have not settled in their minds a rule by which to govern their conduct, and they are not used to bringing their actions to some standard, to judge whether they are good or bad. It is therefore a good direction to propose a rule of life, and then to govern ourselves by that rule. And the direction is still more wise and suitable since the rule it recommends is the Word of God, which is the best rule that can be. We have the excelling properties of this rule elegantly described in Psalm 19:7–9: "The law of the Lord is perfect, converting the soul; the testimony of the Lord is sure, making wise the simple; the statutes of the Lord are right, rejoicing the heart; the commandment of the Lord is pure, enlightening the eyes; the fear of the Lord is clean, enduring forever; the judgments of the Lord are true and righteous altogether." Nor was the world ever favored with so clear and perfect a rule of life as what we have in the word of God. We are here taught the whole of our duty towards God, ourselves, and one another; and it ought to be practiced in every relationship, and under all the varying conditions and circumstances of life. If we follow this direction, making the Word of God the rule of our actions, doing whatever it prescribes and nothing of which it disapproves, we shall not fail to keep ourselves free from sin, and exercise ourselves in all religious services to the honor of God, and our own establishment in grace and goodness. To take heed to God's Word as a rule of life is therefore good advice; a better direction could scarcely

have been given us.

(2) The Word of God offers the most powerful arguments to prevail with us to engage in a religious course; for they are, in short, nothing less than the rewards and punishments of the eternal world.

These sanctions of the law of God were not, I am aware, at the time when David gave the advice in my text, so fully and clearly expressed as they have been since. Yet good men in those days had sufficient reason, from divine revelation, to expect a future state in everlasting blessedness; and the impenitently wicked to dwell with devouring fire and inhabit everlasting burnings.

But however it was then, the coming of Jesus Christ has brought life and immortality to light, an immortality of both happiness and misery. It has scattered all those clouds that hid the other world from our sight, and removed all doubt concerning the future existence of both good and bad men. The kingdom of heaven is now laid open to our view with all the glories of it. Hell also is represented naked and destruction without a covering. And what powerful arguments these are! And what are all other motives in comparison to them? They are certainly, in the wisest manner, adapted to work upon our hope and fear, the two strongest and most leading passions of human nature. And their operation is so powerful that if the fear of eternal misery will not frighten us from sin, nor the hope of eternal happiness encourage us to enter upon a life of serious godliness, we are sunk into the depths of stupidity. More powerful arguments cannot be used with us; and if we won't be wrought upon by these, our case is truly lamentable.

Now this also obviously justifies the wisdom of the direction in my text. For we stand in absolute need of very strong and forcible arguments to prevail with us to engage in the business of religion; and those which the Word of God offers are the most so of any that can be used with us.

(3) In the last place, the Word of God is a most powerful means to purify the heart, and beget and increase in the soul the principle of holiness. It has strong, natural tendency to these ends since it contains that in it which is most suited to enlighten the mind, inform the understanding, convince the judgment, persuade the will, move the affections, and stir up the executive powers. But its chief efficacy to promote real piety lies in its being an instituted means of God's dispensing those divine assistances that are necessary to our being truly religious. Upon this account especially the gospel is called "the power of God to salvation" (Romans 1:16). Our Savior makes this prayer in John 17:17: "Sanctify them through Thy truth; Thy word is truth." And we are said to be sanctified and cleansed with the washing of water by the Word (Ephesians 5:26). All these texts abundantly point out the Word to be a special means that is ordinarily made use of in the work of recovering sinners to God and duty. I do not deny that the Holy Spirit may convert persons without means, but instances of this kind are very uncommon, if there are any such at all. And as the Spirit generally makes use of means, so the Word, both read and preached, is a special means to this end. There are, perhaps, a few persons here who have passed under a work of regenerating grace, and from their own experience are able to say that the Word has been instrumen-

tal herein, and can tell what parts of it in particular were impressed upon their minds by the good Spirit of God.

When the holy psalmist was directing young men in the way to religion and happiness, what more suitable and effectual method could he advise than paying a due regard to God's Word? Since this is naturally adapted to promote this design, and is the very method in which it pleases God ordinarily to bestow renewing, saving grace, what more likely way can be taken to become sincerely pious than by attending to that Word, which God has instructed as a means, which He has given us the greatest encouragement to hope that He will bless to this end? Surely none may be thought to be under a more hopeful prospect of a real, thorough conversion than those who put themselves in the prescribed way of meeting with divine grace by heedfully regarding God's Word.

Now, from what has been said, take these points:

• How great is our indebtedness to God for His Word! Having always been favored with it, we scarcely know our advantage herein, or how justly to prize it. It is truly a rich gift that to us are committed the oracles of God. Oh, let us value this privilege! We can never esteem it too much or be too thankful for it.

• Such deserve a severe reproof who treat the Word with neglect, who seldom or never look into it, and make little or no more use of it than if they had no concern with it. This is the character of multitudes, as is too evident from the gross ignorance of some in the great points of Christianity, and the wretched carelessness of others about eternal concerns. Oh, be admonished for your sin and folly! You are greatly guilty before God of casting horrid contempt on His grace; and not only so, but you hurt your own souls, and lose one of the best advantages that will enable you to be happy forever.

• We should be much in reading the Word; we should have stated times for that, and should not allow ourselves normally to let a day pass without repairing to it. And while we are studying the Word, we should guard against a light, vain, and trifling frame of spirit, which is in no way becoming the importance of the duty. Rather, we should endeavor to compose ourselves to seriousness, getting our minds into a thoughtful, considerate temper. This, doubtless, is a likely method of reading the Word to a saving advantage.

• We should especially attend on the preached Word, making it our care to be always at the place of public worship at the stated times on the Lord's days— and on other days also as our occasions will permit. Nor should we content ourselves merely with an attendance on the Word, but should take heed how we hear. We should attend with reverence and an awakened sense of the awful weight of future and eternal concerns; with desires of and aims at being spiritually profited, that we may be quickened in duty and strengthened to the performance of it; that we may get possessed of sanctifying grace and have it increased in our souls. In a word, we should see that the life of God may be begun, maintained, and carried on in us as much as may be to perfection.

• Finally, let us make use of the Word to the purposes of religion for which it is here prescribed. I will suppose that we are, at least some of us, convinced of the reasonableness and necessity of an early course of piety, and are accordingly resolved to enter upon such a course. And for our direction, let us, as the psalmist has advised, take heed to our way according to God's Word. We have here the great rule of all religion. Let us compare our pretenses to virtue and goodness herewith, and not satisfy ourselves with anything short of that which the gospel calls "pure and undefiled religion." We have here the most powerful motives, and are laid under the strongest obligations to a pious, holy life. Let us here learn our duty and fetch our encouragements, quickening ourselves in the way of godliness from those considerations which are here proposed to us. We have here one special means the Holy Spirit makes use of in converting sinners to God. Let us attend to it as such, humbly waiting and hoping for the manifestations of that power to our salvation whereby Jesus Christ was raised from the dead.

In a word, as the Scriptures are profitable to all saving purposes, and are in every way sufficient to make the man of God perfect and thoroughly furnished unto all good works, let us use them accordingly. Let all our views, all our hopes, all our encouragements and dependencies in and from religion be regulated by the Word. And let us—from the beginning of our lives, and through the whole course of them, under all the changes of time and various distributions of providence—govern our hearts, and order our walk according to the gospel's directions. If we do this, we shall not fail, through the supply of the Spirit of Jesus Christ, to be built up in faith and holiness, till we become possessed of an inheritance among those who are sanctified.

May the good Lord now touch our hearts with a

sense of these things! And may that grace of His, which has appeared to all men, bringing salvation, effectually teach us that, denying ungodliness and worldly lusts, we should live soberly, righteously, and godly in this present world. And may we with comfort look for the blessed hope and glorious appearing of the great God and our Savior Jesus Christ, to whom, with the Father and the Holy Spirit, be eternal praises. Amen.

Letter to a Young Convert

by Jonathan Edwards

(Some time in 1741, a young lady residing in Smithfield, Connecticut, who had lately made a profession of religion, requested Mr. Edwards to give her some advice as to the best manner of maintaining a religious life. In reply, he addressed to her the following letter, which will be found eminently useful to all persons just entering on the Christian course.)

My dear young friend,

As you desired me to send you in writing some directions as to how to conduct yourself in your Christian course, I would now answer your request. The sweet remembrance of the great things I have lately seen at Smithfield inclines me to do anything in my power to contribute to the spiritual joy and prosperity of God's people there.

1. I would advise you to keep up as great a striving and earnestness in religion as if you knew yourself to be in a natural state and were still seeking conversion. We advise persons under conviction to be earnest and violent for the kingdom of heaven; but when they have attained to conversion, they ought not to be any less watchful, laborious, and earnest in the whole work of religion, but the more so; for they are under infinitely greater obligations. For want of this, many persons, in a few months after their conversion, have begun to lose the sweet and lively sense of spiritual things, and to grow cold and dark, and have pierced themselves

through with many sorrows, whereas, if they had done as the apostle did (Philippians 3:12–14), their path would have been as the shining light, that shines more and more unto the perfect day.

2. Do not leave off seeking, striving, and praying for the very same things that we exhort unconverted persons to strive for, and a degree of which you have already had in conversion. Pray that your eyes may be opened, that you may receive sight, that you may know yourself and be brought to God's footstool, that you may see the glory of God and Christ and be raised from the dead, and have the love of Christ shed abroad in your heart. Those who have most of these things have need to still pray for them; for there is so much blindness and hardness, pride and death remaining that they still need to have that work of God wrought upon them, further to enlighten and enliven them, that shall bring them out of darkness into God's marvelous light, and be a kind of new conversion and resurrection from the dead. There are very few requests that are proper for an impenitent man that are not also, in some sense, proper for the godly.

3. When you hear a sermon, hear for yourself. Though what is spoken may be more especially directed to the unconverted, or to those who in other respects are in different circumstances from yourself, yet let the chief intent of your mind be to consider, "In what respect is this applicable to me? And what application ought I to make of this for my own soul's good?"

Though God has forgiven and forgotten your past sins, yet do not forget them yourself; often remember what a wretched bondslave you were in the land of

Egypt. Often bring to mind your particular acts of sin before conversion, as the blessed Apostle Paul is often mentioning his old blaspheming, persecuting spirit and his injuriousness to the renewed, humbling his heart, and acknowledging that he was the least of the apostles, not worthy to be called an apostle, and the chief of sinners. Be often confessing your old sins to God, and let that text be often in your mind which is found in Ezekiel 16:63: " 'That thou mayest remember and be confounded, and never open thy mouth any more, because of thy shame, when I am pacified toward thee for all that thou hast done,' saith the Lord God."

5. Remember that you have more cause, on some accounts a thousand times more, to lament and humble yourself for sins that have been committed since conversion than before, because of the infinitely greater obligations that are upon you to live to God, and to look upon the faithfulness of Christ in unchangeably continuing His loving-kindness, notwithstanding all your great unworthiness since your conversion.

6. Be always greatly abased for your remaining sin, and never think that you lie low enough for it; but yet be not discouraged or disheartened by it for, though we are exceedingly sinful, yet we have an Advocate with the Father, Jesus Christ the righteous, the preciousness of whose blood, the merit of whose righteousness, and the greatness of whose love and faithfulness infinitely overtop the highest mountains of our sins.

7. When you engage in the duty of prayer, come to the Lord's Supper, or attend any other duty of divine worship, come to Christ, as Mary Magdalene did (Luke 7:37–38); come and cast yourself at His feet and kiss them, and pour forth upon Him the sweet, perfumed

ointment of divine love out of a pure and broken heart, as she poured the precious ointment out of her pure, broken alabaster box.

8. Remember that pride is the worst viper that is in the heart, the greatest disturber of the soul's peace and of sweet communion with Christ; it was the first sin committed, and lies lowest in the foundation of Satan's whole building; it is with the greatest difficulty rooted out, and is the most hidden, secret, and deceitful of all lusts, often creeping insensibly into the midst of religion, even, sometimes, under the guise of humility itself.

9. That you may pass a correct judgment concerning yourself, always look upon those as the best discoveries and the best comforts that have the most of these two effects: those that make you least and lowest, and most like a child, and those that most engage and fix your heart in a full and firm disposition to deny yourself for God, and to spend and be spent for Him.

10. If at any time you fall into doubts about the state of your soul, in dark and dull frames of mind, it is proper to review your past experience; but do not consume too much time and strength in this way. Rather apply yourself, with all your might, to an earnest pursuit after renewed experience, new light, and new lively acts of faith and love. One new discovery of the glory of Christ's face will do more toward scattering clouds of darkness in one minute than examining old experience, by the best marks that can be given, for a whole year.

11. When the exercise of grace is low, and corruption prevails, and, by that means, fear prevails, do not desire to have fear cast out by any other way than

by the reviving and prevailing of love in the heart. By this, fear will be effectually compelled, as darkness in a room vanishes away when the pleasant beams of the sun are let into it.

12. When you counsel and warn others, do it earnestly, affectionately, and thoroughly; and when you are speaking to equals, let your warnings be intermixed with expressions of your own unworthiness, and of the sovereign grace that makes you differ.

13. If you would set up religious meetings of young women by themselves, to be attended once in a while besides the other meetings that you attend, I should think it would be very proper and profitable.

14. Under special difficulties, or when in great need of, or great longings after, any particular mercy for yourself or others, set apart a day for secret prayer and fasting; and let the day be spent not only in petitions for the mercies you desire, but in searching your heart, and in looking over your past life and confessing your sins before God—not as is wont to be done in public prayer, but by a very particular rehearsal before God of the sins of your past life, from your childhood hitherto, before and after conversion, with the circumstances and aggravations attending them, spreading all the abominations of your heart very particularly, and as fully as possible, before Him.

15. Do not let the adversaries of the cross have occasion to reproach religion on your account. How holy should the children of God, the redeemed and the beloved of the Son of God, behave themselves. Therefore, "walk as children of light and of the day," and "adorn the doctrines of God your Savior." Especially, abound in what are called the Christian virtues,

and which make you like the Lamb of God; be meek and lowly of heart, and full of pure, heavenly, and humble love to all; abound in deeds of love to others, and self-denial for others; and let there be in you a disposition to account others better than yourself.

16. In your course, walk with God and follow Christ as a little, poor, helpless child, taking hold of Christ's hand, keeping your eye on the marks of the wounds in His hands and side whence came the blood that cleanses you from sin, and hiding your nakedness under the skirt of the white, shining robes of His righteousness.

17. Pray much for the ministers and the church of God, especially, that He would carry on the glorious work which He has now begun till the world shall be full of His glory.

Jonathan Edwards